Altered Creatures Epic Fantasy Adventures
Book 6 of the Thorik Dain Series

Plea of Avanda

Historical Date 2.0113.0804
(2nd Age, 113th Year, 8th Month, 4th Day)

Copyright © 2015 by Anthony G. Wedgeworth

Published by Anthony G. Wedgeworth

Artwork by Frederick L. Wedgeworth

Paperback ISBN: 978-0-9859159-8-8

Altered Creatures Epic Fantasy Adventures
Historical Date 2.0113.0804
Thorik Dain Series, Book 6, Revision 1.0,
Plea of Avanda
www.AlteredCreatures.com

Printed in the United States of America

Dedication:

Thank you for joining me on this wonderful adventure that has forever changed my life for the better. I cherish everyone's support in helping make this a great experience.

Acknowledgments:

My lovely wife, Tami, for putting up with the years of me working in my office on these stories, and for believing in me.

My kids, Alexander, Jessica, and Kimberly who inspire me to make the world a better place, even if only through the stories I tell.

My mother, for nurturing good values and helping me establish a strong moral compass, as well as allowing me to fail at times in order to learn the valuable lessons in life.

My brother, Rick, for pacifying my wild ideas of creating a new land by rendering it in 3D. Thanks for all the years in our youth while playing AD&D and allowing me to explore my creative side. It eventually grew into an amazing set of books.

My sister, Kris. In spite of me torturing her in our youth, as most big brothers due, she still supports me in all my crazy ventures... especially in the seriously crazy ones...

My father, who is truly an adventurer at heart. I watched him throughout my life and I learned how anger issues can make somone become their own worst enemy. I almost walked down this same path behind him until I realized that my fate was in my own hands, and then I chose to forge my own way.

My dyslexia, for this gift has taught me compassion & empathy for others, drive to conquer my struggles, and creativity to survive outside the norm. What a wonderful set of life lessons to have.

Everyone who took the time to read my manuscript to help me work out the details and issues. These include Kristina Walker, JoAnn Cegon, Sarah Wedgeworth, Tami Wedgeworth, Author Lyle Ernst, Author Fred Waiss, Kelly Gochenaur, Darci Knapp, Pat Mulhern, and Dennis Shurson. I couldn't have done it without you.

Altered Creatures Epic Adventures continues with the
following books:

Nums of Shoreview Series (Pre-teen, Ages 7 to 12)
Stolen Orb
Unfair Trade
Slave Trade
Baka's Curse
Haunted Secrets
Rodent Buttes

Thorik Dain Series (Young Adult and Adult)
Fate of Thorik
Sacrifice of Ericc
Essence of Gluic
Rise of Rummon
Prey of Ambrosius
Plea of Avanda

Altered Creatures Epic Fantasy Adventures
Book 6 of the Thorik Dain Series

Plea of Avanda

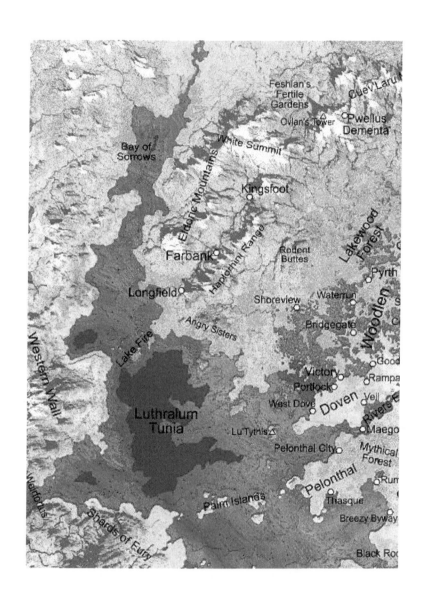

Preface
Homeless

With their city destroyed, the remaining Dolor citizens trekked through the mountainside forest in hopes that Thorik Dain would lead them to safety within Pwellus Dementa'.

This had been the first venture into the wild for the slaves of the mining camp and fear of the unknown consumed their thoughts. Even the cold grey confines of their prior homes seemed tempting, for there was always food, water, and protection from beasts. The forest had none of that. They were exposed to the elements and no wagons of food would arrive at the designated time each day. No, they were now on their own and had to fend for themselves for the very first time in their lives.

The citizens rested their hopes and safety on the outsiders who had traveled back through time and then helped save the Dolor people from certain death. It was now up to Thorik, Avanda, and Brimmelle to guide them to safety. And it would be the decisions that they made that would determine everyone's fate.

Chapter 1
Creature of the Wild

The south face of the Cuev'Laru Mountain Range was unforgiving to any who attempted to scale its steep vertical rocky surface. And yet a large deadly creature raced down its side with the lack of precision and grace of a charging Chuttlebeast. Each step stabbed thick claws into the rocks, sending shards out and then down. With eyes fixed on the leader of the travelers below, the creature extended its long teeth that had been hiding under the gums. Terror was coming and it was in the form of a raging giant lizard-like beast toward Thorik and his followers.

"Run!" Thorik shouted as he quickly riffled through his sad excuse for a backpack, which was stuffed with pouches, cooking gear, and a wooden coffer. Scrolled up parchments extended from various rips as well as the main opening of the pack. Clearly all of these were getting in Thorik's way of finding what he was searching for.

At the grassy base of the mountain the crowd of hundreds began to scatter from the terrifying sight of the creature on the rock wall. Only a few stayed close to Thorik instead of escaping the open area and running into the surrounding forest. These included Avanda and her green dragon, Pheosco, and Thorik's uncle who stood in shock of the approaching creatures.

"There it is!" Pulling out a small pouch of flat stones, Thorik threw his frail pack to his uncle. "Take it to safety, Brimmelle! I'll hold off this creature!"

The punch of the backpack hitting his chest snapped Thorik's uncle out of his fear induced trance. Grabbing the bag out of pure instinct, Brimmelle put the pack's strap over one shoulder while turning and bolting back to the surrounding woods with the others. Nearly there, he met up with Narra, who had fallen onto her knees after running from the danger. "Are you hurt?"

"It's time!" She answered. With a full-term pregnancy, the onset of labor had been induced by the stress. Grabbing Brimmelle's hand, she stood back up to retreat into the forest with his help.

With everyone racing from the open grassy dell, Thorik gave a clear order to Avanda, "You too! Get to safety!"

Already crushing a handful of berries and stink bugs, she smirked at her dragon, Pheosco, less than half her size. "When have I ever let him give me orders?"

"Never, as far as I recall." Leaping up into the air, the dragon spread his green wings and took flight, heading up toward the attacker.

After some quick digging into the pouch of hexagonal stones, Thorik found the Runestone he was looking for and hung the pouch on his belt hook. "I can handle this!" Establishing a firm hold on both sides of the Runestone, he placed his thumbs and fingers tightly onto the small gems imbedded near some of the corners of the flat dark stone. Closing his eyes, he controlled his breathing and relaxed as the stone's energy raced up one arm, across his chest, and then back down the other arm to complete the circle and cause the large crystal in the center of the stone to glow.

Ignoring his instructions, Avanda continued preparing her spell components and began the physical gestures required to activate her magic. "Shoo-ka dar key octay."

Pheosco soared toward the creature's face and veered off at the last moment, causing the beast to snap out at the small dragon while leaping away from the mountain's rock wall.

Missing the green dragon, the creature lost its footing and plummeted directly at Thorik and Avanda; both of which were too busy to pay attention to events above them.

Widening its mouth and claws, it prepared for their capture upon landing.

"Tu Ra Gi!" shouted Avanda upward, effectively causing a spray of deadly poisonous gas overhead within the path of the giant spiked-ridgeback lizard.

Entering the cloud of fumes, the creature prepared its lethal attack until it inhaled Avanda's magical spell. The facial scales quickly began to burn away from the acid vapors and pockets of blood blisters along the gums of the creature immediately burst outward. The creature looked more hideous now than before as it approached the potential victims. The next moment would determine if the spell worked effectively enough or if the creature would kill its prey.

Before that moment could be taken, the creature was flung back up into the air and then slapped hard against the wall of the mountain. The powers of Thorik's Runestone had successfully shot a force of energy out at the lizard-like creature while also knocking Thorik backward to the ground for a few tumbles.

Just inside of the tree line, Narra leaned against a tree as she breathed heavily from the contractions, as she prepared for the birth of her child. "Brimmelle, find someone who knows how to help me give birth. Quickly!"

Attempting to calm her, he patted her shoulder as one would pet a dog. He was completely out of his element, and yet he truly wanted to help. "I've trained others how to help with births, Narra." Hoping to give her comfort, he gave a hard swallow as he looked for assistance to arrive from the rest of the Dolor citizens hiding in the woods from the creatures of the wilderness.

Rolling back up to his feet after his successful use of the Runestone, Thorik smiled while rubbing his neck from the unexpected impact on himself. "It worked!"

"What did you do that for?" Avanda was visibly upset at what had transpired. The soft discolored lines that decorated her body, known as soul-markings, turned a few shades darker.

"What? I just saved us!"

"No, I was about to save us. One more gasp in those vapors and he would have fallen dead at our feet."

"Are you serious? He might have died, but he would have taken us with him. He was going to land directly on top of us."

"You think you know everything, don't you?"

"No. However, I can tell when I'm about to get flattened by a ton of death heading my way."

"I hate to interrupt your little love spat, but..." Pheosco said as he flapped his wings to stay airborne a few yards from them.

"What is it?" They both shouted at the same time, glaring at Pheosco.

"Neither of you succeeded and both of you have made it very angry."

Pulling itself back up onto its feet, the creature appeared more hideous and terrifying then before. Growling, it glared at Thorik and Avanda and it was clear it had only one thought in mind; to devour the food before it.

Thorik returned to his Runestone just in time to block the leap of the creature upon them. The stone's power pushed the beast over and past them, knocking it toward the woods.

Flames shot toward the beast after a quick spell was conjured by Avanda, spraying it with thousands of blazing pebbles. It was just a matter of moments before the creature's scales were glowing from the heat and fire.

Another pounding blow from the power of Thorik's Runestone and another wave of fire from Avanda's spell caused the giant beast to turn and run into the woods. This was the same woods where hundreds of followers had sought refuge and the same woods that were now on fire due to the burning creature racing through the foliage as it attempted to extinguish the flames by rolling in the dirt and brush.

"No!" Avanda could believe her eyes. "Thorik, what have you done?"

"Me? I didn't light it on fire!"

"You practically tossed the creature on top of our friends!"

Pheosco zipped past overhead. "Can I get some help here?" Arching his body, he sprinted through the trees, yelling instructions to help communicate movement to avoid the beast.

As the creature roared in pain and ravaged the forest in search of a way to stop the fire, a crowd of hundreds raced back out of the woods toward safety in the open field. Thorik and Avanda stopped their bickering long enough to race over to help whoever they could.

The citizens of Dolor included all age groups and many species. The majority were Human and Polenum; Num for short. The Nums where about a head shorter than Humans and had dark soul-markings on their pale skin tones. In addition to these two species, there were many Ov'Unday species which ranged from the tall Mognins, who stood twice the height of humans, to the small Quix that were the size of a man's fist.

Thorik and Avanda's large friend, Grewen, coordinated efforts to ensure everyone was safely removed from harm's way. The giant Mognin personally carried over eight people as well as dragged a wagon of supplies into the clearing.

Brimmelle assisted Narra back into the dell with the help of her young daughter, Revi. As he did so, it was obvious that he was searching for someone else to step in and take ownership of the birthing process. Every few steps Narra took, she had to stop from a contraction. There wasn't much time.

There they all stood, watching the wailing beast set the entire surrounding woods ablaze. They were now trapped in the semicircle of fire up against the steep mountain wall, and would have to stay there until the flames died out.

"Gather next to the rocks at the mountain's base!" Attempting to take charge again, Thorik continued to support the young and old out of harm's way.

Avanda helped as well, while Brimmelle and Revi assisted the slow movement of Narra, as everyone was in a rush to move themselves to the small area of safety from the now raging forest fire. Children, the elderly, and those with injuries were assisted along with Narra as they collectively worked together to avoid the danger.

Not being able to see past the first few feet into the woods, it was a surprise to everyone when the beast jumped out onto the grassy knoll. Still on fire, it was going to make one last attack.

Narra screamed and fell to her knees, but her tone was not one of fear. It was one of pain. It was time. She was giving birth.

Brimmelle removed Thorik's backpack from his shoulder, tossed it down, and quickly jumped to Narra's side. As the spiritual leader of his village, known as a Fir, he had trained many Nums on a variety of skills, and yet he had never actually performed most of them. This would include the act of helping give birth. Helpless, he searched for assistance from others.

Grabbing a handful of his shirt and some of his skin, Narra barked orders, "Brimmelle, help me bring this child into this world!"

Nodding, Fir Brimmelle swallowed hard and began the process as a few women surrounded them and fanned their dresses out to give her what little privacy they could while keeping an eye on the battle coming their way.

Avanda and Thorik meanwhile aggressively used their skills to beat the creature back from the travelers. Unwilling to see it suffer any longer than necessary, Thorik caused the final blow to put it out of its misery. Breathless from the battle, they paused for a moment and gazed at one another. Slight smiles and nods told each other what they needed to know and a long firm hug ended their prior argument. They had overcome the threat, and they had proven again how strong of a team they could be.

A woman's voice was suddenly heard above all others. "What are you doing?" The shout was easily heard across the small field, as Narra screamed at Brimmelle. "I thought you knew how this worked!"

His response was soft and nervous. "I do. It's just different in practice than the trainings. It's so much more rushed and emotional."

Grabbing him with a hold that cut off his arm's blood flow, she yanked him in toward her. "If you don't start helping me, you're going to wish you stayed in those woods!"

Nodding, Brimmelle broke free of her tight grip and moved into position. "I'm ready. Start pushing."

"I am pushing!"

"Good. Keep doing that."

Trying his best, he knew he was in over his head. And to his relief a few women from the crowd came forward to help them through the process. There was screaming and crying as it continued, but Brimmelle wiped his eyes clear and tried to control himself as he kept attempting to help.

Narra also did some yelling of her own, and after a while she delivered her son who was quickly cleaned and bundled up in a blanket by various helpers before handing the child to Brimmelle who had returned to her side.

"Here is your son, Narra." Brimmelle lowered the infant and leaned forward to show her the newborn's face. "I'm sorry his father, Gansler, didn't survive our escape from the city to reflect upon this child's beauty."

"It wasn't your fault." Taking the child from him, she pulled the newborn close and breathed in the infant's smell. "It was Thorik who talked Gansler into attempting the escape. Now I will be forced to raise my children in the wilderness instead of the safety of our city and home."

Avanda quickly made her way over to see if Narra and her newborn were healthy. Upon arrival, she beamed with excitement at the sight of the baby. "He's beautiful."

With the creature no longer a threat, Thorik knew they just needed to wait out the forest fire, so after making sure everyone was safe he took a moment to join Avanda in congratulating Narra on the birth of her son. "What a lovely baby. You must be so proud. Greatest of wishes to this child on this special day."

"Greatest of wishes?" Brimmelle reached over and grabbed Thorik's pack, which his nephew had thrown to him earlier. His initial body language appeared as though he was going to heave it at Thorik in anger. Scrolled up papers flew out of the pack and scattered about the ground surrounding Fir Brimmelle. Instead, he slammed it back onto the ground and grabbing several of the scrolls, wielding them like swords at his nephew. "There is no greatest of wishes here, thanks to you. It is because of you that this child will never see his home, his city, or his father." Slapping Thorik with the papers, he continued. "It is because of you that he was born in this wilderness filled with dangerous creatures." Slapping him again with the documents the parchments began to unravel and fall open.

"Brimmelle! Stop! Those documents are all we have from Gansler. Don't destroy them. His written words are all his family has left." Thorik had his hands out to protect himself from the rolled up paper slaps to his head. "Please listen, Uncle. If I hadn't helped these citizens escape they would all be dead right now. Why can't you believe me when I tell you that Deleth had planned to destroy the city and the people within it now that he obtained his crystal for Lu'Tythis Tower? We lost some loved ones in our fight to escape, but at the end of the day we saved these people!"

Brimmelle stood motionless as he stared at the open documents before him until his hands began to shake causing the parchments to vibrate. "You may have saved these people, but you've killed everyone in Terra Australis."

Not knowing what his uncle meant, Thorik didn't know how to respond to the statement. "How exactly did I do that?"

Fir Brimmelle pulled his chest up slightly as he continued to shake. He began to read one of the ancient teachings of the Mountain King scribed on the documents. Word for word, Brimmelle knew that these were the exact lessons he had given his villagers for most of his life.

Thorik recognized them immediately. "The scrolls of the Mountain King? Where did Gansler find them?"

"He didn't."

"If he didn't find them, how else did he come into possession of them?

Brimmelle showed the documents to Thorik.

"Yes. I can see they are in Gansler's own handwriting." Looking down at Narra, he asked, "Where did he copy these from?"

She shook her head in sadness.

"Thorik?" Brimmelle's hands turned to fists and he held out the documents toward his nephew. "Do you understand what you've done?"

"I…I don't think so."

"We've travelled back in time, correct?"

"Yes. The Govi Glade sent us here, thousands of years before we were born."

"Perhaps before the Mountain King came to power and fought off the Notarians, causing us to live free lives?"

"Yes, that's very likely seeing that we haven't met anyone that knows who the Mountain King is."

Straightening his arms toward Thorik with the document in hand, Brimmelle was furious. "These are the original writings of the Mountain King."

"No. They are Gansler's writings." As the words left his mouth, Thorik realized what his brain was trying to block out. "Gansler was the Mountain King?"

"And now that you've taken actions that have caused his death, there will never be a Mountain King. Therefore there will be no great battle for freedom and our kind will be slaves forever!"

Churning through his thoughts, Thorik attempted to prove his uncle wrong, but couldn't. "What have I done? I've killed the Mountain King!"

Chapter 2
Protection

Avanda had led Revi away from the confrontation between Brimmelle and Thorik. She felt someone needed to be thinking of the young girl as Narra's focus was now on the newborn. Knowing what it felt like to be left out, she kneeled down to talk with her about what she had seen. However, Revi gazed past Avanda as though she wasn't even there. Her face turned from concern to horror at what she viewed up above them.

Several yards away, Thorik stood in shock. Realizing his actions had caused the death of the most important figure in history made him blind and deaf to the chaos that surrounded him. Hundreds of Dolor citizens screamed and ran from the mountain's sheer cliff. They quickly moved as close as they could to the forest fire without harming themselves. He was oblivious to the mass chaos until he was knocked over by one of the many people running in panic.

"The E'rudites tried to stop me from my decisions that led to his death. Why didn't I listen?" Struggling to pull himself out of his own state of reality, Thorik started realizing that the Dolor citizens were running in fear away from the rock wall. His first thought was that another giant lizard-like creature was working its way down toward them. Peering up, his heart sank.

"Wake up!" Pheosco flew just over his head, attempting to snap him from his frozen stance, before heading up the cliff.

Well over a dozen of the lizard-like creatures raced down the side of the mountain toward the small grassy area were the citizens were trapped and ready for the eating.

Thorik knew it would be up to Avanda and himself to stop them, for the citizens had few weapons and the skills of miners instead of warriors.

Avanda had just finished a spell encasing Revi within a protective egg-like sphere, which was translucent aside from oily swirls giving away its surface. There hadn't been time for her to get the child to safety so this was her immediate response before addressing the coming attack.

Seeing that Avanda was already preparing a spell on her side of the open area, Thorik began to utilize the powers of his Runestones. Struggling to concentrate, he knew that his Runestones and Avanda's spells would only be able to stop a few of the attackers. If they were fortunate on this day, perhaps a few of the Dolor citizens would survive this slaughter. However, it was unlikely that the creatures would leave anyone alive on purpose.

Glancing over at Avanda, he could see her strong focus and determination in what she did. She had no thoughts of what the most likely outcome would be from this event. As always, she was in the here and now. It was a place that allowed her to handle every situation as it came to her.

The here and now was not Thorik's strong suit. His mind always looked into the future and how his actions could change the options and opportunities. The idea of hope for calmer days and peace were always in his dreams, so close to reality and yet always too far away to reach. Now with the Mountain King gone, it was difficult to foresee any such future.

Pheosco soared recklessly close to the invaders, attempting to cause them to lose focus and trip on their way down the steep rock wall. Whenever given the opportunity, he shot out small sprays of fire at their eyes. His mission was not to stop them, but simply to increase the odds of Thorik and Avanda in their tasks.

Taking Avanda's lead, Thorik gained control over his emotions and focused on his Runestone just in time to utilize its powers to slap back several of the creatures.

A few more creatures fell near Avanda as they gasped for air with lungs that had been eaten away from her magical mist.

Stopping the first wave of attack was not celebrated, for the following wave of creatures were able to learn from the mistakes of the prior fallen beasts. In doing so, they evaded the spells and Runestone powers and successfully landed in the grassy opening before leaping at the citizens of Dolor.

More creatures raced down the wall and only a few were stopped by Thorik and Avanda. The ones that made it past them were now engaging the crowd and leaping at their first victims.

One of the first raced to Revi and slapped its massive mouth around her from both sides. The powerful jaws and sharp teeth of the creature pressed hard against the protective semi-transparent shell Avanda had placed around her. Too large to swallow, and too hard to crush, the creature began slapping the sphere against the rock wall to break open the magical eggshell while Revi screamed from inside the giant lizard's mouth.

Grewen and the other giant Mognins attempted to block their paths or grapple with the oncoming beasts, but the creatures were too hard to restrain for just one Mognin.

Blocking an attack onto the citizens, Grewen used his size and weight to knock one of the attackers to its side. However, it quickly rolled to its feet and jumped upon the Mognin, pinning him to the ground. Grewen grabbed the creature by the neck to keep it from biting at him until he was able to maneuver his legs under the lizard. He then pressed with his massive legs upward, catapulting the creature into the forest.

Narra held her newborn son tight as one of the creatures raced forward and leaped directly at her.

Uncharacteristically, Brimmelle stepped in front of her to block the attack. It may have been the first selfless act he had made in a decade and it would appear that it would be last time he would ever have the opportunity to do so.

Revi screamed in fear as the giant lizard continued to pound her protective shield against the mountain's wall. Each strike caused the oily swirls to spin fasted on the shield's mostly transparent surface. It was unclear how long it would take the creature's abuse before collapsing.

Grewen was too far away to help save them, and Thorik and Avanda were busy dealing with more creatures arriving. Brimmelle was on his own to save her, as he braced himself for the creature's impact upon his body. Even if he could save Narra and her son from this attack, there were far too many creatures to stop them all.

It was then that all of the creatures froze in their tracks and even in midair. Each and every one of them became motionless as though time for them had stopped while time continued on for all others.

Brimmelle slowly opened one eye to find a large claw only inches from his head. The beast it belonged to was mid-leap and ready to pounce on him. The weight of the creature would have crushed the Fir as well as Narra and her child, should time have continued equally for all. Gathering Narra and her son, he removed them from the creature's trajectory just in case the beast's state changed back to normal.

The only thing in the air still moving was a confused green dragon, who continued to circle the dell, waiting for the battle to continue.

Avanda searched to Thorik for answers, but his confused look told her that this event was not of his doing either.

What seemed like several minutes of uneasy quiet, was truly only seconds before the forest fire was unexpectedly extinguished, followed by the arrival of the E'rudite, Wyrlyn, and his apprentice, Irluk. Their powers were far greater than Thorik or Avanda could comprehend.

The E'rudites would easily protect the travelers from the dangers in the wilderness.

Relief flooded the emotions of nearly everyone at the sight of the two individuals entering the grassy clearing on a Faralope-pulled wagon. Lying between them on the wagon's bench, a young black panther snuggled up next to her owner, Wyrlyn.

Ending the protective spell surrounding Revi, Avanda lowered the girl from the open mouth of the beast before heading toward the E'rudites.

Brimmelle was one of the few that were not so pleased. "Where have you been?" he shouted. "We were nearly killed!"

The young black panther, Pantera, hissed at the approaching Num.

"See, I told you that they wouldn't be thankful." Lightly running her thumb up from the bridge of the cat's nose, Irluk stroked the cat's face to calm her down before looking back into her book. She ignored the people she had just helped save as their wagon continued to roll forward into the clearing.

Wyrlyn gave a soft smile. "You have always been too quick to judge. Fear is expressed in many ways. Many lash out in response to this emotion. It doesn't mean they are not thankful, and even if it was true we should always do what is right, regardless."

Avanda couldn't get past how many of Wyrlyn's facial features and body gestures were so similar to their friend, Ambrosius; an E'rudite that they had befriended thousands of years in the future before falling back in time. "Thank goodness you've returned. And just in time."

Wyrlyn stopped the wagon near the center of the open area. "You were not at the designated rendezvous, so we surmised that you were having some difficulties."

"Difficulties?" Brimmelle's voice was overly sarcastic as he glanced about at the still frozen creatures in mid-attack mode. His wide soul-markings grew darker than normal as his anger increased. "You call preparing to be eaten by beasts or racing from them into flaming woods as some *difficulties*?"

Irluk peered over the top of her book at him. "As minor as they are, yes."

Avanda could see that Fir Brimmelle was straightening his shirt and preparing for a verbal assault, so she stepped in to prevent it. "Well, we're thankful for your timely return. With that said, I think we'd all be more at ease if we could leave this area before these creatures regain their momentum."

Brimmelle wasn't going to allow her to speak for him. "If you're so powerful, just get rid of these beasts. Snap your fingers and end their existence."

Watching the cat leap off the wagon to stretch her legs, Irluk turned to her master. "Brimmelle has a lot of anger in him for a Num. Weren't they designed to be more passive?"

Wyrlyn nodded as he stepped down from the wagon. "Yes. However, there are always outliers within every species developed. It could be caused from variances in diet, or the onset of malnutrition, or perhaps even issues of inbreeding. More study will have to take place to tell for sure."

"Inbreeding? Inbreeding!" Brimmelle's pale skin turned a bright red as he digested the comments.

Ignoring Brimmelle, Wyrlyn addressed Avanda. "I suggest we continue on to Pwellus Dementa' in order to determine what will be done with them."

The Fir was not about to be dismissed. "What? You can't be serious. We've been hiking for days and these people are exhausted. Narra just gave birth, she's not fit to travel. Besides, it's nearly evening and this is one of the few clear settings we have run across. Why don't you just kill these things so we can stay?"

Wyrlyn calmly turned to address the questions. "This is their territory which you have entered. I see no justification to kill a creature for being itself and protecting its land. We are the invaders in this situation and we shall leave these creatures to their own. Those who wish to stay may surely do so, with the understanding that once I leave the area all time will flow at the same speed for all walks of life."

Before Brimmelle could respond, Avanda resolved his main concern. "We'll have Grewen carry Narra and her children the rest of the way to ensure they have time to rest."

"I don't understand why we have to do everything his way," Brimmelle responded to her.

Wyrlyn gave another soft grin. "You don't have to do anything I say. You were designed to have free will and I encourage you to utilize it. However, if you wish to continue to receive my support, then you will follow my lead. I didn't ask you and your people for help. It was the other way around."

"Designed?" Brimmelle was horrified at the concept. "Polenums are not some breed of grazer that is selectively bred to our needs!"

Wyrlyn appreciated the comparison. "That is an excellent analogy as to how the Notarians altered native Thrashers to create the more docile species known as Polenums."

The Fir was aghast at the notion. So much so, that he couldn't even begin to explain how wrong the concept could be.

"Brimmelle, I think it's best if you focus on helping Narra right now." Avanda attempted to be compassionate to his feelings about the subject for Narra's sake. "Once we reach Pwellus Dementa' we will be safe from the wilderness and we can determine what to do next."

Tossing his hands in the air, Fir Brimmelle gave up on the discussion and returned to Narra and her children.

Nearby, the black panther hunted about for her next meal. Chasing small little Quixes from time to time, the little marsupials quickly scattered, avoiding the cat. Pantera settled for a stray squirrel that had evaded the fire.

"We are very thankful for what you have given us," Avanda said to Wyrlyn. "You've provided us guidance and route to a protected city. We're in your debt."

"No debt. I do, however, have a question for you."

"I'll answer if I can."

"You appear to have taken the lead of this collection of species." Glancing off to side, Wyrlyn could see Thorik away from all the rest, down on one knee and with his head hanging low. "Has Thorik been defeated in some way that provided you with authority?"

Avanda gave off a quick unexpected burst of a laugh before replying. "First of all, who is to say he was ever leading the citizens of Dolor? I'm the one that led them to their final victory in our escape from that mining city."

"I was not aware of that. So, why does he appear to be in a state of grief and solitude?"

Avanda followed his gaze to Thorik and sighed. "He just found out that he is responsible for the death of the Mountain King who was supposed to lead a war to free all of the slaves from the Notarians."

"I've never heard of such a tale."

"That's because it hasn't happened yet for you and those that live in this time."

"Apparently nor will it, seeing that the King is now dead." Stepping away, Wyrlyn headed toward Thorik.

Avanda scrunched her nose at his comment. "How is that possible?"

"How is what possible?" Irluk said from behind her book.

Popping her head up, Avanda could see the apprentice sitting cross legged on the front bench of the wagon while her long dark hair waved in the breeze. "How is it that the King has died and will not win the war, and yet I still know of him?"

Setting her book flat on her lap, Irluk's face was serious and cold. "By you returning to your history and changing it, you have created a rift that is racing through the years toward your own existence. Once it reaches you there is a very good chance you will never exist, causing you to never have returned to this time and Thorik never killing the King. This in turn will cause you and Thorik to be born and kill the King again, creating an endless paradox that will eventually fold in upon itself and destroy time itself!"

Avanda didn't understand half of what was just said. However, the other half was extremely frightening. "Is that true?"

"I have no idea. The killing of this King could also just create a new timeline of its own causing this future to be different than yours."

Letting out a sigh of relief, Avanda felt a little better. "That doesn't sound as bad."

"Absolutely. It only means that you're now stuck in this timeline and will never be able to return to your time and home, because it doesn't really exist anymore. And it most likely means the war you were talking about never happens and the Notarians stay in power."

"You're just a fountain of good news. Do you have any spells in that book that can make this scenario any better for us?"

Looking up from her book, she smiled. "Spells? What do you know of spells?"

"Some. Enough. Why?"

"Spells are a forbidden topic to the E'rudites."

"I'm sorry, but I assumed you had spells."

Glancing up to make sure her master was out of earshot she nodded. "I do, but we are not to discuss them in front of Wyrlyn. The last time I attempted to explain the value of them to him he nearly ended my apprenticeship."

"I didn't realize it had to be hidden."

"Well it does, but I have a new technique that is allowing me to practice without being caught." Patting the seat next to her, she invited Avanda up onto the wagon.

Accepting the offer, Avanda climbed up into the wagon to see what Irluk had been hiding.

Pulling a large leather bound book out from under a few blankets, Irluk placed it on her lap and unfolded the first flap before opening the front cover. "I call her Vesik."

Avanda's eyes widened larger than they had ever before as she stared at the book that she became addicted to back in her own time.

After opening the cover, Irluk began flipping through the blank pages. "It looks empty, but I already have embodied it with several special spells. No one can see them without our permission."

"Our?"

"Vesik and mine. I've given it a life of its own."

Avanda's eyes gazed at the book and her hands trembled slightly. "How did you create life?"

"Well, I didn't actually create life. I just gave it a small piece of my essence."

Slowly, Avanda reached over to feel Vesik's leather cover. It was a physical touch that she had missed so much.

Irluk quickly slammed the book shut and tied the outer leather strap tight before hiding it back under the blankets. "Not here. I don't want my Master to see us looking at it."

Avanda was in slight shock. She had assumed she would never see the book again.

Sitting back up straight, Irluk opened her prior book. "So, tell me about your spells. What have you learned?

"Thorik?" Wyrlyn strolled over, only to find his panther coiled up and sleeping against the Num.

Sitting at the base of a rock near the cliff wall, the Num lifted his head to see a man resembling his good friend, Ambrosius. Tall and lean with mahogany colored hair, his stride and facial features were uncanny similar. "Don't come any closer, Wyrlyn. You don't want me in your company."

A slight grin was exposed while finding a comfortable place to sit on a nearby fallen boulder. "And why is that?"

Waking from her owner's voice, Pantera stretched and moved over to him.

"I'm a menace. My presence acts as an epidemic that kills all that comes near. Everything I've touched my entire life has ended in ruins."

"Surely you're overstating the issues."

"No. Not really. When I was young, I attempted to save my parents in a mudslide which caused my mother's death in her attempt to save me. When I tried to help Ambrosius stop the destruction of the Dovenar Kingdom, it ended in his own demise, only for him to return later to stop me from causing the death of the Mountain King, which I did anyway." Lowering his head into his hands, he continued. "I am a death sentence to all that are near me. So perhaps it would be best if I stayed behind while you helped these people who no longer have a home because of my actions."

"If that is what you wish." His words were casual and without emotions.

"No, that is not what I wish. But the danger of me being around is too great for you to take any other actions."

"I see. You feel your decisions will destroy me and my civilization. I had no idea that you were this powerful."

"That's not what I meant, and you know it."

"Thorik, I do not know your history, but you do not strike me as one who willfully plans to hurt others. Irluk and I healed your Dolor battle injuries prior to leaving the Govi Glade and we're more than willing to assist with any new wounds. Everyone is healthy enough to travel, so I suggest you continue with us to Pwellus Dementa' and then you can determine your destiny from there."

Taking a moment to look back up at the creatures still floating motionless in time during their attack, he nodded. "Agreed. I don't really want to be here when they continue their hunt for food."

Standing up, Thorik began brushing off his clothes before he noticed a large brown dragon and a colorful bird flying into the clearing. "Chug and Granna have returned!"

The beginnings of a growl from Pantera was softened to a purr once Wyrlyn placed a hand down to gently touch her head as they all watched the two new arrivals make their way into the opening, as they scouted for Thorik.

Landing in his typical clumsy fashion, the Chuttlebeast-sized brown dragon was very uncomfortable with the motionless giant lizard-like creatures in the clearing. With heightened cautious instincts he made his way to the Num and planted a quick slap of his tongue upside Thorik's head, nearly knocking him down.

"It's good to see you, Chug." Wiping the saliva from the side of his face with one hand, he petted the dragon with the other. "Were you able to salvage anything for us from within the city of Dolor?"

Lowering his head, it was clear that they couldn't.

"The glacier had collapsed and the avalanche completely buried the city, dear. There is nothing left of the city of Dolor to salvage." The answer came from the large multicolored bird that casually landed on one of the arms of the frozen ferocious lizards. With two oversized eyes that worked independently on her bright orange and red feathered head, the odd looking bird jerked its head about as it talked.

"Thank you for checking, Granna." Catching the questioning look upon Wyrlyn's face, Thorik leaned over slightly to pose next to the bird over half his height before making his attempt at dry humor. "What? Can't you see the resemblance between my grandmother and me?"

Chapter 3
Pwellus Dementa'

Thorik Log:
It's been weeks since the Dolor city miners found the Keystone for Deleth, and he showed his appreciation by destroying the city with a cave-in of rock and ice. A large part of the city's Mognin population transported the giant crystal to the Lu'Tythis Tower, seeing that they were the strongest of the citizens. Fortunate to escape with our lives, Wyrlyn and Irluk are leading the remaining of them to the Notarian city of Pwellus Dementa' so they can live safe from the creatures of the wild. I am pleased they will find what they are looking for, but I am doubtful that I can ever be truly happy again, knowing that I am responsible for the Mountain King's death.

Spruce and evergreens filled the lower regions of the snowcapped mountain river valley that followed the river back and forth around foothills and outcropping. Life of this river was born from a mountain's glacier and a series of waterfalls, each of various heights, as they fed a small lake below them. Upstream and on the far side of the lake was an opening, not a cave or inlet caused by erosion or water flow, this was a glacier crafted into a grand entrance of geometric designs. The dense ice gave off bluish hues and exposed long thin crystals which carried light throughout, inviting safe harbor to all who wished to enter.

As Thorik and Avanda followed the wagon that Wyrlyn, Irluk, and Pantera rode upon, their initial assessment of the opening's size was vastly underestimated. The base width alone was at least one hundred yards across, and every inch of its flooring was meticulously etched in fractal patterns.

The cool air of the glacial entrance felt refreshing against their exposed skin after a long day of traveling. Searching forward, the length of the entrance was difficult to measure as it slowly ramped upward before leveling off a mile or two up the way. Clean and free of any signs of life, or even dirt from other travelers, the glowing passage felt holy in nature.

Avanda grabbed Thorik's hand. She was obviously excited and nervous at the same time. They had seen many wonders of the world, but none such as this.

Cautious as usual, Thorik felt comfort from Avanda's hand as he jerked his head from side to side and front to back, waiting for something to go terribly wrong. "Calm before the storm?"

"Calm before the grand, my dear." Gluic had been riding on the back of the wagon enjoying the sights. "I'm so glad to be back."

"Back? Granna, we've never been here before."

"You haven't, dear. But your grandmother has a few more miles on her than you may be aware of."

Eventually, the long entrance opened up into an underworld filled with a pure white light that emanated from six grand angled columns that reached down from the cavernous ceiling to the center of a beautiful city. Each of these light blue shafts glistened and sparkled from their base all the way up until they merged into the ceiling. The columns themselves were slightly translucent crystals and had grown from a single region within the city, currently out of view.

The city itself was built with the finest of white and black marble stones, some the length of the buildings themselves. Green, blue, and dark red marble had been used as accents and to distinguish individual buildings. Decorative wall surfaces over entrances were filled with carved statues that bridged over the smaller stone columns of each building, which impressively still rose over thirty feet into the air.

Water fell from the high cavernous ceiling, landing perfectly into open pools and grand artistic stone fountains at the crossroads of several streets. Art and function acted as one for the public while other waterfalls descended directly into some of the larger buildings. Various statues lined the streets with candles and melted wax upon them. All unique from one another, they each had a pocket or pouch that held paper, ink, and a quill.

Grewen reached his long Mognin arms out to catch the falling water in his oversized hands before hitting one of the fountains. Pulling it back in and tasting it, he was satisfied enough to fill a few barrels for the thirsty travelers.

Aside from the newcomers, the streets were filled with local Humans, Nums, Mognins, Gathlers, and many more who were all dressed with fine clothes and jewelry. Most buildings along these streets appeared open to the public. However, a few structures were guarded by tall red Blothruds or various types of Dragons between the size of Chug and Pheosco.

Most of the local residents were busy hanging bright and colorful banners and streamers from the buildings and over the streets. The vibrant cloths played off the contrasting black and white marble structures, giving them a celebratory feel.

Leading the Dolor citizens down the primary street, Wyrlyn smiled at the decorations as he stopped the wagon in the street halfway down a block. "The Freedom Festival appears to be taking everyone's mind off of their daily duties."

Thorik overheard the comment as he approached the side of the wagon. "Festival? For what?"

"Soon, the rest of the Notarians will be arriving to colonize this land. This event is how the locals have chosen to spiritually purify these lands so that the future is bright for all to enjoy."

Wyrlyn snapped the Faralope's reins and pulled the wagon into a stable area filled with a variety of other wagons and coaches. Stepping down from his ride, he pulled a lantern from a shelf, lit it, and placed it in the hand of a nearby statue.

A sickly green glow grew from the lantern's flame. As it did, the statue that was now carrying the lantern began to move. And with its free hand it reached up and grabbed the reins of the Faralope. The statue then continued the process of putting the Faralope in one of the stalls before pushing the wagon against a far wall.

As the statue performed its duties, Pantera causally worked her way into the street before abruptly being surprised by Chug's face poking in the doorway. The cat's quick reflexes dodged the dragon's lick before arching her back and hissing at him.

Amused, Pheosco was calmly perched on the brown dragon's neck. "I've told you not to play with your food, Chug," he said as the panther worked her way into the crowd.

Meanwhile, Wyrlyn and Irluk grabbed their items and walked back out to meet Thorik and Avanda, who had both been watching the stone statue come to life.

"Master, I must be going if I am to study the effects of the Keystone crystal now that it is installed in the Lu'Tythis Tower." Irluk was clearly in a hurry to leave. "I missed the installation, but I do not wish to miss its calibration."

"Understood." Wyrlyn nodded his approval. "It may take a few weeks for the harmonics to stabilize, so ensure you give Deleth the needed resources."

"I will." She hesitated before continuing. "May I take an assistant to support my collection of information?"

"Do what you must." Wyrlyn turned back to the hundreds of displaced Dolor citizens. "I will inquire about the options available for our followers." Pointing down the street to direct the green dragon, they began to lead the massive group further into the majestic city, all following Pheosco on his winged mount.

Near the front of the parade of visitors, Avanda was pulled from Thorik's hand and then off to the side by Irluk. "You're not going with them."

Nodding back to Thorik that all was well and for him to continue, Avanda then turned to Irluk. "What's going on?" She then gave a quick glance to see if Pheosco had seen her removal from the parade down the street. He had not.

Thorik looked back twice for reassurance that all was fine before stepping up near Wyrlyn in the lead.

"You're coming with me." Grabbing Avanda's hand tightly, Irluk began leading her on a brisk walk under one of the many festive decorative banners and down a side street.

"Where? How long will we be away?"

"Only for a few hours. They are safe here in this city. It will give us some time alone to discuss...things."

Avanda considered the idea. "I should at least see if Thorik or Pheosco want to join us."

"No. I don't know how they feel about spells or if they will alert Wyrlyn of my spell book, Vesik."

"True. I don't believe they would be very supportive of such actions."

"Agreed. Then let's be on our way."

"Wait! I need to at least let them know where I'm going."

"Then you might as well not bother coming with me. I've seen the way Thorik and Pheosco look at me. They don't trust me for some reason. The moment you tell them about our side trip, it will be over for you."

Tightly pressing her lips together, Avanda was frustrated at the fact that she knew Irluk was correct. "Well, I can't just disappear. I need to let them know I'm safe."

"Not a hindrance to our plans." Stopping at one of the many statues along the sides of the streets, Irluk pulled out the needed supplies from the open sack carved against his side and quickly wrote a note before she placed it in the statue's hand. She then lit a few of the many small candles randomly placed upon the statue. Once the sickly green light emerged from the oil-based candles, the statue came to life. "Give this note to Wyrlyn. He will be at the city's pantry."

Once she ended her instructions, the statue calmly turned and slowly headed back down the street from where they came.

Putting her papers back in her pack, Irluk turned to her new friend. "There, now that that's taken care of, we need to make haste. We are missing a one-time experience. You will be one of the few in history to witness this amazing change in our world."

Taking her by the hand again, Irluk led Avanda down several more streets filled with larger than life structures and artistic creations. It was everything Avanda could do to keep up as she continually turned back and forth to inhale the fragrances and sights along their speedy journey.

It wasn't long before they came to an open grassy piazza filled with art far superior and grand than any Avanda had ever seen. Paths circled the large open lawn and a few led directly to the center which housed an enormous dark grey hexagonal stone platform with tall glowing crystal columns at each one of its six angles. These were the columns that crisscrossed and then spread out and connected to the ceiling of the underground city, which they had seen when they first arrived.

Each side of the platform had two wide steps leading up onto the platform. Decorative and perfectly cut, they had been etched with various scenes.

Running up to the open structure, Irluk pulled Avanda around to the far side. "If we want to go to the Lu'Tythis Tower, we need to enter from the correct side."

"Correct side?" All sides looked identical except for a few small colored marble blocks, perfectly inlaid in each staircase.

"Of course." They stopped at the side with a blue veined marble slab built into the platform just past the steps.

"Let's go!" Stepping up to edge of the platform, she waited for Avanda to join her.

A blur of images raced through Avanda's mind from the past few minutes of running. "Go?" Slowly she stepped both feet onto the first step, and then the second step as she looked at the local residents in the piazza who were not paying any attention to them. "Go to the tower from here?" No passages were obvious as she looked between the crystal columns to other parts of the city.

Reaching out with a smile for reassurance, Irluk waited for her to take the final step.

One last glance around, she took a breath and grabbed Irluk's hand tight while stepping next to her.

Reaching around Avanda's waist, Irluk led her to the center of the hexagon platform before they stopped. It was then that Avanda realized that the opening between the two columns in front of her as well as the rest of the openings had been completely altered.

The one to their right appeared to be the inside of a temple, while the one to their left looked like the inside of the Weirfortus Dam.

Before Avanda had a chance to look at the rest, she was pulled back to the far right opening and through the two columns on the platform. Once they passed the threshold, they arrived inside a large round ash-black room with a staircase spiraling down as far as they could see. Aside from the stairs, a small ledge kept the two from falling down the open center of the room's stairwell. The two columns they had just walked through were now half merged into the wall, next to a metal doorway that shared the ledge.

The unexpected view of an endless pit before her caused Avanda to freeze for a moment to gain her bearings. "Where are we?"

Irluk took a few steps and opened the metal door to let in some sunlight and a view over all of Terra Australis. "We are on the top of the Lu'Tythis Tower, of course."

Chapter 4
Lu'Tythis Tower

On a small island in the enormous lake of Luthralum Tunia, the ash-black Lu'Tythis tower stood several thousand feet above its slightly wider base as though a limbless tree had grown from the earth. Looking over the distant Weirfortus Dam to the west, the White Summit's dormant volcano to the north, the faraway sharp Shi'Pel Peaks to the east, and the weatherworn Broken Walls of Farowcomp to the southwest, the tower was visible from most locations within Terra Australis.

Stepping outside onto the gallery deck surrounding the tower, Avanda was captivated by the view before her. The sensation of viewing the land from so high above was more than she had imagined. "This is amazing!"

Irluk looked down and shrugged. "It will be once we're finished with it."

"Finished?"

"Yes, the Keystone has now been installed." Pointing up above them, the only level higher than their deck was one supporting a massive crystal pointing directly up in the air.

"The Keystone." She quickly recalled seeing the crystal that was found in the Dolor mines. "What's its purpose?"

"It has a few. First of all it is an anchor and support."

"For what?"

A surprised expression swept across Irluk's face. "The dam, of course."

Avanda looked out at the very distant line in the horizon along the western edge of the lake. "Weirfortus?"

"Yes. The Keystone will push against the inside wall of the dam to give it strength as the water in Luthralum's lake is a few thousand feet lower than the ocean on the other side. Once the Keystone is proven to be in place, our fellow Notarians can return home from reinforcing this side of the dam and the lake can finish rising."

"Why is the water rising?"

"You really know nothing about this, do you?"

Still amazed at the sights of distant mountains and valleys, she smiled. "No."

"Well, in short, this entire area was an ocean inlet. The Weirfortus dam was built to keep the salty seawater out. Then the water inside the valley was pumped through the dam and back into the ocean on the other side. Through a process within the dam, salt water is now converted to fresh water and released into Luthralum Tunia until it provides enough fresh water for the valley without flooding more newly regained land than necessary. And just like that, we have a new livable valley paradise reclaimed from the sea to be used for our future."

"I understand about Weirfortus, but not about the Keystone."

"All things have energy. The energy and lattice structure of this giant quartz crystal provides the perfect harmonics for our needs. First, it has the ability to push upon objects. In our case, it is now starting to push on the dam to keep it strong against the ever pressing ocean on the far side."

"Wouldn't that cause this tower to tip over?"

"Exactly! That's why it also has to push against objects on the other side such as the White Summit and the Shi'Pel Peaks to balance it out."

"So, it's a brace of sorts?"

"Yes, but its magnetism also changes the weather in this region. Aside from the mountainsides, Terra Australis is a dried out barren ocean outlet. We are expecting that large portions of the current dry lands and deserts you see below us in every direction will begin to grow forests and grasslands once the weather has been modified."

"You can control the weather?"

"No, but the Keystone can increase or reduce the chance of rain in more consistent intervals. Without the Keystone, the majority of the regions will remain dry. If all goes well, periodic rains will come and go in controlled patterns. If the Keystone is not installed and aligned correctly or if the stone is ever damaged, our weather will become chaotic and immense storms will take the lands, preventing us from utilizing them. It's all about paradise, you know."

"Paradise?"

"Yes. That's the entire purpose of the Notarians coming here in the first place, in search of a location to create a paradise for themselves."

Taking out a small black leather book, Irluk began taking some notes about the cloud structure in each of several key regions. "It appears that only a few regions are starting to receive the planned weather patterns."

"So it didn't work?"

Laughing at the idea, Irluk placed her notes aside for the moment and removed Vesik from her pack. "I'm confident that it will function as planned seeing that this was Deleth's personal project. Although it could take several weeks before we will know for sure if the patterns begin to form properly. If so, I can start to monitor them once a day instead of several times a day."

Avanda was no longer listening to Irluk as she gazed at the book of spells.

"Hello? Are you going to be sick from the heights or something?"

"What? No. I'm fine. I'm just excited about seeing Vesik."

"Just so you know, Wyrlyn would not approve." Giving Avanda a devilish smirk, Irluk winked and opened the book for them both to view. "What he doesn't know won't hurt him."

Chapter 5
O'Gee and ZiXi

Streets were overflowing with the entire Dolor citizenship parading through the underground city of Pwellus Dementa', following Wyrlyn and Thorik. Pheosco continued to ride upon Chug as Grewen made his way up to them to view the path ahead. The walk was slow and steady to ensure no one fell behind; and in doing so it allowed for many to investigate the new location and residents while enjoying the amazing decorations being hung for the upcoming festival.

Brimmelle carried Narra's infant son while leading her and her daughter, Revi. He had become very attached to the newborn and proudly puffed up his chest as he marched toward the front. For the first time in his life he suddenly felt part of a family. Respected and cared for, Narra gave him a new purpose in life. After all of his years fighting for respect, the feeling of being a father trumped his old tired ways, even though he had no biological relationship.

"Oh, a baby!" a local youth cried out. Light brown hair and a fair complexion, even for a Num, the girl ran over to see Narra's child.

"Careful now!" Brimmelle protected the baby from misguided playfulness. "This is not a toy."

Stopping just before him, she gazed up into his face as though she was determining if he was joking or not. "I'm pretty sure I know the difference. May I see him?"

Instinctively pulling back a bit, he felt a soft touch of Narra's hand on his back, assuring him that there was no danger. And after fighting off the temptation to order the girl to leave, he opened his heart just a crack to lean down enough for a peek at Narra's infant.

"Oh my. He is a good looking lad. He must take after you, sir."

Brimmelle was struck with pride, embarrassment, and confusion. Even though the child was clearly not his, he had marched around as though it was. He struggled for words on how to respond.

"Thank you," Narra said. "He definitely is a handsome gentleman." Patting Brimmelle on the back, she smiled at his reaction.

"I'm O'Gee. Who are you?" Her clothes were clean and of the finest of cloths, but were in disarray much like her hair.

"This is Narra, Revi, and Revi's new brother. I'm Fir Brimmelle Riddlewood the Seventh of..." He failed to finish his sentence as he watched a small six-legged hairy creature crawl out from under her hair and onto her shoulder. "What in the name of the King is that?"

The mouse-sized marsupial had large eyes and a small puppy nose. "ZiXi. I go by ZiXi," it quipped back to answer his question.

O'Gee reached up and stroked her finger over ZiXi's little head. "Haven't you seen a Quix before?"

Brimmelle pulled the infant slightly away from what he considered to be a rodent. "No."

"Really? Just where are you from?" The girl started walking with the Dolor citizens as they meandered through the streets.

"Well..." Brimmelle readjusted his shoulders back to their normal square stance as he thought about the question. "Most everyone here is from the city of Dolor, a small mining location many days walk from here."

Reaching up to touch the baby's outstretched arm, O'Gee nodded. "I know where it is. But you're not from there, are you?"

"That's correct. I'm from a village called Farbank."

A puzzled look crossed her face. "I know of all sites created by the Notarians and that is not one of them."

"That is because it does not exist yet. I come here from a different location as well as from a different time. My grandparents originated from the base of the White Summit, where the great Mountain King statue was carved into the side of the mountain, standing over a thousand feet tall."

"That's sounds wonderful. Why would they leave such a place to live in Farbank?"

Brimmelle's voice changed to a story telling theatrical tone. "There was an event that changed their lives."

The girl had nearly forgotten about the infant as she and ZiXi were holding onto his every word. "An event?" they both said at once.

"Yes, according to family legend. It was the only time in history when the great solar eclipse coincided with the Seedtime Comet. The dusting of the comet's tail under the moon during the eclipse was told to be the most spectacular event of all time as the darkness lit up with an astonishing shower of falling stars."

"That must have been amazing!"

"Falling stars?" ZiXi rushed back under O'Gee's hair.

Enjoying the response of his small audience, Brimmelle continued entertaining them. "My grandparents took it as a beautiful sign that their world was about to change dramatically, and it did. A voice instructed them to travel downstream and start anew. They did just that and then raised a daughter who married the Fir of Farbank who eventually became my father."

O'Gee laughed with delight. "I would so very much have enjoyed seeing the day of the eclipse and comet event."

Puffing up his chest, he smiled proudly. "It was surely the most spectacular experience that ever happened, aside from the triumph of the Mountain King."

"Who's this Mountain King you keep talking about?"

Brimmelle realized they were starting to fall behind, so he started picking up the pace of his walk. "Oh, if you only knew the stories I could tell you about the Num who changed history."

"Do tell! I love good stories."

"Well, we don't have the time to stop and tell you everything."

"No need! I'll walk with you."

"Yes, we'll join you," said the small pixie voice of ZiXi, who was now cuddled up against Narra's infant, under the blanket.

Shocked by the unexpected guest in his arms, Brimmelle shot a glance of concern over to Narra.

Placing a calming hand upon him, she reassured him that all was well. "I've never met a Quix that was malicious; overly inquisitive and frequently playing pranks perhaps, but not dangerous."

In order to gain control over his instincts to save the child from the creature, he avoided looking at ZiXi while he started weaving the tales of the most courageous Num in history as they followed Thorik and Wyrlyn through the city and eventually out into an area without structures.

Chapter 6
Food for the Taking

W yrlyn led Thorik's party and the citizens of Dolor into a large open area reaching all the way back to the cavern walls over a mile away. This area was filled a third of the way to the walls with hearty crops and orchards being harvested while seeds were being planted by those that worked the sections of open fields.

An unnatural illumination of light from above gave off a warm refreshing feeling upon Thorik's face as he breathed in the smell of freshly tilled earth. Closing his eyes, he could swear he was standing outside in a farm.

Grewen grinned at the sight. "It reminds me a lot of how the city of Trewek was designed. The only thing missing is a hole in the ceiling to allow the sunlight in, but it appears they found a better option."

Crates and barrels filled with produce were stacked in long organized rows to the side waiting to be shipped. Unmanned wagons sat idle at one end while their deep wheel tracks ran up and down the aisles between the endless nutritional options.

The E'rudite turned around and lifted his arms to the crowd following him. "Take what you need for the moment. All we ask is that you do not waste or hoard. There will be more available for future meals." Giving a slight grin, Wyrlyn waited to see who would be the first to partake in his gift.

Intimidated by the entire city as well as the bounty before them, the citizens of Dolor were weary of stepping forward and just taking something to eat. Generations of slave labor had taught them that there was no such thing as an endless buffet of food.

Brimmelle, on the other hand, had not been subjected to this lifestyle. "It's about time! We're starving." Leading Narra and her children out of the crowd, they headed to the first set of crates. Pulling out an apple and taking a bite, he sighed at the fresh taste swirling around in his mouth before he swallowed and took another.

Chug followed closely behind with Pheosco still perched on his head. Even with his long and wide wings pulled tight against his sides, the large brown dragon bumped his way down the path, knocking over crates and barrels of food.

Citizens of Dolor needed no further coaxing as they flooded their way into the aisles of fresh fruits and vegetables as they began pulling items from various containers. A few began to fill their pockets and pouches, but for the most part they respected Wyrlyn's request and only selected what they needed.

Following the rush of Humans and Polenums, the giant Mognins and Gathlers approached the food storage area. Being larger than their counterparts, they politely lifted large crates and barrels down for others to have access to them. They were also the ones needing the most nutrition to replenish their large bodies. Grewen led the other Mognins in organizing the feeding of the Dolor citizens as they enjoyed their own handfuls of vegetables.

Pantera stalked her way toward the gathering to find her own meals, as she watched the little Quixes race about and leap from crate to crate. Patiently she waited in her hunched position until several of the six-legged marsupials gathered in one place not far from the cat's hiding place between a barrel and a crate. It was a clear attack, and a meal the cat could have within moments. Leaping forward, Pantera was within inches of her prey before she cried out in pain and stopped in midair. She twisted around to see who had a hold of her, only to find that twine had been quietly and every so lightly been tied around her tail. Upon leaping, the snare had tightened up and prevented her from her meal.

Several Quixes laughed from above the crates; pointing at the panther while doing so. To make it more humiliating, the gathering of Quix in the street had been a setup and they too were having a great time with the prank.

With a quick slice of her claw, she freed herself, the Quixes scattered, and the race was on.

Still standing near Wyrlyn, Thorik recognized the design of the containers and wagons as those which were used to deliver items to the city of Dolor before it was abandoned. "That's why we couldn't find any farms near the city. You shipped it from here."

"We exported goods to all six construction settlements. However, they are closed now so we have more than enough." He scanned the Dolor citizens. "It's fascinating to observe the relationship various species have with food; some respect it, others attempt to control it, while some simply enjoy it." He watched for a few more moments before nudging the Num toward the food. "Go ahead. Take what you need."

Even with the lack of food in his system, Thorik simply wasn't in the mood to eat. "I'll have some later." His eyes lowered from the sight of the famished Dolor citizens filling their stomachs. "I'm not hungry right now."

"Thorik, there is a weight upon your shoulders that prevents you from enjoying even basic pleasures, such as eating."

"True enough. To be honest, I simply can't get over the fact that I'm responsible for the death of the Mountain King. I know I've made mistakes throughout my life, but nothing to this extent. Now, because of me, our entire culture will never know the teachings of the King. Our festivals to honor him and the games we play will not exist. Our relationships and beliefs will no longer be based on his writings. This is the weight I feel upon me; a weight that causes my heart to hurt and my mind to not think straight. Was this my fate all along, to destroy the very culture I have grown to love?" Pulling his backpack off, he held onto it from the bottom in order to minimize the risk of the fabric giving way and his items falling out. The corner of his wooden coffer poked out one large hole while his pouch of Runestones was exposed through another.

"It appears that your pack is in the very state that you are. It needs some mending." Wyrlyn eyed the ripped seams of old worn material and wondered how it was holding itself together. "I'm sure I could acquire a new one for you."

Grasping it tightly to his chest, Thorik had never given such a thought to it. "This pack will be with me until the day I die."

"Understood." Placing an arm around the Num, Wyrlyn led him from the area. "Come with me, my friend. I have something to show you that may free your mind from these painful thoughts."

A few minutes of quiet walking through the underground city led the two past several grand buildings, fountains, and art that stood twice the height of his friend Grewen.

"Over there is the Hall of Harmonics, where we E'rudites go to focus our craft." Wyrlyn said, pointing at a distant building from one of the larger intersecting streets. "Many of the homes here are vacant, but they will be filled soon enough. We nearly have everything built and cleaned for the rest of the Notarians to arrive."

Continuing to stroll down the streets, they finally came upon an open piazza area filled with many works of fascinating art. A large hexagonal platform was in the very center of the open grassy lawn as walkways were artfully placed for those entering. Glowing crystal columns grew out of each angle of the hexagonal stone as steps lead up to the platform between each of the columns. The thick long crystals reached up and crisscrossed each other before extending out and up to the cavern's high ceiling where a cluster of quartz populated the junction's proximity. The intersection of the six crystals was so tight that over a third of each crystal was imbedded into one or more others.

Unknown to Thorik, it was the same platform Avanda had entered earlier in the day.

Thorik began to walk up one of the staircases to the platform, but was stopped prior to entering.

"That entrance will leave you stranded." Walking to the far entrance, Wyrlyn waved Thorik over, signaling the Num to walk around instead of directly through the empty platform. "The entrance you select provides different options once inside the Portibule."

"Portibule?" Scratching behind his ear, Thorik looked through the open platform at Wyrlyn before finally following orders and walking around the entire platform. He was not in an inquisitive mood, but the question was obvious.

"Think of it as a vestibule with access to various portals. The way you enter defines the options you have before you." Wyrlyn waited for Thorik to step up next to him. "In a way, isn't life much the same?"

Arriving, Thorik looked back through between the crystal columns to the other side where he had originally been standing. Nothing appeared different. "In what way?"

"The way we approach life, as well as every challenge, provides us with different options to move forward. Your perspective determines your opportunities."

Confusion about why he couldn't enter the platform from the other side added to the grief he still felt about the death of the Mountain King, he pacified the E'rudite. "I suppose."

Walking up the steps and to the center of the platform, he turned and followed the E'rudite back out between a different set of crystal columns. It was then that Thorik began to pull out of his self-induced depression and notice his surroundings.

Stepping between the crystal columns that had suddenly changed to carved stone, they walked into a granite hallway leading to a gigantic structure built in the shape of a massive bowl. Without warning, fresh cool nighttime air blew across their faces as the stars shined above the outdoor arena.

A few more steps down the entrance corridor and the entire coliseum could be seen to them as hundreds of spectators found their seats and prepared to be entertained. Following suit, the Num and E'rudite found a place to sit down in the mostly empty venue.

"Apparently this was built larger than needed," Thorik mused as over ninety percent of the seating was vacant.

Glancing at the unused seats, Wyrlyn shook his head. "Perhaps now. However, it is the correct size once the remaining Notarians arrive to populate these fertile lands."

The open outdoor seating structure was built in three segments within its oval shape with three large entrances into the main dirt-filled floor of the arena. Various statues filled the center of the arena as well as the wall around it. The first level of seating on the far side was more decorative and held several Notarians who sat quietly waiting for the event to start. The remaining seating was populated by various species, including Humans, Polenums, Blothruds, Mognins, Dragons, and many more.

The Notarians semi-translucent skin clearly set them apart from the other species, unlike the E'rudites who looked Human. If it hadn't been for the fine clothes they wore, one would have to wait to see if they used the powers they had learned from the Notarians.

"I recognize this place." Thorik's eyes spied about. "I've been here. This Coliseum is in the Woodlen Province. This is a barbaric place filled with creatures fighting to the death. Why have you brought me here?"

"Relax, my friend. This province you speak of does not exist yet and I have no knowledge of what they will utilize this structure for, but I believe you will find this to be less barbaric."

Unsettled, Thorik worried about the events that would unfold. What level of fighting would the Notarians require to be entertained?

A female Notarian stepped out into the Notarian seating area with a style and elegance above all others around her. Upon her arrival the entire audience hushed.

"Ovlan?" Thorik's attempt to be quiet failed in the now silent stadium.

Impressed at Thorik's knowledge, Wyrlyn nodded that he was correct.

Waiting for creatures to race out of the three entrances into the sandy arena, Thorik had flashbacks of the last time he had been there and the concern he had for his friend fighting for his life. His memories quickly turned to visions of seeing his friends and family being herded out into the arena for battle as Thrashers raced in to rip them apart limb by limb and Chuttlebeasts stampeding over them. His heart raced at the ideas. However, what he saw was completely different.

Ovlan finished her walk, which looked more like a glide, to the center of the Notarians before she raised her arms straight out in front of her. It was followed by the other Notarians standing up and doing the same.

Seconds later, a flash of light appeared from an unknown source, hovering over the center of the arena. Like a distant star, the light twinkled and flashed various colors while floating at nearly eye level.

Flashes of brighter light began to occur at regular intervals and pulsed like a heart, each beat giving off waves of energy that could be felt by the audience. Deep and low tones followed the segments of time between the flashes.

It was then that Thorik realized that there weren't bright flashes causing the waves and tones, it was the compression of light between them that did.

As the bright mass hovering in front of them grew larger and larger, each containment of the energy provided deeper tones and more powerful shock waves which flooded over the structure's walls and out into the wilderness beyond.

Beat after beat, the size and the power grew and the stress of attempting to contain its energy could be felt by all watching.

His amazement began to change to worry as the sheer power before Thorik was appearing to become unstable. If they were unable to control the energy, what damage could it do? It would surely destroy all who had attended, and most likely the building as well.

"This is insane." Thorik's heart pulsed faster. "Why would they put all of us in danger?"

A final suppression of the energy gave off a vibrating glowing mass waiting to explode. Trembling from the internal pressure, it finally burst outward into glowing gaseous forms in every direction.

Wyrlyn smiled at the sight before them. "The beginnings of all life…"

Contained within the edges of the arena, just before the seating area, small pockets of gas swirled and formed spinning balls of light, many of which slammed into one another giving off great shows of various shapes and colors in the extinction of both objects or the birth of greater ones.

It was a sight that Thorik could never forget as he gazed in silence.

"I thought this would take your mind off things." Wyrlyn smiled at the Num before returning his attention to the events before them.

It was several minutes before the amazement and bewilderment in Thorik's mind softened enough to all him to speak. "This structure was designed for this?"

"Yes, this and other creations. Beautiful, isn't it?"

"Now I'm confused."

Still enjoying the sights, Wyrlyn smiled at the comment. "About what?"

"History. I mean my history, where we are today. Aside from what Deleth was doing at Dolor to create a slave labor camp to mine out the Keystone, why did the Mountain King wish to see all of this end? Pwellus Dementa' is a paradise and this coliseum is used for art instead of brutal killings."

"Art? Is that all you see?"

"Um…yes. What am I missing?"

"As a Num, you have excellent eyesight, but you often don't see what's before you."

Thorik doubted he had missed anything. In spite of that, he searched again for something more without any new findings.

"Dare to see beyond what others only view. This accomplishment being displayed before you isn't just for enjoyment. It's more than just a show of light and sound. Real science is happening before us as well. This is just as much a study of our surroundings as it is beautiful. It is Harmonic Synergy, shown here in the TriSyn symbol." Pulling out a metal crafted item, he handed it to Thorik. It showed three rings equally intersecting one another.

"What does each circle symbolize?"

"Science, Art, and Spirituality. To be an E'rudite, one must by centered with all three."

Tracing his fingers over the circles on the TrySyn medallion, the Num thought about each zone. "You said Harmonic Synergy. What do you mean by harmonic?"

"All things have a harmonic nature to them. Light, gravity, time, space, and even life itself. All energy has a harmonic wave to it. The Notarians have taught the E'rudites how to tap into these harmonics."

"All things?" A skeptical eye peered up from the Num.

"Yes. From the very stone you sit on to the water racing down the river just outside this structure. Even things a Num can't see have a harmonic tone unique to them."

Thorik searched his memories for such instances. "The green burning oil from Bakalor causes stone statues to come to life. Is this a case?"

"Yes, if the stone statues have been embedded with the proper harmonics."

"Embedded?"

"Stones have a low slow pulse which varies based on the type of stone, but none of them would allow stones to conduct actions. Additional energies must be stored inside to be activated by a catalyst such as the burning of the unique oil you speak of. Some types of stone are better at retaining memory. Crystals are very good at storing large amounts of memories and energy harmonics."

"Okay. I think I may understand. But I'm still confused as to why the Mountain King would want to destroy all of this knowledge and culture."

"I don't know. It hasn't happened yet in our time."

"And thanks to me, it now won't happen in mine either."

"Is that such a bad thing? You, yourself, are questioning his motives. This is just the beginning of the Notarian civilization. The first phase was completed once the Weirfortus Dam was built, the sea water was removed from the ocean inlet, Lake Luthralum was filled up with fresh water, ecosystems were established, and the Keystone was finally placed in the Lu'Tythis Tower. The second phase will be to populate this new land recovered from the ocean and we are fortunate enough to be a part of it."

"So, paradise has been created and we are on the threshold of entering it."

"That is a fair summary." Wyrlyn enjoyed the view out over the arena for a few more moments. "Why does your statement bother you such? Do you not wish to live in peace?"

"Just the opposite. I have been looking for such a place my entire life."

"Then you should be pleased you have finally found it."

"Agreed. I should be...and yet I'm not. Something's just not right. The Mountain King would not have wanted to destroy this that I see before me. I must be missing something."

"You can find fault in anything if you strive to. But the question you must ask yourself is why are you attempting to do so?" Taking in the view, he nodded to himself. "It is nearly time we return to Pwellus Dementa'. Your uncle and the Dolor citizens should have had plenty of time to fill their needs…and pockets." Nodding to the Num who now seemed impressed with the light show, he continued. "No rush. Before we take our leave, absorb a few more moments of what is offered here before you. Enjoy the sensations without searching for any faults within it."

Chapter 7
Pheosco's Flight

Chug's sense of smell had led him and Pheosco to the large hexagonal platform in their search of their friends, Avanda and Thorik. Pacing around the perimeter of the open column structure, Chug was nervous about stepping up between any of the columns and onto the top of the dark platform.

"They're not here." Pheosco looked onto the empty platform and then through it to the artistic shapes that filled the open piazza. "I don't like this place." Bowing his long thin green dragon neck, he searched their surroundings. "It appears too perfect, too enlightened. These Notarian's are hiding something and I plan on finding out what it is."

Pulling his green wings out to his sides, he lifted off of Chug's thick head and up into the air. "Stay here, Chug, just in case they do show up. This city appears a little too harmonious for me. I'll return once I have a better idea of how this city really functions."

Obedient as always, the large brown dragon stayed on the ground instead of following his friend. It wasn't long, however, that he became bored and he began scratching his back against various art fixtures. Toppling over a few of them, he eventually found a comfortable location on the steps of the hexagonal platform to take a nap on his back. His tail then casually wrapped around one of the crystal columns that extended to the cavern's ceiling. Snoring, before he had even fallen asleep, he enjoyed the peacefulness of the piazza as he waited for his friend to return. Water slowly drained off his body from his quick bath in the local fountain before his decision to rest. Aside from fallen objects and the fountain now shooting its spray off to one side, the piazza was mostly undamaged.

Flying to the higher regions of the massive cavern, Pheosco could see that the city extended for miles in every direction. Crystal columns appeared to hold the cavern's roof from falling while also providing light to the city made of marble and various other well-crafted stones.

The Dolor citizens could be seen near the fields of food, while local citizens made their way around town performing their duties and preparing for the upcoming festival. "Where are the Notarians?"

Lowering his altitude a bit, he glided over the city to inspect the streets a little closer. Various species filled walkways and open forums in random groupings as individuals and small groups headed to their destinations.

"What's this?" Pheosco noticed a change in the pattern he was getting used to. A group of Blothruds marched down a street as the other residents moved out of their way to open a clear path for them.

These large beasts ranged about eight feet in height with large powerful wolf legs that supported a red muscular human torso and arms with spikes growing out of their back and arms. Brawny necks supported their heads which appeared to be a cross between a dragon and a hairless wolf. These creatures were designed for battle.

Pheosco glided overhead. "You seem a bit out of place. Let's see what you're up to," he said to himself.

Following the group of five Blothruds around a few more corners, they eventually stopped at the bottom of the steps leading up to an impressive black and red marble structure guarded by other Blothruds. Four of the five stopped and joined the existing guards by facing the street while the fifth one walked up the steps, past a few more Blothrud guards standing near the building, and then into the oversized doorway that led to a great hall beyond.

Unable to see inside from his angle, Pheosco flew around the building a few times looking for a way in without having to fly through the guarded main door. Unfortunately there didn't appear to be any obvious options.

Keeping his flight near the roof of the building, the green dragon picked up speed and rounded the corner to the front where the Blothruds stood guard. Utilizing the curve of his entire body to change direction, he avoided flapping his wings to minimize his chances of being noticed. Soaring over their heads, Pheosco angled down just enough to snap his small body under the frame of the doorway and into the room beyond.

Successfully inside, he latched onto the backside of a stone column within the room, and waited a moment to ensure he had entered undetected. Once he felt he was unseen, Pheosco released his grip on the column and flew along the outer wall near the ceiling to investigate the goings on.

Lined with columns on both sides and an arched ceiling above, the great hall was empty except for the Blothrud who was standing at the far end of the room talking to an unknown leader. Thin long crystals pierced through the marble ceiling, extending a few feet into the room and allowing light to beam down to specific locations in the great hall; several of which were focused on the Blothrud who was providing information or status on an event. Residual light revealed a large throne raised several steps above the main floor level, however no crystals provided light to the far end where the mysterious creature sat.

Pheosco flew from column to column near the ceiling as he worked his way closer to hear the conversation and see who was on the throne. Being cautious was not his area of expertise, but he was not foolhardy enough to just plow forward and be spotted. He typically left that to Chug.

Attaching himself onto the final column in the row, he worked his way around as he grasped onto the vertical ridges carved within the marble. Reaching only his thin head around the side, he had a clear view of the Blothrud and could hear his conversation.

"Yes, Master. I informed Deleth of your demands and the consequences of not reaching an agreement. He does not see us as a threat, or as an equal. He views us as his personal army to do his bidding. His arrogance and omnipotence will be his downfall if he does not realize your power. Perhaps it is time to demonstrate it."

A low growl emanated from the darkened section of the room where the throne rested. Then a deep rumbling voice finally spoke. "Not yet. We must allow him to assume we are still in good standing with his efforts." Standing up from his throne and stepping forward into the light, a giant of a Blothrud came forth. Nearly one and a half times the height of the first Blothrud, his massive torso appeared strong enough to lift the stone building he stood in.

"Ergrauth?" Pheosco said under his breath without thinking.

The massive creature standing in the room snapped his head toward Pheosco.

The green dragon had been heard.

"Capture the spy!" Ergrauth ordered.

Wasting no time, Pheosco leaped from the column and flew to the doorway as fast as his small wings could take him. Unfortunately, the doors slammed shut before he could reach them, trapping him in the great hall with a Blothrud and the demon Ergrauth. Escape was unlikely. Surviving was even less.

Chapter 8
Home Away From Home

Stepping out of the hexagonal platform, Thorik nearly tripped over Chug's wing that had flopped up onto the steps as the brown dragon slept with all four feet in the air. "Chug. Wake up!" The Num attempted to be firm as he suppressed a laugh at the sight.

Rolling away from the platform, the large Chuttlebeast-sized dragon rolled himself upright, stood, and stretched out his wings with a loud yawn. The stretch that accompanied his after-nap routine included his shaking of his body and an ejection of brown gas from his backside. The process always left a smile on Chug's face.

"Sorry about that," Thorik apologized to Wyrlyn while reaching over and scratching Chug's head. "He's always had a little challenge with his digestive system."

Wyrlyn peered across the piazza at the toppled artistic sculptures and the fountain that now sprayed off to one side. "It would appear that he has more challenges than just that."

Following the E'rudite's line of sight, Thorik quickly realized what he was referring to. "Chug! Did you do all of this?"

Chug smiled and gave Thorik a large slobbery lick, knocking the Num off his feet.

Wiping his face with his sleeve, Thorik stood back up and glanced back at Wyrlyn with his head slightly lowered. "Again, sorry about that."

"If that is the worst thing that happens in our life, then we have been given quite a gift."

Relieved to hear the response, the Num smiled. "True enough."

Smiling at the happy brown dragon, Wyrlyn gave it a slight grin. "I will ensure accommodations are ready for the citizens of Dolor. Return to where we left them and I will meet you there with instructions."

Nodding, Thorik leaped up onto the brown dragon and patted him on the side. "Okay, friend, do you remember where the food is stored?" Receiving Chug's smile and a nod at the thought of more food, Thorik added, "Excellent. Head back there."

Without waiting for another order, Chug plowed his way forward until he had enough speed to lift off and fly them out of the piazza and back toward the farmlands.

After they cleared the area, Wyrlyn took another look around him. Focusing on each piece of art at a time, he used his E'rudite powers to stand them back up in place before repairing the fountain. Once all was back to normal, he calmly walked out and then down one of the streets.

Returning to the Dolor citizens, Thorik and Chug landed near the food containers and began the process of getting everyone to help clean up and organize the baskets, sacks, crates, barrels, and stacks of food that had not been eaten or taken for future meals.

Most citizens followed Thorik's lead and assisted with the task while just as many started preparing to leave the area per the Num's orders. Thorik Dain had led them from curtain death in Dolor to safety and plenty of food. Respect had been earned and his requests were being followed. At least most of the population followed.

Brimmelle stood off to the side, surrounded by dozens of children and elders who were all hanging onto his every word. Raising his arms in grand gestures he spoke of a Num that clearly rivaled the meek Thorik Dain. His bigger-than-life tales of the Mountain King's accomplishments were almost unrealistic. Yet no one wanted the amazing stories to stop. This King was a hero they could all follow and who was superior to any mortal Num. A godly touch must have been within him to provide the King with such wisdom and the ability to defeat the Notarians and Altered Creatures.

Thorik considered breaking up the theatrical event in an effort to help finish packing up, but stopped just short of approaching them. He suddenly had a vision of Brimmelle turning and pointing at him while explaining to the crowd that Thorik had killed this new found hero. A mob scene was not what he wanted to bring to this peaceful city, nor was it an event he was confident he could escape.

By the time everything was in order, and Thorik felt comfortable that they had left the area in as good of shape as they had found it, Wyrlyn had arrived to take them to the next location.

"Hello, Wyrlyn." Thorik ran over after straightening up the last few boxes of grapes. He always felt better when things were tidy and organized. "Have you found a place for the Dolor citizens to live?"

"Yes."

"Excellent!" He had taken Wyrlyn's advice and was starting to focus on the wonderful world that existed before him. Knowing he still had to deal with the idea of the Mountain King never arriving, he had hid those emotions down far enough so the others could not see them. "Have you seen Avanda? She has not returned yet."

"Irluk and Avanda sent a messenger and I sent one back. They will be waiting for us. Is everyone ready to travel?"

"They are. Lead the way." Climbing up on Chug, he waved his arms to alert the citizens to follow. He then jumped down off the brown dragon and helped Narra and her children up onto Chug's back for the ride.

Brimmelle pushed Thorik out of his way before climbing on Chug as well.

Parading everyone out of the farmland, Thorik followed Wyrlyn down several large streets and then out toward the outskirts of the city where Avanda and Irluk stood waiting for them.

"Avanda!" Thorik ran forward to her. "Where did you go?"

Hugging him, she smiled. "Everything is fine. Irluk was just showing me around."

A concerned eye glanced over to Irluk as Thorik unconsciously showed his concern.

Kissing him on the lips, she broke his gaze at Irluk. "I'm fine. Trust me. You don't need to worry about me."

"It's not you I'm worried about," he said softly.

Leading Chug and the citizens forward, Wyrlyn caught up to Thorik and Avanda. "We're almost there."

Heading out of the city, the environment changed. It was slightly darker as they moved away from the city to the outer cavern where they eventually stopped in an open unmodified area. The ground was comprised of rock and dirt instead of stone streets, piazza's grass yard, or fresh farm soil. Water fell from the cavern's ceiling into shallow pools before running off into a small underground stream.

If seen a week prior, Thorik would have been thankful for having a safe place to sleep without the worry of being enslaved by Deleth or eaten by creatures of the forest. However, after spending the day in the city of Pwellus Dementa' it was very disappointing. "Is this our new home?"

"For now." Wyrlyn's answer was perhaps more sharp than he had intended. "This is a place to sleep during your stay with us. You have fresh water and safety. I will have blankets and meals delivered to you until we leave."

"I thought you said there were empty homes."

"There are, but those have been painstakingly prepared for the Notarians."

"We wouldn't cause a mess, and what we do we will gladly clean up."

"That is not an option. You may stay here for now and we will determine the long term plan for your accommodations after we leave."

Thorik was clearly confused. "Where are we going?"

"We will be departing for the White Summit Quarry."

"These people aren't welcome to stay here in this city?"

"No. This city was designed for the Notarians, not the citizens of Dolor."

"But there is plenty of room for all of us."

"Currently. However, not once the remaining Notarians join us. They will fill this city rapidly."

"So, we are being sent to another mine? Another slave camp? How can you do this? Why would you send us to some desolate lifeless gloomy site?"

Wyrlyn's eyebrow raised at the narrative portrayal of a place the Num had never been. "Careful, Thorik. You are describing my home. I have lived at the White Summit Quarry for most of my life. Are you suggesting such a location is not good enough for you and these people?"

Thorik's soft soul-markings turned a shade lighter. "Oh…I had no idea."

"That's correct. You didn't. You shouldn't be so quick to judge, especially after all that you have experienced today. Is there no way for you to believe this existence is safe?"

Thinking about it, he agreed. "I'm sorry. I appreciate your hospitality. You have done nothing to cause me to doubt you. My past has been riddled with people that have deceived me and it has become difficult to take anyone at face value."

Most of the Dolor people had already started setting their goods down, as they created groupings around various water pools. Mognins pulled the wagons to a stop for distribution of supplies, while Gathlers performed the duties of handing them out and organizing the needs of the less fortunate.

Pantera raced through camp chasing several Quixes, while ZiXi rode on her back like a miniature jockey. Children laughed and followed the entertainment, while the cat raced under wagons and between legs, knocking over several people along the way.

Helping Narra and her children down off of Chug, Avanda searched the air above them. "Where's Pheosco?"

"I thought he was with you." Thorik also began peering up toward the cavern ceiling for a small dragon hovering above, but found nothing.

Irluk gave a casual uncaring glance around. "I'm sure your friend is simply exploring. I'll track him down if it would put your mind at ease."

"Thank you." Pulling Irluk slightly off to the side, Avanda wanted a moment of privacy. "I had a delightful time today." Lowering her voice, she quietly added, "When can we look at Vesik again?"

Smiling, Irluk nodded. "Stay with me and help me with my studies. Once completed we can use the Portibule to meet your friends at Master Wyrlyn's home around the same time that they will arrive. Perhaps we'll even arrive before them."

"I don't feel right about not traveling to the new home without being around to help protect everyone."

A suppressed laugh escaped Irluk's lips. "I'm confident my master is up to the challenge of keeping everyone safe. Besides, the Portibule has a pathway to his home, however he does not have a returning portal. If you go, you will not be able to just step back here and join me."

Avanda's eyes darted about as she weighed her options. "I need to talk to Thorik first. I can't just disappear and send him a note as we did today."

"I understand. In fact, you should take him to the far edge of the cavern." She pointed out beyond their new cavern campgrounds. "There is a small lake that you two will find most..." She searched for the right word before continuing "...romantic." And with that, she turned and caught up to Wyrlyn who had already started his walk back to the city. Pantera was already halfway up to him as she dragged several long lines of twine behind her.

Avanda watched their silhouettes move away against the bright glow of the city.

"What did Irluk want?" Thorik's voice gave away his concern.

"She was telling me about a place you and I should see. It's here in the Pwellus Dementa' cavern."

Shrugging his shoulders, he didn't think much of it. "We should help everyone unpack. If we have time tomorrow, a group of us can explore."

"I don't want anyone but you and I to see it first."

"Avanda, we are needed here. There will be a time and place for such things."

"No there won't. There never is. We are always so busy with life's chores and helping others that we truly never have any time to explore us." She continued to gaze out at the surreal white and black marble city with crystal columns reaching out of the center and then touching the ceiling. It was still breathtaking.

Reaching into a pocket, Avanda pulled out a small blue crystal shard. "Do you recall when we found this?"

He softly responded, "Yes." She had gained his attention. "We were trapped in Della Estovia, the underworld, surrounded by the spirits of the dead and hunted by the demon, Bakalor."

"We've promised ourselves that if we should ever survive such a place we could survive anything, but I no longer think this is true."

"Why would you say this? We continue to overcome every threat thrown at us."

"Not every. In our efforts to do so, we continue to miss the opportunities to be with one another. Just us, Thorik. Alone. No one else. In all these years, we worked together to solve everyone's problems without ever focusing on our own relationship."

"I know. It just seems as though one event simply leads us into another. There never seems to be a good time."

"Then we must make the time." Avanda gently placed the blue glowing crystal in his palm. "When have we ever been in a better situation that the two of us can just leave to explore for a few hours?"

Thorik could come up with dozens of reasons why they should stay and help those who needed it, but he also knew she was correct. He had continued to tell her to wait and she had been patient enough to do so. It was time he gave her the time she deserved. It was time he gave himself to her. "You're absolutely correct, Avanda. Let's have some time for us. Where would you like to go?"

Taking in the moment she had been waiting so long to have, she relished it with a lasting light kiss against his lips before grabbing his hand and leading him to the outer cavern.

As they proceeded forward, it continued to get darker the farther they were from the lights of the city. The sand and rock floor was becoming more difficult to see and an occasional trip would catch them from time to time, but none that caused them to fall.

Just as the darkness fully enveloped them, they arrived to an unseen ridge. A few yards below the ridge was a shallow bed of water which would have been unnoticeable if it hadn't been for a very slight glowing of the hundreds of small fish swimming near the shore. In addition, a few tiny flying insects gave of a random glow as they fluttered about the water.

"This is amazing," Avanda pulled at Thorik to make his way down the ridge to the water's edge. Once there, she dipped her hand in. "It's warm. Nearly bath water."

Thorik peered about to see how far the water went each way along the cavern's outer wall. "This must be part of a hot spring." Squinting, he attempted to see even further. "I wonder if it surrounds the entire city, such as the waterway around the city of Trewek."

By the time he stopped his investigation, he turned back to see Avanda removing her sandals and placing her feet into the water. "Avanda, it might not be safe."

"Sit down Thorik and stop protecting me long enough to enjoy our time."

The quiet setting was one of the least threatening they had been in for a long time. If there was ever a time to heed her words, it was now. "You're right." He began taking off his boots to dip his own feet into the water as well. Once there, he could feel the relaxing sensation she had already been enjoying.

Soon a school of the tiny glowing fish worked their way toward their feet and eventually one pressed its lips up against one of her submerged feet. In doing so, a thin layer of dead skin peeled off and floated about. Another fish did the same on the other foot, and then a third. Each small kiss gave off a small tingle that ran up Avanda's legs as the fish slowly ate the dead skin cells. It wasn't long before the rest of the school joined in and began enjoying the free meal on both Nums.

Thorik pulled his feet out for a moment at the thought of being eaten alive, but soon was reassured by Avanda's giggling that all was well. Placing his feet and legs back in the water, half of the school surrounded his extremities exposed to the water. "It kind of tickles."

"Especially when they get between my toes."

"It looks scarier than it really is."

"Most things do, Thorik."

"True enough." Taking in a deep breath, he enjoyed the fish pedicure. "Most things in life seem to feel scarier than they really are."

Avanda reached forward and allowed the tiny fish to clean her hands and arms as well. "Such as us?"

Enjoying the tingling sensation, he leaned back on his elbows. "Yes. Especially us."

"Why?"

"Sometimes I'm afraid you'll reject me."

"Why would I reject you?"

"Look at me, Avanda. I'm at my parent's age at the time I lost them, and I finally started receiving my soul-marking which have yet to fully develop. You've had yours since you were in your teens like most Nums."

"You know that doesn't matter to me. I've never said anything about them. Surely there's more than that. What is it that you're afraid of?"

"I don't know. Maybe everything. Perhaps nothing. Sometimes I'm afraid to get too intimate with you because it might break my heart if you are taken away or leave me."

"Thorik Dain of Farbank, there will be times that we will be apart, but I'm not planning on leaving you."

"Life is uncertain. You may be taken away against our wishes. Accidents happen."

Pulling her hands out of the water and away from the fish providing spa treatments, she sat back up and traced his jaw with the back of her hand. "If you're talking about death, we will all die eventually. We can't live our entire lives fearing lost loves and missing out on our relationships."

"I know. And I don't want to live that way any longer." Placing a hand behind her head, he pulled her toward him and they lost themselves in a long emotional kiss. Arms wrapped around each other, legs were withdrawn from water, and their bodies embraced.

Away from prying eyes, they were finally able to show the love and passion they had wanted to share after all the years of restraint.

Chapter 9
Enchanting

The main chamber doors opened with the large black and red marble structure, revealing a tall ceiling and long slabs of stone running the length of the hall. The black marble utilized had veins of red and white throughout the columns on both side of the center walkway, which led up to a massive throne at the far end, hidden mostly from the light.

"Ergrauth?" Irluk said from the doorway, as two Blothrud guards stood at attention behind her.

A low growl emanated from the throne and echoed within the chamber for several moments. "Irluk, what brings you to my meager haunt?"

Stepping forward, she waited for the guards to close the doors for privacy before she casually made her way across the room toward him. "I am in search of a small green dragon, and I believe he is here with you."

"Dragons? You are in the wrong house, apprentice. Has your master not explained that dragons are not welcome in my house, just as Blothruds are not welcome in Rummon's?"

Each step she took appeared amplified in sound in the nearly empty chamber. "I'm aware of your disputes with one another. It is as though the two children of Deleth are arguing over who has the best toy or competing over who is the strongest. I think it boils down to something as simple as who needs to prove that father loves him best."

Leaping from his throne and into the light, it only required the demon a few steps before meeting her in the center of the room. "How dare you come into my home and insult me! By all the rights, I should rip you limb from limb!"

Calmly standing her ground, she turned her head slightly to the side from the heated vapors spraying from Ergrauth's mouth. "It's just my opinion. Surely I'm still allowed that."

"Keep your opinions and thoughts to yourself! Deleth may have created both of us, but it is clear he designed me to rule on his behalf. Rummon, on the other hand is a creative weapon to be harnessed and utilized at my call."

"I see." Her calm tone worked to unnerve the giant. "So he is but a tool of war for you to wield in battle?"

"That is exactly what he is."

"And what if he chooses not to be your weapon of choice? Brothers can often be difficult to work with."

Puffing up his chest, he scoffed at the idea. "Then I will utilize his dragons without his blessings." Slowly circling Irluk, he eyed her small fragile body. "Your search here was not for a green dragon, was it?"

Standing firmly in her original direction, she answered calmly. "I don't follow your meaning."

"End these charades! You are here to ensure that I will follow Deleth's lead even if Rummon does not join my efforts. And to this, I have passed your little test."

She nodded with satisfaction. "I'm pleased you have answered well. My report to Deleth will be positive."

Crouching down from behind her, he placed his dragon-like head nearby to intimidate her. "Don't ever test me again, apprentice, for I will eat you the moment you step one foot in my halls again."

Several uncomfortable moments went by while hearing his powerful breath rush past her face and blow her hair about. She was not used to being threatened. "Understood. I will not return. However, before I leave, Deleth and I have been working on something that I believe you will want to see."

"Then show it to me and then vacate my premises!"

Nodding, she obeyed and reached into a pocket and pulled out a metal brooch with gems and a symbol across the front showing a hand with lips within the palm and rings upon the fingers. Tracing it with her own fingers she did not appear to want to show him what it was.

"Give that to me!"

Slightly reluctant, she reached out with open palms for him to take it. Once he did, she placed her empty hands onto her face for a moment and sighed while waiting for him to inspect it.

"What is it? Jewelry?"

"Yes, but much more. "It is an enchanted item."

"Enchanted?" Pulling it slightly away, he became hesitant of it. "It was my understanding that Wyrlyn stopped your alchemist ideas of giving inanimate objects powers to be activated by anyone."

"Oh, he did. However, Deleth does not agree with his logic."

Pulling it closer to his face, he looked at the symbol. "What are these markings?"

"Spells require three primary components; a gesture, a physical component, and speech. To symbolize these I created this symbol with a hand, the rings, and a mouth."

Pulling it even closer, he looked at the details. "What does it do?"

"This specific enchanted item is able to control the minds of others."

"You mean I could use this to make Rummon do as I please?"

"Yes, along those lines. It can also cause them to forget the actions you instructed them to perform."

"Excellent! This will make my plans much easier."

"I'm pleased you find this useful."

"Very. How does one activate it?"

"That is the tricky part. The one you wish to use it on must take it from you or at the very least request that you give it to them."

Nodding, Ergrauth thought of ways to deceive Rummon. "And happens once he has taken it?"

"Then the one casting the spell must place their hands over their eyes for a moment as they visualize their victim."

"Understood. Is there a verbal command? If so, I will need that as well."

She agreed. "As long as the item is being touched your victim or at the very least nearby your victim, you may take control with a simple single word."

"And that would be?"

Stepping a few steps away from him, she then turned to watch his intrigue at the item. "It had to be an odd word that wouldn't be used often, otherwise the spell could be inadvertently started by anyone in the area. In fact, I used a word that Wyrlyn often spoke when it came to me straying into these unknown concepts."

"Fine! It's a unique word. Just tell me it so you can leave and I can plan accordingly."

"Are you sure you wish to have this? Last I recall, you sided with Wyrlyn when it came to my spell casting."

Growling at her, he clutched onto the brooch with one hand and reach down to grab her with the other. "Enough of your games!" Picking her body up to his eye-level, his tolerance had been taxed. "Give me the last component!"

"Blasphemy!"

Ergrauth stopped all movement and his face muscles loosened up. He was still fully there, however his anger at her suddenly ceased.

"Set me down," she ordered.

He did as she commanded before standing back up. "So, that is all I need to do to utilize this on Rummon?"

"No, Ergrauth. You will not be using this on Rummon. I would never give you such power."

Nodding, the demon understood. "Then why have you given this to me?" His voice was still powerful, but it was no longer filled with aggression toward her.

"I did not give it to you. You took it from me, and now you are under my power of suggestion."

"I understand." His eyes darted about as he attempted to fight off her control. "May I ask, how will you prevent me from retaliating once you no longer have me in this situation?"

Grinning at the idea, she straightened her clothes from the unnecessary grabbing and lifting into the air. "Simple. Before I leave I'll relax your mind and have you fall asleep. By the time you wake up you won't recall any of this had happened."

Glaring at her, he attempted to move his hand to crush her, but it simply didn't follow his thoughts. "Why have you done this?"

"Two reasons. First, I simply wanted to see if it would work on something more than Wyrlyn's panther, which it has like a charm. But more importantly, I want a straight answer from you."

Still fighting to say what was truly on his mind, he was unable to act physically against Irluk's wishes. His mind was his own, but his actions were not. "What is your question?"

"I came here looking for a green dragon. Where is he?"

Chapter 10
Caverns Have No Stars at Night

Thorik's Log:
It would appear that giving people what they want does not make them happy. The citizens of Dolor wished for freedom from slavery. Once they obtained it, they wished for the safety they once had as slaves without going back to it. Then, we arrived in Pwellus Dementa and received freedom, food, water, and a safe place to sleep. And yet, the rumblings of discontent continue to grow over and fester as new levels of need emerge. Even Uncle Brimmelle has been caught up in the emotional rhetoric. I'm unsure how to address it before it's out of control.

The glowing crystal columns reaching up and out from the city's centrally located piazza gave the structure of Pwellus Dementa' an omnipotent and godly feel to the citizens of Dolor. Their camp area was out of the city limits on untouched cavern floors. A few days ago, they would have wished for such safety, but now with the resources of grand comfort within view, their desires and expectations had raised to a new level.

Grewen woke from his sleep to find that ZiXi had coordinated a full scale capture with his cohorts. Twine had been crisscrossed over and around every part of his body by the little band of fun-loving hooligans.

Climbing up onto the Mognin's large nose, ZiXi raised a miniature flag in triumph. "I declare this the living land of Zi!" Shouts of praise came from all of his little followers who were holding the twine firmly down. "You are now our slave and you will take us where I order!"

Blowing ZiXi off his nose, Grewen sent the little Ov'Unday flying, nearly landing in Chug's open mouth. The drool from the sleeping brown dragon had thickened on the cavern floor, acting like a syrupy mess which ZiXi was quickly stuck in.

Rolling over to one side, Grewen went back to sleep as dozens of Quixes were catapulted in the air, landing in the water as well as into packs and barrels. One unfortunate little guy landed on the back of a very upset Num, charging his way through camp.

"Thorik, this is inexcusable!" Approaching his nephew, Brimmelle was not shy to complain as he said what those following him were already thinking. "They have better food and lodging which should be shared. Why aren't they?" Seeing the little Quix, he quickly swatted it off his shoulder.

Thorik had returned from the water at the edge of the cavern and had just finished helping others prepare for the night when his uncle had abruptly stomped over to him. Holding up his hands to calm Brimmelle and his small group of angry Dolor citizens, he maintained a composed voice. "We did come unexpected and they didn't have time to make plans for us. We should be thankful for them taking us in. They have provided bedding, blankets, water, food, and supplies."

"They have enough to feed the residents of this city fivefold. Giving us these things didn't mean they went without. It was extra they would not use anyway. So don't make it sound like they have done us any favors."

"Uncle, they could have left us to be meals for the woodland creatures. They didn't have to take us in at all."

"They're selfish greedy people who are enjoying the comforts of civilized living while we're laying on rock and dirt like Fesh'Unday!"

"Are you suggesting they should simply divide everything they have and share their homes with us? They must have worked for years to obtain what they have. Who are we to expect them to distribute their resources above and beyond what they already have?"

"The Dolor people deserve more than blankets and food after living in such terrible conditions for so long under the Notarian's rule." He then pointed across the camp at Narra and her children to make a point. "We have an infant and his sister and mother all shivering and struggling to survive day after day, while the people of Pwellus Dementa' live in wealth and happiness from our labors."

"Our labors? Uncle Brimmelle, you are not even from Dolor."

"I was there long enough to understand them. I understand how they have been repressed by the Overlord and used as cattle to obtain their fortunes. This city you see in the distance was built by the labor and lives of people such as us."

"First of all, you don't know that to be true. For all we know the Notarians waved their hands and used their powers to create all of this. And second of all, I think we're allowing jealousy to validate why we deserve more. What they have is amazing. How they came to have it is unknown to us. What they have given us is a peace of mind that no dangers will attack us at night and no one will go hungry. So, I'm asking you, Uncle, please go back to sleep and let us see what tomorrow brings with fresh heads after our first full slumber in a long time."

Grumbling, Brimmelle turned from his nephew and walked away with his group of disgruntled men. It was clear that their minds had not been changed.

Disappointed in his uncle's misguided thoughts, Thorik finished his rounds to see if anyone else needed help before returning to Avanda and their small campsite. Sitting down next to her, he pulled his coffer out of his beat-up old pack and opened the wooden lid. After digging through several of the loose pieces of paper inside, he eventually selected one and thought about what he should write for his daily log.

"What was all that about?" Her eyes never opened as she lifted the blanket up so he could get in and keep her warm.

Sighing, he just couldn't motivate himself to write, so he put his logs and coffer away. "You know my uncle. He's never satisfied with what he has if he finds out others have more than him." Lowering himself to the bedding, he rolled under the blanket and faced her. "So, when are you going to tell me about what you and Irluk did today?"

Inching forward until their nosed touched, she opened her eyes wide and stared into his for several seconds. Smiling, she started to giggle. "You know, when we're this close your eyes blend together and you look like a cyclops."

Thorik closed one eye. "How about now."

"Ew! Now it looks like I can see through your eyelid and see your cyclops eye." Her smile never faded. "I love you, Thorik Dain of Farbank."

"And I love you, Avanda Frellican of Longfield."

Rolling over, she snuggled her back up against his chest. "Goodnight, my love."

Quiet fell upon them for only a few minutes before Thorik spoke up. "Seriously?"

Ignoring him, she smiled and closed her eyes tight.

"You're not going to tell me what you and Irluk were up to all day? What's with all the sudden secrets? Are you doing something that you know will upset me?"

Without opening her eyes, she softly asked, "Don't you trust me?"

"I could ask the same of you. You aren't trusting me enough to tell me where you went with the Death Witch."

Rolling back over to face him, she was no longer showing signs of playfulness. "Her name is Irluk."

"And at some point she will become the Death Witch."

"But she isn't at this point in history. So don't call her that."

"Avanda, I don't trust her. We've seen what she can do."

"She hasn't done any of those actions yet. That's thousands of years in the future. Who knows what she goes through between now and then."

"I do. She creates spells, Vesik, and a following of Alchemists who battle Wyrlyn and the other E'rudites in a war that changes this land forever."

"Who is to say Wyrlyn is right and she is wrong in this?" Avanda's tone had become sharper as they talked.

"You know, I can't." Calming his own speech, he continued. "We haven't been here long enough and the events we're talking about haven't even happened yet. I just have a feeling that she's going to be a bad influence on you."

"You have a feeling about her. That's what this is about?"

"Yes. I know it carries no weight, but I don't want anything to happen to you. You've come to mean everything to me and I just can't bear seeing someone hurt you."

Another soft quiet moment fell upon them until Avanda finally spoke. "Lu'Tythis Tower."

Thorik was clearly not understanding what she meant.

"That's where we went."

"But, it is a long journey to the tower from here. Weeks if I recall correctly."

"I've always loved the sight of the tower in the distance. Irluk brought me to the top of Lu'Tythis to see where the Keystone had been installed. We used some type of Portibule in the park to get there."

"On the Hexagonal platform where the crystal columns branch out from?"

"Yes. Have you seen it?"

Thorik nodded. "Wyrlyn took me through that same Portibule to the Coliseum where you and I saved Grewen several years ago…or should I say several thousand years from now. I'm still struggling to keep this all straight."

"Isn't it all so amazing, Thorik? We have finally found a place we fit in. We can live with Wyrlyn and Irluk and learn so much from them. We don't have to keep traveling and fighting to stay alive. We can finally settle down and eventually have a family of our own."

"A family?"

"Haven't you ever thought about having a little Avanda running around the house terrorizing Pheosco, while a cute little Thorik goes off exploring with his sidekick, Chug?"

"No, I haven't, but I get the feeling you have."

Taking in a deep breath of Thorik's scent, Avanda held him close. "Yes, dear, I have."

"And where is this place that we will live with this family?"

"I always assumed we would return to Farbank."

Thorik grinned at the unrealistic idea. "Unfortunately, Farbank doesn't exist yet."

Smiling ear to ear, she gave him a wickedly sexy smile. "Well, perhaps we'll have to create it and start populating it ourselves."

Laughing at her idea, he held her close. "I like that idea. We've fought our battles. It's time for us to start enjoying our lives. We'll head out to the base of the White Summit and once we help everyone settle in, we can start planning our own future."

"I like that. You and Wyrlyn can lead everyone across the mountains. I'll meet up with you at Wyrlyn's home."

"Meet us?"

"Yes, I'm going to stay here and help Irluk monitor the Keystone for a little longer. I'll use the Portibule to travel there. In fact, I'll most likely be there before you will."

"Absolutely not! I don't feel it's safe to leave you here."

"Thorik Dain. How can you say that traveling out in the wild provides me more security than staying here in this safe haven?"

Thorik's face turned red as he attempted to contain his anger and fear of her staying with the Death Witch.

Softly touching his face, she traced his cheek with a single finger. "Please Thorik. This is something I will never have a chance to do again. Once I arrive at the Summit, I'm yours for the rest of my life. I promise."

His temper slowly subsided as he gazed into her eyes and considered her proposal.

The moment of calmness was short lived as Narra approached the two. With infant in hand and her daughter clasping to the fabric of her dress, Narra raced up to them. "He's gone! They left!"

Releasing each other, Thorik and Avanda sat up to address the situation.

"Who's gone?" Thorik replied.

"Brimmelle and several of the other men."

Avanda quickly scanned the camp. "Do you know where they went?"

"Yes. They went into the city to gather what they believe is rightfully ours."

Thorik bit his lip upon hearing their location. "They're going to steal?"

"They said we should stand up for ourselves and not be treated as slaves while they live life as overlords. They are planning to take what is fair."

"When did they leave?"

"I don't know. The last I saw them is when they talked to you. I expected him to return, but when he didn't I started asking around. Others told me they had seen several of them head to the city."

Chapter 11
Caught in the Act

Thorik and Avanda rode the large brown dragon to the city in an attempt to prevent Thorik's uncle from doing something foolish.

Chug was too heavy to simply glide, even if he wasn't carrying two Nums on his back. The slow and powerful flaps of his wide wings kept them at a high vantage point as they searched for Brimmelle and the others.

"Where are we going?" came an unexpected voice. Hidden in the dragon's ears, ZiXi awoke to find his sleeping quarters had been moved.

"Not now, ZiXi. We need to find Brimmelle in the city."

"Alright, but keep it down, I'm trying to sleep." Coiling back up into Chug's ear cavity, the hairy little creature shook a few times before relaxing. "Wake me when we land."

Even in the late hours various workers moved about the city and a few stray children played quietly with each other. Being underground, the concept of night and day was blurred. Calm and orderly, there was a level of grace and charm in every aspect of Pwellus Dementa' and those who lived there.

"Thorik." Avanda nodded down to a side street where she had seen something out of the ordinary.

Instructing Chug to land quietly in the next block was filled with good intentions, especially knowing that Thorik had never seen him land without a loud thud or crash. That being said, the street was wide and vacant of crates and wagons which should have made it easy. However, upon setting his feet down, Chug heard a loud scream in his ear.

"Stop!" ZiXi shouted. I missed my street!" A scream from a Quix is not loud, unless they are shouting from within your ear.

Losing his focus and tripping, Chug tumbled past the block and then the one following before coming to a halt, on his back. All passengers had been sent flying in one way or another somewhere down the street.

Impressed that he and Avanda were not hurt from the rough landing, Thorik ran to Chug's side to ensure he was okay. "We're all alive, my friend. At least I can say that."

Swinging his head about, he gave the Num a large sloppy lick. The joy of being praised worked its way down his body and escaped him in a brown cloud of toxic fumes.

Stepping out of the area, Avanda shrugged. "So much for this city being angelic and divine." She then watched as the little Quix raced down the street they had planned to go.

"Hey, it's not his fault." Thorik shook his head and ran to catch up to her just before they both made it to the corner and peeked around the building. There in the smaller side street was a child that Thorik recognized from the small group that listened to Brimmelle's stories of the Mountain King.

The child laughed as she talked to a large bird with orange and red feathers. "I understand." Nodding, she then reached around and gave the bird a strong hug. While doing so, ZiXi leaped up onto the girl's leg and then under her outer cloak.

The bird's eyes spun in different directions and its feathers rustled up a bit. "Thank you, my dear. Now, before you go, I'd like you to meet someone very special to us." The bird's head rolled backward and hung from her long neck like a weight. With her head upside-down, her eyes worked together as they focused on the new arrival. "Thorik Dain of Farbank."

Releasing the bird, the small child stepped back and gazed at him. "He's the one?"

"Yes, dear. He's the one I told you about." Pulling her head up straight, the bird shook her feathers back into the mess they normally were in.

Thorik glanced at Avanda and then back at the other two. "Granna, what have you been telling this child?"

"Only the truth, dear. Only the truth."

Walking slowly forward the girl stopped and gave a quick curtsy. "It's a pleasure meeting you. I'd like to thank you for saving me, when the time comes."

Nodding back, he grinned. "Granna, who is this?"

Strutting over next to the girl, her head was nearly the same height. "This, my dear, is Ovlan's daughter, O'Gee."

Clearly surprised by the news, Thorik's brow raised and lips tightened. "Why does she think I'm going to save her?"

"Surely, dear, you don't think I had something to do with that?"

"No, I think you had everything to with it. Granna, I love that you believe in me but you can't go around telling impressionable children that I will be saving them."

Avanda nodded. "He's right, Gluic. I don't even expect him to save me."

Swinging his head back to her for a moment, he rolled his eyes at her. "Thanks for the support."

"Always here to keep you humble."

"That you do." Turning back to the child, he bent down on one knee. "I'm sorry for what my grandmother has told you, but I'm not some type of saint."

Laughter erupted from O'Gee as well as Gluic and Avanda until the girl contained herself. "I never said you were a saint. I just thanked you for saving me." Glancing back over her shoulder, she looked at Gluic. "Are you sure this is the one?"

"Yes, dear. He's the one. Just remember what I told you and let it unfold. Enjoy the adventure."

Walking back to Gluic, the child placed a hand upon the bird's back and allowed ZiXi to hop off onto the bird for a quick hug before it leaped back onto her arm and scurried up under her sleeve. "Thank you for finding me." Turning back to Thorik and Avanda, she waved one last time. "It was a pleasure meeting you. I look forward to seeing more of you." And before another question could be asked by the two Nums, the child skipped off down the road.

"Granna, how can that be Ovlan's daughter? She looks as much of a Num as you and I."

"She is, dear. Ovlan created the Nums, just as Feshlan created the wolves and the grazers, and Deleth created the Blothruds and all those other nasties. The difference is that she wanted a species that had a soul and culture that represented her for all time. In doing so, she fell in love with one of the Nums she had created and had a child half Num and half Notarian. O'Gee appears Num, as Ovlan had planned, but she still has some of the Notarian talents. Ovlan gave this land a gift called the Polenum species. So you see, dear, there is a little of her in us."

As Thorik and Avanda took in her words they quietly thought how much they owed Ovlan for their own existence.

"Of course," Gluic interrupted the solemn moment in carefree tone, "She also created the Myth'Unday which has nearly done you in a few times. They are a chaotic bunch of sprites and pixies aren't they?" With eyes independently darting around again in different directions, she stretched out her wings, took a few steps, and launched herself into the air before bumping against the building on her way up and over it.

"Why didn't you ask her?"

Thorik looked confused.

"Why are we here, in town, at this late hour?"

"To find Brimmelle! Oh no! I should have asked her if she knew where her son was."

"You're quick."

"Hey, you could have asked."

"I'm not the one that's going to save everyone. What did you call yourself? A saint?"

"I didn't call myself a saint."

"I'm pretty sure you did."

"No, I said I'm not a saint."

"Okay, if that makes you feel better."

"Seriously, just ask. I have two witnesses!"

Looking around the empty street, she nodded. "Are these witnesses invisible?"

Turning slightly red, he attempted to defend himself. "You know exactly what I said."

Laughing at his response, Avanda smiled and placed a loving hand around his back. "You know I'm just teasing you."

Taking a deep breath, his lips loosened up. "I know."

"Right now we need to find Brimmelle…then we can let him know about you becoming a saint."

"Perfect."

Returning to the main street, they found Chug a few blocks down with his head deep into a barrel while eating its contents.

"Chug!" Thorik rushed over to the brown dragon.

Raising his head at the sound of his name, the barrel stayed firmly attached to his head, preventing him from seeing who was approaching. Panicking to get the barrel off, Chug shook his thick head and neck until the barrel crashed against a wall and shattered the bottom and one side off. In doing so, the metal bands were now bent, preventing it from sliding back off over his head.

Avanda laughed at the sight of the wooden helmet held firmly by metal bands to his head, protecting his eyes and forehead as though the dragon was preparing for battle. "Looking good, Chug."

Straightening up, the dragon smiled at the compliment.

"It's not funny, Avanda. Help me get that off of him."

Just then, they both heard festive chatter from down the street as several of the Dolor citizens crossed the intersection with handfuls of clothing and décor.

"No, time. We'll remove it later." Thorik hopped up onto Chug's back and then reached down to pull Avanda on as well. Once situated, they launched forward on their dragon steed to stop the theft of goods.

Galloping down the street, Chug used his wings to help turn the corner without having to slow down, allowing them to quickly catch up to the dozen Dolor citizens racing out of town with arms filled with supplies, food, and home decorations.

Within a few moments they had caught up to the thieves and made a leap into the air, allowing them to fly long enough to land directly in front of those escaping the city.

"Stop!" Thorik raised one hand to add to his command. "You must not do this."

The small group of citizens were comprised of Humans and Nums. Brimmelle was not among them. Clearly nervous about being caught, a few of them dropped their treasures and ran for their temporary campsite outside of town. The others clung to the items and refused to give them up. "We need these to survive!" one shouted at Thorik.

Climbing down from the dragon, Thorik approached the man who had spoken up. "I see, so the food, bedding, and blankets were not enough to keep you alive for the night?"

"I have a family. They need more."

Glancing at the items clutched by the man, Thorik shook his head in disappointment. "So your family requires fine silk sheets instead of the wool and cotton ones we were given?"

"My wife deserves the best."

"And your family needs that dinner chime and those fine plates?"

"We are not beneath them! We deserve them just as anyone else does."

"I'm not arguing whether you deserve these items. My concern lies with the fact they are not yours and you are stealing from others."

"The population of Pwellus Dementa' have obtained these off the labors of my people in the mines. We have already earned them. It's now up to us to take what's rightfully ours."

"I can't allow you to do this."

Sizing up his group against the two Nums and their dragon wearing a broken wooden barrel for a helmet, he shook his head. "If you're not with us, then you must be with them, which means you're part of the problem."

"What?"

"We've seen how Wyrlyn and Irluk give you two special treatment. You aren't from Dolor and you didn't live through what we did. You are outsiders who have chosen to side with those who repressed us. We are no longer slaves and we don't have to take your orders." Nodding to the others, the group marched off with their stolen goods back toward the temporary campsites outside of the city.

Shell-shocked by the statements, Thorik silently stood as he wondered if the words spoken were valid. Had he chosen sides? Had he not fully understood their suffering? Or had the world gone mad where criminal acts were justified due to feeling victimized.

Arms filled with fine cloths, Brimmelle rounded the corner and was surprised to see his nephew standing in the middle of the street near Chug and Avanda. "Excellent. You came to give me a ride home."

"No, I came to stop you from performing a crime!" Charging up to his uncle, he blocked his path. "What has possessed you to steal from these people?" He was furious and shouted less than a foot from his face. "How can you call yourself a Fir by leading others to commit such acts? Have you suddenly lost all memory of the meaning in the King's words?"

Dropping his items, Brimmelle grabbed two handfuls of Thorik's shirt before pushing him up against a nearby wall. "I'm not the one with a memory issue, Nephew. Perhaps I need to remind you that the Mountain King is dead! You killed him! There will no longer be a Mountain King to follow or wise words to guide us. It will never exist! We've been following a spiritual leader that was nothing more than a foolish Num that was killed in Dolor. He has no validity any longer. Why would we follow such meaningless words?"

Knocking his hands off him, Thorik turn the tables by grabbing his uncle by the shirt with both hands, swung him around, and pushed Brimmelle up against the same wall he had just been at. "Meaningless! Meaningless? That's been your problem all along Brimmelle. You aren't understanding the meaning! Spirituality is not just to be read or taught. It must be lived in every breath and action you take. It must exist in your thoughts as you live each day. It must be there when we wander from our paths in order to guide us back to it." Thorik firmly kept his uncle up against the wall as he continued. "It should have never been about the King himself or any other idle such as Runestones or scrolls. It's about the morals and ethics of doing our best and supporting one another…and showing respect and kindness to each other."

"You call this kindness?" Brimmelle spat back while still pinned to the wall.

Pushing him harder against the wall one last time before releasing him, Thorik stepped back and stared down at the more robust Num before him. "How sad it is that you know so much about the Mountain King and his words and yet you never took the time to truly understand them or live them out. Our faith is a belief in a concept of trust, which does not dim in light when the one speaking about it no longer is there to be heard. Your faith was obviously a superficial memorization of policies to use when it was convenient and when you felt the aura of the Mountain King looking over your shoulder." Stepping back once again, he distanced himself from his uncle. "How miserable it must be for you, Brimmelle, to have been blessed with a perfect memory, but no depth to understand and appreciate what it is you're viewing."

Unsure how to react, his uncle stumbled on his words as he started several sentences without being able to complete them.

Climbing back up onto Chug, he turned back to Brimmelle. "This is not over, Uncle. I expect you to collect all those goods and bring them back first thing in the morning." Then, leaving Brimmelle standing in the small side road, they lifted up into the air and returned to their camp.

Chapter 12
Time to Leave

Morning came without sunrise within the enormous cavern. Instead, it was in the form of Wyrlyn standing next to Thorik and Avanda's sleeping bodies. "It is time for you to leave."

"Leave?" Thorik rubbed his eyes as he attempted to shake out the cobwebs of his dreams. "Right now?"

"Yes. It was a mistake to trust these people to be here in the first place."

"What do you mean?"

"We have provided safety and provisions and in return we received theft and looting. Apparently, there is no trusting some cultures."

Standing up, Thorik became defensive. "Wait a moment. There are many very good people here."

"People that break into homes and take what is not theirs are not what I classify as good."

"It was only a dozen men who were involved."

"How do you know how many there were?"

"It's complicated. We were all in the city last night and…"

"I'm disappointed to hear that you were a part of this."

"No. you don't understand. I was trying to stop them."

"But you failed to lead these people to a more civilized way of life?"

"I wasn't able to talk them out of it."

"Then they truly are leaderless. Another reason they must leave here."

"That's not fair."

Wyrlyn looked down at the Num's eyes. "Nor is the fact that I placed my trust in you and placed my reputation on the line with Ovlan to allow the Dolor citizens to stay in our home, only to be proven that my trust was misplaced."

Realizing that Wyrlyn had disappointed Ovlan, Thorik lowered his head.

"We do not need these issues, especially this close to the date of the rest of the Notarian's arriving to occupy this city. You have one hour to prepare before we leave the city."

Nodding, Thorik agreed without complaining.

Wyrlyn then addressed Avanda, "Irluk has requested that you stay behind and assist her with her studies of the Keystone."

Glancing back and forth from Thorik to the E'rudite, she was unsure how to respond at first. "Yes, I'm grateful for the opportunity to help. May I ask, why can't everyone take the Portibule so we don't have to travel in the wild and around the mountain?"

"It is not safe to have more than one or two use it at once and it should be given time to regain its power prior to the next use. It would take too long. Besides, we must conserve its energy as we prepare for the colonization of this city." Turning, Wyrlyn had one last comment before walking away. "One hour, Thorik."

"What if the Dolor citizens won't go?"

Without looking back, the E'rudite spoke clearly and calmly. "Tell them not to test us. It is in their best interest to take this opportunity before Deleth becomes involved."

Taking a deep breath, Avanda smiled at Thorik. "I'm going to go with Irluk and find out more about this time and place. I will be at Wyrlyn's home waiting for you when you arrive."

Thorik clearly didn't like the idea. "I still don't trust Irluk."

"I'll be fine. You only have to trust me, not her." She then grabbed her gear, stood up, and then hugged Thorik before giving him a kiss. "I love you. Nothing will ever come between us. I promise."

"I hope that's true," he mumbled under his breath as he watched her catch up to Wyrlyn.

The hour quickly passed and many were still attempting to pack up their items as the mass majority had started to leave. Slowly walking the perimeter of the city, they eventually came across the primary street that had lead them out of the cavern, through the tunnel, and back to the foothills of the Cuev'Laru Mountain Range.

The cloudy day helped make the transition easier on their eyes, while the sudden realization of surviving out in the wilderness was now upon them again. It would be long days of walking for all involved.

Leading the group, Wyrlyn and Thorik sat in the wagon filled with supplies. Behind them, several more wagons were also being pulled by Faralopes, but were driven by Dolor citizens and filled with food, cooking gear, blankets, and tents.

Grewen led a pod of Mognins who carried the weak, hauled heavy gear, and pulled wagons. Their ten to twelve foot tall thick bodies where designed for hauling heavy stone blocks, so these tasks were of little challenge.

Thorik glanced back and watched Brimmelle, Narra, and her children rest within Grewen's safe arms. "I don't understand him anymore."

"Pardon me?" Wyrlyn glanced over at Thorik and then back to Brimmelle. "Oh, your uncle."

"Yes. I thought he had grown so much and had finally found some peace of mind. Then the next thing I know he's leading an angry mob into the city."

Wyrlyn thought about Brimmelle before replying. "You say he's been a spiritual leader all of his life?"

"That's correct. My grandfather passed away when Brimmelle was very young, so he had to take over."

"So his adult life has been dedicated to the teachings of the Mountain King."

"Every single day."

"Is it truly surprising that he is having trouble coping with the loss of the one he has been following his entire life? Even more than the king's death, the king may never even have existed in the first place. This sponges away the stone-carved rules that he has taught for decades. Brimmelle's view of the world has been torn apart. For the first time in your uncle's life he is untethered from these restrictions and internal guidelines he's placed upon himself. My guess is that he is confused as to how to act and he's fearful of the future without his teachings. There will be void in his life as he slowly starts to trust his own moral compass." Glancing down to see Thorik in deep thought about his comments, he knew he said enough. "He will need love and compassion from his family and friends to help guide him through these difficult times."

Thorik glanced back again. His uncle held and rocked the infant to sleep in his own arms as though it was his own son. It was clear that he truly cared for the child as well as Narra and Revi. "I wish he would have shown me that side of him."

"It is because of you that he can give Narra's family such love."

Scrunching his lips to one side, he attempted to determine how. "Are you suggesting he can because my actions caused Gansler's death, leaving emptiness for a father figure?"

"Yes. That's the obvious reason. But the deeper one is his life has changed from one of cold hard rules and structure when he lived in Farbank to one of being engaged with his fellow people. Your decision to leave Farbank caused him to grow."

"Just how do you know of Brimmelle and his past?"

"Let's just say a little bird told me."

Thorik eyed the E'rudite's face for any games being played. "You wouldn't happen to mean a bird with orange and red feathers would you?"

"Your grandmother has come to be quite helpful in bringing me the appropriate information needed to make sound decisions."

"She has always had a way about her…And just what has she told you about me?"

"Enough to learn you are doing well with your training."

"Training?"

"Do you have the Runestones with you?"

"Yes. What do you know of them?" Reaching into his pack, Thorik pulled out the sack of Runestones and set them on his lap before reaching in and pulling a few out to show Wyrlyn. "Granna told you about these?"

Keeping one hand on the reins, Wyrlyn reached over with his other hand and selected one of the dark flat hexagonal stones with a round crystal in the center and gems at a few of the corners. "They are very old, but they should still teach the basics."

"The basics of what?" Thorik was slightly nervous at first about someone else holding his mystical stones, but Wyrlyn did not appear to have any interest in stealing it.

"What you have in your possession are training tiles for young apprentices to learn the ways of the E'rudites."

Chuckling under his breath, Thorik disagreed. "These are not E'rudite tools, they are Runestones, each with their own meaning and each one corresponding to specific scrolls created by the Mountain King."

"That might be true a few thousand years from now, but currently these are created by E'rudites to teach their apprentices how to access the harmonics of nature. Each harmonic is identified by the color of the central crystal, the number of gems surrounding the crystal, and the design of the raised ridges on the surface. These are clearly the markings of specific powers to tap into."

Thorik gazed at the Runestones that he had received so many years ago. "My mother and father found them near my home of Farbank. It cost them their lives to get these for me, and I've often regretted the fact that I encouraged them to find these sacred and mysterious Runestones that were once owned by the Mountain King." Feeling its weight in his hand, he traced one of the ridges with his thumb. "Now that you inform me they aren't truly Runestones and they were never used by the Mountain King, I must tell you that I feel saddened to hear they are not real."

"They may not be what you thought them to be, but they are real." Still holding onto the one he had taken out of Thorik's hand, Wyrlyn slid his thumb across the ridges in a specific sequence. Once completed, the sunlight surrounding the wagon and the Faralope dropped down to that of a few candle wicks burning in the deepest of dungeons. "These are still very powerful tools to teach E'rudite powers."

After a few moments, Wyrlyn removed his thumb's pressure he had been placing on the Runestone and the sunlight and its heat returned to normal. "What I don't understand is how you are able to utilize them."

"I didn't have an E'rudite teacher. Granna was able to teach me the essentials."

"It's odd that she would know how to teach you. However, what I was referring to was you are a Num. Num's have never been able to tap into nature's harmonics. This was a gift that was only given to Humans by the Notarians. You should not have this ability. Was there ever a Human E'rudite within your bloodline?"

"No, of course not. My parents, grandparents, and great grandparents were Polenums."

"It had to have been within a few generations to carry any of the markers from an E'rudite to you." Wyrlyn's brow lowered in thought. "You are a puzzle Mr. Dain. That you are."

Chapter 13
White Summit

Thorik's Log:
We are heading home, so to speak. Farbank won't be built for hundreds if not thousands of years from now. However, the city of Kingsfoot is the oldest known Polenum structure I know of, and it sits at the base of the White Summit. Wyrlyn tells me that this is the site of one of the rock quarries used to collect enormous building blocks for the Weirfortus Dam. I am also hoping the city that I recall when we first left Farbank has been built and is available for our living.

Weeks of slow travel in the foothills led Wyrlyn, Thorik and all of the Dolor citizens around the mighty White Summit Mountain and to the overpass. The summer days allowed for snow free travel up and over the nearly hidden path which led from the south side of the Haplorhini Range to the open valley on the north side.

The slow trek down into the valley showcased a variety of landscapes and ecosystems. Glaciers covered sections of the majestic exposed rocks along the peaks, while small plants and patchy grass led way to thick pine forests on the way down the mountainous slopes.

At the base of the valley were lush grasslands with a lake on the right side that pushed up against a rock quarry. On the left of their path was fast swirling river filled with water from the distant melting mountain glaciers. Whitecaps splashed about from the rocky base as the river headed toward them, past the lake, and then turned downstream between high cliffs. Their path would lead them between the river and the lake and over a bridge that spanned the lake's water outlet.

The quarry itself was a slice of the mountain that had been cut away into large blocks of stone that had been carried down the river in order to build the Weirfortus Dam. This left an unnatural two-thousand foot tall cliff with the large lake at its base before the water slowly drifted through an outlet stream into a fast-moving large river and then downstream.

On the far side of the half-circle lake was a structure designed to appear as a scaled down version of the towering White Summit Mountain, several miles behind it. This structure was in fact the creation and living place of none other than the E'rudite heading toward it.

Wyrlyn was clearly pleased to see his home. "The lake is a temperate mineral water which flows out of the White Summit's volcanic base."

"Yes, I know…" Thorik stared in awe at the sight. "This is the future home of Kingsfoot. That cliff face will be smoothed out with a giant statue of the Mountain King with his hands out before him, inviting all to join in his spiritual beliefs. The lake will be a half moon with tall statues of Fesh'Unday reaching up to the King. And the city of Kingsfoot will be our greatest sanctuary for his teachings."

Attempting to visualize Thorik's memories, he reminded the Num of recent changes. "With the Mountain King dead prior to him being victorious, I don't foresee the future unfolding the way you remember it."

His words stabbed Thorik like a knife. His chest tightened and his stomach felt sour. His decisions had changed history and therefore would prevent everything he loved about his culture from ever existing.

Noticing the distress in the Nums body language, he apologized. "I meant no malice."

Thorik nodded lightly. "I know."

"How exactly are you responsible?"

"He asked me to help him rally a rebellion for freedom and he died in the act."

Wyrlyn appeared puzzled. "How is this your fault?"

"He was clearly not well in the head. His actions were erratic and his wife, Narra, pleaded with me not to encourage him on such a dangerous venture…and yet I did."

"I see." The E'rudite nodded with a better understanding of the conflict.

After they traveled down the mountainside and past the mineral water lake, the path ended at the city structure on the far side. They had passed many clusters of wooden shacks which housed the lingering workers of the abandoned quarry. They also passed the remainder of raw materials stacked up waiting for the next catwalk or scaffolding to be built but was never needed. Huge blocks of stone that had been cut from the mountain wall had been left in and around the lake. Once the word had come that no more blocks were needed, all mining and shipping came to an immediate halt.

With the task completed, the local workers turned to other tasks such as farming, fishing, hunting, and building their own community.

Reaching the large structure on the far side of the lake, Wyrlyn pulled the wagon across a stone courtyard up to a set of wide stairs leading to the main entrance. "Someday I envision having this entire courtyard at the base of these stairs designed to appear as enormous E'rudite symbols, just like the Runestones you carry." Holding up the Runestone he was still in possession of, Wyrlyn smiled and handed it back to Thorik. "They may not mean what you thought they did, but they still mean something very important."

Relieved to have the full set back again, Thorik tucked it away with the rest of them.

By the time they both got down from the wagon, many of the Dolor citizens had caught up to them and were looking about for what to do next.

Wyrlyn walked up the steps and waved at the group to move in and listen. Without shouting, he used his powers to ensure they were clearly heard even to those in the back. "Welcome everyone to your new home. You are now officially White Summit villagers. Understand that this is my home, my lake, and my land. I'm willing to share it with you as long as you do your part. You may fish, hunt, and build homes as well as places of business. All I ask is that you earn your way. There are no free handouts here. No wagons of supplies will be making their way down that slope to feed you and replenish your supplies. What you have in these wagons and on your backs is all that you have. If you work together, you can build a successful culture. If individual greed and malice win over, all of you will starve come winter."

The words shocked the crowd, who didn't know how to react.

"You can't expect this from them." Thorik ran up the steps next to the E'rudite. "They have always been given food and goods as long as they worked in the mines. They don't know how to suddenly change."

Wyrlyn grinned at Thorik. "Do you and your companions from the future understand this concept?"

"Well, of course."

"Excellent. Then I will place you in charge of educating them and leading them into a new era for their future." Turning back to the confused faces in the crowd, Wyrlyn spoke again. "Thorik Dain will be your liaison to building this new civilization. If you have any concerns, please bring them to him." Glancing back to Thorik he nodded. "You are in charge, Thorik. Let's see what you can do with it."

Chapter 14
A New Beginning

Grewen and another Mognin lifted a roof up and onto the frame of yet another new home as the quarry lake valley was being transformed into a village of wooden homes stretching from the mineral lake to a river that flowed down from the melting glacier high on the mountain peaks. Coping with the new concept was going well for most, but there was a complete change in mindset and culture that would need to be made for the community to survive and thrive.

Luva slowly painted a mural of the various species upon the longest side of the community center, built for those still without shelter. As a Gathler, his giant sloth-like body moved slowly, so his completion of the art would not be for quite some time. That said, Gathlers were also known for their patience and quality. Luva definitely had both of these qualities, but it was his artistic talent that was currently in question. His portrait of Grewen appeared to be more like a giant brown toad standing upright while wearing a bathrobe.

Brimmelle sat with Narra and several children while he continued his teachings of the Mountain King and all that could be learned from his wise words and actions. Several of the youth had just returned from a hillside of purple berry bushes and were passing them around for all to enjoy. Unfortunately, the sweet treat was also very messy as the thick sticky juices stained anything they touched.

Narra laughed at the sight of the purple faces of the children until she glanced over to see the same upon Brimmelle's fingers and hands as he feverishly attempted to clean himself up.

Fortunately Chug had been nearby and quickly jumped in to start licking the Fir's face clean, even against the Num's protest.

Everyone was starting to find their place in the new society even though they all knew they had just begun to prepare for what was needed to survive the winter.

Unlike most of the White Summit villagers, the first week had been stressful for Thorik as he was pulled into every question and concern by every member of the Dolor citizens. It wasn't until Thorik utilized the talents of those he could trust to take the lead in many areas before the Num could get a good night's rest. He had placed Grewen in charge of construction and Brimmelle in charge of farming. In addition to overall direction, Thorik was in charge of disputes and new rules as well as unifying the Dolor citizens with the Quarry Valley workers into the new White Summit villagers.

After a long day of coordinating events, Thorik sat upon the wide steps staring out past the courtyard and grassy field, beyond the new wooden homes, and downstream into the river valley. Far out of view was a place he missed and memories he wished he could step back into in Farbank.

"You have done well, Thorik." Wyrlyn had stepped out of his stone structure and walked up near the Num. "Why the long face? You should be proud of your success. You have learned to delegate and coordinate. It is a fine quality of a leader."

"Thank you. I am pleased how things are going." Brushing off dirt and wood shavings from his pants, he never looked over his shoulder at the E'rudite. "I'm still upset that Avanda did not arrive as promised. Not only did she not show up prior to us, she hasn't shown up at all."

"We've had this conversation a dozen times. The installation of the Keystone is critical to our lives and it is unknown how long it will take to ensure Deleth has it perfect. I'm sure she is only delayed. Besides, you have tasks here to perform that are required for this community."

"I know you've explained that the Portibule only has a single path to this location, unlike the dual path to the Coliseum. Without a returning doorway, we simply can't step back into the city to ask if all is well. However, if she does not arrive soon, I will forgo my duties here and fly back on Chug to investigate."

"You're worried about her safety."

"Absolutely, I am."

"There has not been a death within the Pwellus Dementa' for years. The city is a safe haven and she has Irluk to watch over her."

"It's the latter that bothers me." Wiping sweat from his forehead, he stood up and faced Wyrlyn. "I know I shouldn't be telling you this, but in my past Irluk turns against you and starts a war which neither of you win. I don't know what happens to you, but she ends up as the Death Witch and escorts our souls to Della Estovia for Bakalor to devour. So, no, I don't trust her."

A few moments of reflection upon the subject were taken by Wyrlyn before replying. "I cannot foresee the future. I know that she can be argumentative and strong willed at times. We have even had words about her straying from my teachings into dangerous concepts. However, since then she has not attempted to perform such blasphemy against our E'rudite beliefs." He gave a thoughtful pause before continuing. "No, Thorik, she is not my foe and she hasn't shown any signs of harming anyone. Your past may very well not be our future now that you have made changes to our current situation." Not receiving a response, he continued. "Irluk is my apprentice. Until she proves otherwise, I trust her with my life. Surely we can trust her with Avanda's."

It was clear that Thorik did not have the same level of faith in her.

Wyrlyn watched the various races and species working together to build a new life for themselves. "Are you done for the day?"

"I'm never done. But, yes, I don't have any tasks that must be done before nightfall."

"Good. Please come with me into my home."

Startled at first, he thought he had heard incorrectly. No one had been allowed into Wyrlyn's home. The massive structure had one set of large double doors which were locked to all but the E'rudites. Thorik had nearly given up on the idea of ever entering.

"It's safe. Please enter with me."

Nodding, Thorik walked over to the open door and peered in. Every floor, wall, and ceiling was carved out of stone. The structure itself was a single gigantic stone which Wyrlyn had been spending all of his time carving out to make rooms and corridors. Not just square block rooms. These were each carved out differently in an unending level of details. Floors were carved out to appear as such things as a forest floor with twigs and leaves. If not for the colorless palette, there would be no way to determine if it was real without attempting to pick up a leaf.

Walls appeared to be bark, ferns, or even beehives. Ceiling designs ranged from cavernous to the inside of a giant beast with exposed ribs and tissue between them. Each room was different in textures and in general shapes. Getting lost would be expected seeing that there were few normal construction angles to gain one's bearings.

"I remember this place as the city of Kingsfoot." Thorik smiled as memories flooded his head of his first exposure to the city with his companions Emilen, Wess, and Ambrosius. "No one knows why it was built this way or who built it."

"I've been working on this off and on for most of my life. Since my sabbatical from Weirfortus, this has been my primary focus with the assistance of Irluk. It's my home, as well as Irluk's, and some day it will be our training monastery for all E'rudites. It's a reminder of what we have. As the Notarians terraform the land and species of animals and plants come and go, I want to have a catalog of all that exists so that future generations can know what has been before them."

"When I was here the Nums lived within these walls and had filled it with furniture, shelves, and décor to make it more colorful and inviting." Touching the floor with his fingers, Thorik smiled at the feeling of every leaf and blade of grass lying flat on the floor. "This is the first place I experienced the yellowish green Notarian oil."

"Ah, Bakalor's oil." Closing the main door, the room became completely dark until a single flame appeared in Wyrlyn's palms. Instantly filled with oil, he cupped his hands to keep it contained. The sickly green light lapped at the ceiling, walls, and floor. Once their eyes fully adjusted, he tossed the oil from his hands across the floor near the Num.

Still burning, the oil's light caused the carved forest floor to come to life. Each step Thorik took caused the rustle of twigs and leaves to blow to the side. The stone carvings were as real as any forest floor Thorik had been in.

As the oil burned out a new light appeared. This time it was a single white light glowing from a ball of warmth, floating in the center of the room. Wyrlyn used his powers to establish the light level he wanted in the room before addressing the Num. "Gluic has told me enough about you to pique my interest. I wish to see the extent of your E'rudite powers."

"I don't have any E'rudite powers. My dear friend, Ambrosius has great powers. He could easily pass as your brother. I, on the other hand, am just a Num."

"You are able to use your Runestones by accessing their harmonics?"

"I can use them, yes. But I know nothing about harmonics."

"Please demonstrate."

"I don't use them very often. Uncle Brimmelle warned me about their dangers for so long that I eventually got into a habit of only using them when we were in great jeopardy or he wasn't around."

"Your uncle is not here. Use one of the stones so I can understand how a Num can do such a thing."

"Okay." He could see the sack of stones through several rips in his old tattered backpack. Pushing the main flap open, he reached in past his coffer and grabbed the bag of stones. Pulling out one of the Runestones, Thorik placed a hand on each side and closed his eyes. Relaxed, he allowed an electrical vibration to race up one arm, across his chest, and then back down the other arm and into the stone. Opening his eyes back up he could see the ball of light created by Wyrlyn being pulled toward the Runestone.

Wyrlyn tightened his focus to pull the sphere of light back into the center of the room, but struggled to keep it from moving closer to Thorik. His clothes began to flap forward as though they were also being dragged toward the Num. It was at that time that the E'rudite adjusted his stance to prevent himself from sliding across the floor against his will. "That will be enough, Thorik!"

Letting go of one side, he broke the connection with the Runestone and ended the force pulling everything toward it.

"You are no Num."

"What? How can you say that?"

"Because it's true!" Stepping over, he grabbed Thorik's head and gazed into his eyes. "What are you? Were you created by Deleth to spy on me? No. That wouldn't be characteristic of his approach to resolve issues."

"I'm just Thorik Dain. I'm just a typical normal Num."

Storming out of the room and down a hall, the sphere of light followed closely behind him until it eventually hovered over his head. "You're anything but normal!"

Puzzled, the Num didn't know what to do. So, before all went dark, he raced after the E'rudite. "Wyrlyn, what does this mean?"

"It means, my dear oddity, that I will fulfill my promise to Gluic and train you to control these powers so you don't end up killing someone with them."

"What exactly did Granna ask of you?" The Num continued to rush along the corridor to keep up with the fast paced man as his sphere of light led the way. "What is there to train? I already know how to activate the Runestones."

"Activating them is only the first step. You must learn discipline in understanding what you are influencing so you can skillfully control nature if you are to become an E'rudite." Turning abruptly, Wyrlyn continued in full stride down yet another winding corridor.

"An E'rudite? I never said I wanted to become anything."

"It's too dangerous to allow you to stay at this junction. Either we take those Runestones from you and you halt all interactions with these forces, or I train you to handle them properly. Leaving you to your own devices surely would lead to you recklessly invoking harmonics." Stopping abruptly, he turned to Thorik and leaned forward as his sphere of light hovered just above his head. "Which path do you wish to take, Thorik Dain of Farbank?"

"My parents gave their lives for these Runestones. I'm not giving them up to you or anyone else."

"Then you are choosing to be trained." With a slight wave of one hand the E'rudite caused a large door to swing open just prior to their arrival. Inside was a large room, filled with statues of various creatures in mid-stride as well as many more etched into wall carvings. The ceiling was carved out to be the underside of a forest canopy with some larger limbs exposed below the more flat ceiling surface. In the center of the room was a short column with an oil lamp resting upon it. The lamp itself had solid panels on five of its six sides.

Thorik stopped at the door. He knew this room would be filled with dangers once the lantern was lit with Bakalor's oil. On the far side of the room were doors leading out to an exterior deck. With the natural sunlight beaming in through the far doors, Thorik walked directly to them. Once there, he knew the white light of the sun would cancel out any green light from the lantern, preventing the stone figures from harming him.

Wyrlyn watched Thorik leave the room and walk out to the overhang. It was clear Thorik was not ready to start his training this very second.

Stepping to the edge of the deck, Thorik rested his arms upon the stone railing and looked out over the valley. Below, he could see the locals working hard as he felt Wyrlyn's presence walk up behind him. "They are not only constructing new homes. They are building a new way of life for themselves."

Wyrlyn stepped up next to the num and observed the various species working together. "Isn't it about time you began doing the same for yourself? It's time to become the person you were meant to be."

"I've heard that so many times through my life, but who am I supposed to become and how would you possibly know?"

"Gluic hasn't told you?"

"Granna? No, she's been guiding me, but has never revealed any specific future for me."

"Hmm, perhaps she wishes you not to know." He stroked his chin at the thought.

"If she has given you the slightest idea of my future, you must tell me. What am I being groomed for? Why am I the only Num who can activate the Runestones? Why has my life been one trial after another? Who am I, Wyrlyn?"

Wyrlyn stepped closer and looked him square in the eyes, as though he was assessing the Num's ability to handle the truth before him. "Why, Thorik Dain of Farbank. According to Gluic, you, my little friend, are the legendary Mountain King."

Unable to rationalize the idea for several moments, the Num stood dazed at the concept. "That's not possible."

Shaking his head in disbelief he began pacing. "Gansler wrote the scrolls. He was the original leader of the Dolor citizens. He had to have been their king in order for me to know about it in the first place."

"True. Gluic did tell me he was the original King, but your actions caused his death."

"Yes they did. So how could I be?"

"You have changed your past and yet your past still has the great spiritual leader in your history. It would seem logical that someone else took Gansler's place to become the creator of this spiritual system."

"I don't believe it. Why me?"

"Why any of us? We are all created with great potential and yet so few take these natural abilities and make something out of them."

Still in denial and shock, Thorik turned back toward the railing to gaze over the valley and the workers below. "I don't know if I have what it takes to lead these people."

"You already are leading them. Now you must hone your abilities to ensure they are properly used to protect your followers instead of causing more chaos by activating Runestones you can't control."

"Why wouldn't Granna tell me years ago about my future?"

"I know not of her ways. However, I'm sure she had her reasons." Wyrlyn gazed out across the workers as they built their village. "Perhaps she felt it was more about the journey then the destination. If you had focused on living up to the Kings expectations you may not have become the man you are today."

Thorik let the wise words sink in as he reached back into his thoughts of all the lessons he had learned since leaving Farbank. "Perhaps the journey was to prepare me. Do you think Granna may have had this all planned out?"

"That crazy old bird?" Laughing at the thought, Wyrlyn continued. "I'm not sure she thinks past the moment."

Chapter 15
Vesik's Touch

Standing at the top deck of the Lu'Tythis Tower near dusk, Avanda's powerful Num eyes gazed out over the land she had traveled in for so long. And yet it was different then she remembered it to be, not just because she was now seeing it from several thousand feet above, but because the borders of Lake Luthralum were different due to the water levels. In addition, the cities and great Dovenar Wall hadn't been built yet to keep out the Altered Creatures.

Irluk made a few more entries into her log while chatting with Avanda. "As expected, Deleth installed the Keystone perfectly and the climate is changing just as he had predicted. With his precision, this could keep Terra Australis in perfectly controlled weather forever."

Turning back toward the Human, Avanda nodded. "What you have shown me is amazing, Irluk."

"And you have enlightened me with a few of your own spells. I especially like the one you taught me about creating an invisible egg-shaped protective shield around me."

"I'm pleased you have enjoyed our time together as have I, but even with that said I truly miss Thorik. We're later than I had promised and I'm sure he's worried. When will we head to Wyrlyn's home?"

"I'm sorry this took longer than I had expected. We can leave after my final recordings in the morning. I'm sure my master explained that I've been known to not always show up on time."

Before Irluk could start to clean up her gear and logs, a stone messenger arrived. Unlike most of the statues with dried candle wax dripping from various parts of it, this once was clean and held an oil lantern that gave off the greenish glow.

Collecting the note from its hand, Irluk read it to herself. "Deleth wants a moment of my time."

A concerned scrunch of Avanda's lips and eyes crossed her face. "Another delay?"

"Perhaps." Irluk nodded at the messenger and then glanced back at the Num. "Can you clean up here and meet me back at fountain?"

Nodding, she gave a weak smile to her friend. "I've been through the Portibule enough times to know how to use it."

"Excellent. Hopefully this won't take too long." Leaving with the attendant, Irluk went inside the tower and then returned to Pwellus Dementa though the Portibule.

Walking the perimeter one last time, she knew she may never see the land from this vantage point ever again. After a few thoughts of Thorik, she smiled and suddenly didn't care if she would ever return here.

As she started putting away Irluk's tools to measure and record the weather, she noticed that Irluk had left Vesik in her sack. The two of them had spent many evenings talking about magic spells and thumbing through the book of magic.

Glancing up one last time to assure herself that she was alone, Avanda sat down and pulled Vesik up into her lap. Hesitant at first, she traced the leather binding with a finger until she slowly peeled back the first of two leather covers. Checking over her shoulder one more time to ensure no one was around, she pulled the second leather cover off in the opposite direction.

"Vesik, I've missed you." Smiling at the sight before her, she was excited about finally being able to pull a spell from its pages. Her familiar touch allowed the writings upon the pages to come alive and visible.

Carefully turning the pages, she found the one she had been looking for. "Controlling Time. I wasn't able to read all of your pages back in my time, but now that your pages are more flexible and Irluk's ink is fresh, I finally have what I need."

Reading through the spell, she began to practice some of the verbal commands needed to summon the powers of time.

Avanda had known the book intimately and had intertwined her essence with it. Unfortunately, those events happened during the 4th Age of the land, before Avanda had traveled back in time. Currently, in the 2nd Age, Vesik's exposure to Avanda was limited to a few dozen views and soft tracing of the pages while being held and protected by Irluk. This was not the current situation. Irluk was not there as the spells were being read so the book of magic reacted to protect itself.

Lightning strikes raced from the book up in the air and out in every direction. Bolts struck Avanda, knocking her across the walkway and over the ledge of the top of the tower. Vesik continued shooting electrical charges in random directions, slapping the tower and the Keystone several times.

Shaking off the effects from the sudden jolt, Avanda found herself hanging off the ledge of the tower's top platform. Her strap had caught on the railings and prevented her from falling thousands of feet to her death. Without thinking twice, she began to climb back up and stopped once she could see the danger still being shot out from the book of magic.

It was then that she witnessed the final powerful snap of power from Vesik as it blasted the underside of the Keystone, causing a long fissure to be formed into the mammoth crystal. After that, Vesik snapped itself shut, then the two leather flaps covered its front and the leather strap tied itself closed.

It was now safe to climb back up, which Avanda did quickly. It wasn't until she stood up that she noticed the damage done to the Keystone and the effect it was causing.

Ribbons of translucent reds and greens flowed from the Keystone out across the lands. The new crack had caused a defect that would be visible across Terra Australis every night.

Avanda's heart raced as she ran over and tossed all of the gear into the appropriate bags. Stuffing in the last few items, she turned to race off of the tower and back through the Portibule to Pwellus Dementa'. One last item remained to be picked up and placed away before leaving, Vesik. She opened her bag and scooped up the book on her way out. However, she never made it a full step with Vesik still in her hand before Irluk and Deleth rounded the corner and saw her next to the cracked Keystone.

Avanda's heart sank as the two stared at her for an answer.

Chapter 16
Growth Comes from Within

Thorik's Log:
Wyrlyn's training of me has been relentless as he drives me to my breaking point over and over again to see what I can sustain. I would have thought broken ribs and an arm would have ended sessions early, but Wyrlyn simply heals the damage and tests me again. However, the pain remains and I'm learning to shut those sensations off in my head. And yet with all of the strengthening of my powers, I hold but a candle to the likes of Wyrlyn. So, how could I possibly be the one to save everyone when others are so much more powerful than I?

"**Y**ou're not focusing!" Wyrlyn yelled at Thorik as the Num attempted his physical and mental connection to one of the Runestones. They were once again inside Wyrlyn's residence as the training of E'rudite powers continued. "Preconceived ideas prevent the obvious solutions. You must stop attempting to utilize this specific power as you have the others!"

Sweat poured down Thorik's face as he had been straining to force the Runestone to come alive with its hidden power. "I simply don't understand. I pushed everything I have into this and still haven't seen any results. Are you sure this Runestone isn't broken?"

"You're making excuses!"

"I've attempted to use this one several times over the years and it has never worked."

"You are the problem, not the stone."

Defensive, he fired back at the E'rudite. "How do you know? Prove it!"

"Your own words have given it away. You're pushing!"

"I've tried pushing to get what I want as well as pulling. It makes no difference! I've attempted various plans to activate it with no luck."

"It won't. You must stop with this idea that you can make something happen by planning every action."

"What's my other option? Do nothing and wait for it to reveal itself?"

"Now you're just giving up!"

"I don't want to but you're not making any sense to me. What am I missing?"

Wyrlyn sighed and waited for the Num's tense shoulders to relax. "Many events in our lives are not achieved by trying to determine how to accomplish them. You must visualize the end result of what you want and then manifest it."

"You mean just wish it to come true?"

"No. You must visualize it as being true and truly trust that it exists in every way. You must allow yourself to expand past this moment in your life and experience the future where the action has taken place."

Thorik struggled to understand.

"If you knew for sure, without any doubt in your mind, that something was to take place, how would you act?"

"Confident"

"Yes, but you would also have a clear picture of that moment. It is this vision that you must have in order to manifest your surroundings and your future. Once you do, the paths needed to achieve this will show themselves."

Attempting to understand, Thorik took in a deep breath before slowly releasing it again. "If I understand you correctly, I need to visualize the creation of pure harmonic energy and then in order to manifest it I must expect it to occur as though I already know it will happen."

"Exactly."

Closing his eyes, Thorik relaxed every part of his body and mind as he held onto the Runestone with the black crystal in the center. Calmly he focused as he had been advised. Unfortunately, moments went by and nothing in the room changed.

"Trust that it will happen," Wyrlyn said softly. "Believe that it already has and you have returned to watch it play out once again."

A fluttering of Thorik's eyes could be seen before his muscles eventually relaxed and his struggles vanished. With a light smile he slowly opened his eyes to see a glowing mass in front of him pulsing in tone with his own heartbeat. He had conquered his challenge and opened a new reality of thought for himself.

Chapter 17
A Question of Timing

Gazing out over the landscape filled with a broad palette of colors, Ovlan stood near the elegantly designed railing with her arms tightly behind her with her fingers interweaving and clasping together. The view from Ovlan's Tower was from such great heights that she could practically see all the new lands recovered from the ocean inlet. Cold winds drifted across the mountains, up to the exposed stone peaks, and then onto the highest of tower's platforms causing her foliage-made gown to flutter to one side along with her hair. A sudden shiver shook her from her gaze, and yet it was not from the climate.

"Mother?" O'Gee stood at a distance, watching with concern. She had just arrived via the Portibule. "What's wrong?"

Abruptly untangling her fingers, Ovlan turned and wiped tears from her eyes before addressing he daughter with a strained smile. "How has my lovely little one been?"

"I am well." Spanning the open walkway hanging over the mountain's edge, she approached her mother. "Why do you cry? Are you ill? Have you been harmed?"

"No, dear. I am of strong health." Pulling in a cleansing breath of the frigid mountain air, she calmed her body with a soft smooth exhale. "I have had some visions recently of current actions that are not to our favor."

The child blinked several times before looking into her mother's eyes. "Should I be worried?"

"No, my dear. Worry impedes yours thoughts and your ability to prepare for the future."

"Shall we take action then?"

Stepping forward, she kneeled before her daughter and softly cupped her hands on the sides of the Num's face.

"Yes, dear. We will closely listen and diligently observe all that is around us. Not to just the words and actions, but also to the aura and vibration within these acts. We shall also send out positive thoughts to summon others to assist us to the task. We are not alone. In fact, we are never alone."

"Never?"

"Not even when we block all others out. Our perception that we are alone is a false illusion of our own making." Watching her daughter digest the words, she smiled with pride. "What is on your mind, my little G?"

"I've met some travelers from the city of Dolor. There is one Num named Thorik Dain that seems to be leading them. I was told he came here from our future. Could that be true?"

"Anything is possible." Brushing the Num's long brown hair out from her eyes, she could tell the girl was deep within her own thoughts. "Surely you did not come here to my tower to discuss my vision."

"True." Relaxing her face, she quickly changed subjects. "I came to ask about the Portibule. Can it be set to move us through time as well as space?"

"What an odd question. Do you plan on going someplace?"

"No, but I have a friend that I would like to help in returning him to his own time."

"Manipulating time is a very dangerous, which is why the Portibule was designed to only push us forward in time, instead of backward."

"Perfect! That's what I need."

"It's not as simple as that, my dear. One must understand what time and location they wish to travel to."

"I understand, mother."

"I don't think you do. Seeing that you haven't existed in the future, there is no way you could know what the specific location would exist as at that time in history. If I were to travel right here, a hundreds of years from now, I would have no way to know if this tower still existed. I would fall to my death. Or if a glacier grew upon this very peak, I would be crushed as I appeared inside of it. There are many risks and variables. It would be wise to tell your friend to stay here in this time. Besides he should have never put you in such a position to do such a thing."

O'Gee lowered her eyes. "He hasn't asked me to make this happen. It was to be a gift in return for all of his wonderful stories he shared with me."

Raising her daughter's face back up, Ovlan gave off a slight glow of love at her soft Num face. "You are very special. Give your friend your love and that will be all he will need."

Nodding, she held her hands against her mother's. "Will that make him happy?"

"It will surely help." Leaning forward, Ovlan kissed her O'Gee's forehead. "And it is all you can truly do, for it is up to your friend to define his own fate." Standing back up, she gave a proud smile to her daughter for her caring for others.

Nodding at her mother's words, she glanced over the railing at the distant valleys. "Mother, before I head back to the city, may I stay here with you and watch the sun set over the mountains?"

"Yes, my dear." Placing an arm across her back, she led her daughter to the railing. "Take in every magical moment of life you can, for you never know if this will be the last sunset we will have the opportunity to experience."

Chapter 18
A Change of Heart

In a small poorly lit cell within Pwellus Dementa', Irluk clung to the book of magic, Vesik, as she scolded Avanda. A strong smell of various chemicals wafted through the air from the large laboratory in the next room. She had seen the tables, cages, and magical components as she was dragged along the floor on her way to her cell. But more frightening was the body parts from all types of creatures that had been used for experiments.

"How could you do this, Avanda? You not only damaged Deleth's Keystone, you also broke our trust and friendship!"

"I didn't mean to-"

"You didn't mean to?" Irluk interrupted. "Are you telling me Vesik leaped out of my pack and into your hands, then forced you to open her up and start casting spells?"

"No. Of course not-"

"Don't you understand that Vesik is a part of me? You've violated me by simply opening Vesik without my permission. I'm furious! Now my master, Wyrlyn, will find out and he will remove my privileges or even end my training. What were you thinking?"

Avanda had had enough of the one sided verbal battle. "If you'd let me finish, I'll tell you!" She paused to ensure she would be given that chance before continuing. "I know what I did was wrong. I shouldn't have ever touched Vesik. I know it, you know it, Thorik knows it. Everyone knows it. But that doesn't make it easy for me to resist the temptation. She draws me in with the feeling of power, never to fear anything once I have her in my grasp. I understand that I'm obsessed with that rush of confidence she gives me, but it's so difficult for me to resist."

"That gives you no right to touch-"

It was Avanda's turn to interrupt. "You're correct. It doesn't. I realize that I have a fear of being controlled by others. However, even though Vesik gives me the confidence to overpower this fear, Vesik actually gains control over me. It has been a challenge of mine and I must learn to deal with this issue of power. I apologize to you once again for your pain and misguided trust in me. Just know that I had no malice in mind."

"Then what was it you were trying to do with Vesik?"

"I wanted to fix this."

"Fix what?"

"We're here in the Second Age of our land because of me. We shouldn't be here. I'm trying to get us home. I want to see my parents again. I want to marry Thorik and live with him and our children in his small cottage near the King's River. I just want to go back to Farbank and not have to fight to stay alive every day for the rest of our lives." Avanda lowered her eyes. "I know I shouldn't have touched Vesik. I'll never touch her again. I meant no harm."

A moment of silence filled the warm dry air in the large uncluttered room, as they both looked each other over.

"Avanda, you have no idea what you've done. Even if I were to forgive you, which I will not, you've damaged the Keystone. This took decades to locate, mine, and set in place in order to reinforce Weirfortus, protecting us against the ocean reclaiming these lands. Deleth would be here making you suffer if it wasn't critical that he work to minimize the damage you've done. It's not clear if it can be fully repaired, but once he stabilizes the damage, he will surely return here to take out his vengeance upon you."

"Is there nothing you can do to help me?"

"Help you? The damage is far beyond our friendship and trust. Wyrlyn will be told of Vesik and I will be removed from the E'rudites. I'm only halfway through my training and cannot finish on my own. Deleth is my only ally now, assuming I can regain his trust. I will need to be his greatest supporter if I wish to grow to new strengths."

"Don't just leave me to his devices, Irluk. He will surely kill me or torture me for my lapse in judgement in allowing my cravings for Vesik to skew my actions."

An evil grin grew upon Irluk's face. "Cravings? Perhaps if Deleth returns to find you being punished for such inflictions, he would see the value of my powers."

"I will tell him it was grueling, or whatever else you wish of me."

"Oh, my stupid little Num friend." An underlying laugh mixed with her words. "This is no longer about you. He will see right through any lies and I will not place myself at risk for your well-being. It's best that I actually perform the punishment to ensure he values my loyalty to his cause."

"Don't do this, Irluk. Please just release me and send me to the White Summit. Then tell Deleth you killed me. I beg of you. Don't take away my life with Thorik."

Stepping toward her within the dark cell, she replied to the Num's comment. "You can see your partner in the afterlife."

Chapter 19
Missing Love

Thorik's Log:
All I think about is Avanda and how long it's been since I've seen her beautiful face. Wyrlyn ensures me she is safe, but I can't get her out of my thoughts. I love her. I miss her.

Weeks of practicing went by as Thorik struggled to refine the powers with the Runestones in order to complete specific tasks for Wyrlyn. Dangers were created within the training room as the E'rudite held up the lantern and pointed the open side at various statues and wall carvings. The sickly yellowish-green light would cause vines to reach out from walls, trees to shower the room with fruit, and creatures to come alive. All without warning, Thorik was forced to quickly adapt and grab the appropriate Runestone and engage the situation.

Shining the oil lamp upon a mound in the corner, hundreds of large insects poured out of the various holes and raced toward Thorik with their pincers snapping up in the air.

Tossing the last Runestone away, he missed his pouch, causing it to tumble across the floor. Distracted by the mistake, he paused before haphazardly grabbing the next Runestone required. Immediately activating it, a thick cloud engulfed the room, making it difficult to see beyond a few feet.

Penetrating the cloud, the greenish light kept the insects on course as they quickly climbed up Thorik's legs.

Dropping the Runestone, the num grabbed another and immediately activated it, causing an electrical charge to burst forth and hit his own leg.

Biting and pinching the Num, the insects worked their way up to his arms, neck, and head and then began climbing into his ears and nose.

The extreme pain caused Thorik to drop the Runestone in order to free his hands so he could pull several bugs off of his face. However, their grip was too tight as the clamped onto his soft skin. More could be felt climbing up his legs and inside his trousers. Attempting to block out the pain, he reached into his pouch and retrieved another Runestone to concentrate on.

A gust of wind raced from the stone in his hands. Instead of heading down in an attempt to blow the insects off his body, the wind was focused directly to the light source. And a moment later, the sickly green light went out, causing the insects to return to their static stone state.

"Where's your head today, Thorik? Your reaction time and Runestone selection is not at the level I've trained you for. You've easily met these challenges before." With a wave of his arm, the thick cloud disappeared and the doors to the deck opened, allowing the sun to shine into the room.

Pantera was coiled up and sunning herself on the deck as the Num worked his way out to the daylight. It was the safest place for her to be from the playful Quixes and to watch the evolution of Luva's mural of various unrecognizable species.

Thorik was covered from head to toe with stone insects latched onto his clothing and skin. "I can't concentrate." Pulling each insect off one at a time, he was left with red marks and skin tears needing attention. "It's been too long."

"This is about her again, isn't it?"

"I can't just assume Avanda is safe. I have to find out if she is in trouble or being held by the Notarians."

"And what are you going to do about it if she is?"

"I'll use my Runestones if I have to!"

"They are no match against Notarians."

"I don't care. I'll devise a plan as events unfold."

"Like you just did against these stone insects?"

"That's not fair."

"Life isn't fair. It may be wise to return to Pwellus Dementa' to determine her whereabouts, but you are going there looking for a fight in a city created and run by beings much more powerful than us. You will lose."

"I would rather search for the truth and fail than turn a blind eye and hope all is well."

"So you're finally going through with it this time."

"Yes, it's been far too long since I've heard from Avanda and I cannot sit idly by while waiting for her. I will be taking Chug to fly the distance, making short work of the trip seeing that we aren't traveling around every mountain foothill in these parts."

"I understand. Just don't jump to conclusions. Understand the greater events happening prior to you burning everything down."

Nodding, he walked back into the room to pick up the Runestone he had dropper earlier. "I appreciate what you've taught me so far. I look forward to learning more from you once I return."

"You know, Thorik, the Mountain King is a spiritual leader and symbol for generations to come. What you do now will define the future. Do not start a war if none is needed."

Pausing, the Num looked back at Wyrlyn standing in the doorway to the deck. "I understand."

Chapter 20
E'rudite versus Alchemist

Standing at a window, Wyrlyn stroked the back of Pantera's neck as he watched Thorik and Chug fly up toward the mountain pass. Unsure about the Num, he stood at the end of the corridor as he attempted to uncover the secrets of why Thorik was able to tap into the E'rudite powers of the Runestones. "He is quite the mystery, my friend."

Pantera glanced up at him, before turning her head down the hall and giving off a short burst of caterwauling.

It was then that he heard a knocking at a door. It was clear enough for him to know the sound was nearby and not a knock at the front gates.

Glancing one last time at the distant image of Thorik riding upon the brown dragon, he turned from the window and calmly walked down the corridor with Pantera as the knocking continued in a steady rhythm.

Turning a few corners, he stepped up to the set of large doors that the noise was coming from. No changes in strength or speed of the noise had been noticed while he approached. Upon opening the door the knocking finally stopped and the sound of stone sliding on stone could be heard. A messenger stone statue from Pwellus Dementa' stepped forward. One hand held a lantern burning an ill-green light, and the other held a small parchment tied around a cylinder shaped black rock.

"Ah, a message." Wyrlyn stepped into the large open hall and pulled the paper and rock from the statue's hand. "From Deleth, himself," he said to his panther. Empty of furnishings, each step and word caused an echo to bounce about the room, carved to resemble the inside of a giant whale.

Releasing the black rock from the paper, he stared at the finely polished cylinder for a moment. "This is never a good sign." He then read the note silently, his frown increased upon his face. "My assistance is needed elsewhere, Pantera."

The cat rubbed his back against the E'rudite's leg with little interest to his master's words.

Pulling a fresh roll of parchment from the statue's pack, Wyrlyn penned a few words on it before placing it in the messenger's hand. "Take this to the villagers outside my front gates. I will not be returning any time soon. Deleth's summon to assist him in the repair of the Keystone will most likely be a long engagement."

Accepting the message, the green light continued to embed the statue with life as it then walked down the corridor and out of sight.

Wyrlyn then thumbed the black stone in deep thought a few times before tossing in the air before him.

It was there that the stone stopped in midair and began to spin in a circle faster and faster as the darkness bled off the stone and into the surrounding air until this area increased to the top of a sideways vortex. Once fully developed, the now white rock was sucked into the vortex and immediately disappeared.

The black panther had seen these before and knew what to expect.

Stepping forward, Wyrlyn and Pantera followed the white rock in.

Appearing in the main entrance of Deleth's home, the E'rudite had anticipated seeing the Notarian standing impatiently for him, as usual. Instead, in his place, Irluk stood slightly exhausted resting on the spiral staircase that went up to the higher floors. "Is everything alright?"

She was slightly shocked from his arrival, and yet appeared somewhat relieved that it was him. "Wyrlyn! What are you doing here?"

Pantera strolled over to her and rubbed her face against Irluk's dress.

"I was summoned by Deleth. Did the installation not go well?"

"No, the installation was perfect. You know Deleth. Every structure he creates is exactly as he had planned." Petting Pantera, she added without thinking, "If only his Altered Creatures were of the same level."

"Excuse me?"

"Nothing." Straightening herself up, she approached him. "I was actually expecting Deleth instead of you. He must still be on Lu'Tythis Tower."

Out of the corner of her eye, she could see Pantera sniffing at a set of double doors. Moving over to her, Irluk attempted to distract the panther. "How have you been, girl? Has Wyrlyn been treating you right?"

"Apprentice, why are you here in Deleth's foyer instead of on the tower assisting Deleth?"

"He has informed me that he no longer needs my help."

"And yet he now needs mine?"

"I don't know, master. He doesn't consult me on such plans." Continuing to distract Pantera, she lowered herself onto one knee.

"Irluk, I feel there is more at play here than you are saying. Is there a challenge I should know about?"

"In what regard?"

"Let us not mix words, Irluk. Have you been testing your skills at Alchemy again?"

Dropping her eyes to stare at the panther instead of her master, she wanted to avoid the discussion. "What makes you say that?"

"I knew it. You have started experimenting behind my back!"

Calmly standing back up, her face finally rose up to look him square in the eyes. "Yes. I have."

"Why have you disobeyed my direction?"

"Because it is short-sighted! You don't understand what this means for our future."

"I know exactly what this means. It is you that has no gauge on the ramifications of unleashing these powers."

"You mean sharing these powers!"

"Sharing? E'rudites spend their entire life learning about the harmonics of nature. Few can master more than one set of these forces within a lifetime. And yet you wish to hand these over to anyone who can obtain a charmed item and learn the instructions!"

"What is so wrong with having the powers without wasting your life to obtain them?"

"This is an old argument of ours that never soaks in!" Racking his hand down his chin and pulling slightly at his beard, it was clear he was upset. "It's not just the time it takes to learn the craft, but it's about understanding and respecting these forces. During these decades, we become more at one with the vibrations of all life and grow to be more responsible with these powers. We do not utilize them on a whim or to gain power over others."

"Who is to say others will do so?"

"Who is to say they won't? I've see common folk allow power to corrupt them. Look at Thorik's uncle, for example. What would happen if he would obtain an item with embedded powers of the forces of nature? He may use it to obtain his dominance over others."

She shook her head as she replied. "And he may use it to feed his people. You don't know!"

"Nor do you, and there lies the issue of releasing such powers to the general public."

"Are you saying no E'rudite would ever do the same?"

"No." Wyrlyn took a brief moment to calm himself and his voice. "I am not implying it could never happen. However, decades of focus on discipline and discretion provides each of us with more respect for these abilities. The strict controls and training required to be an E'rudite has been able to weed out those who are likely to conduct such behavior."

"And there lies the issue with your old way; your fear of not being in control. You select a few E'rudites to help control who can enter this special collective with powers that are forbidden from the rest of society. You have determined the fate of the upper-class citizens in our future instead of allowing everyone to have a chance. And because of this I choose to continue developing a way for the rest of us from becoming second-class."

"What has caused you to go down this dangerous path? You started out with such promise. I implore you to end this immediately or I will have to end your apprenticeship!"

Irluk allowed a quick burst of laugher to snap back at his statement. "It ended long before today, Wyrlyn. You have just been blind to it."

The tension was thick as the two stared at each other. Even Pantera had climbed up the spiral staircase to avoid the friction.

Taking in a deep breath, Wyrlyn calmed himself. "Irluk. I understand your position and we need to work this out. Unfortunately, Deleth is still waiting for my arrival. Please return to the Hall of Harmonics and spend some time reflecting on my words as well as your training. I will be available to discuss this in more detail once I am finished supporting Deleth's requests."

Chapter 21
A New Challenge

Flying out of the valley and around the White Summit Mountain, Chug carried Thorik back toward the Notarian city where they had left Avanda. They had spent many days traveling and camping along the way to reach their destination, but it was still much faster than taking a wagon around the mountains.

On this specific morning, the shallow sunlight allowed a beautiful view to the south as glowing ribbons of light were visible from the Lu'Tythis Tower. To their north was a long series of tall mountain peaks, housing Pwellus Dementa' deep inside its hundreds of miles of solid rock. The range was crowned with a ridge of sharp peaks along its crest and upper foothills. On top of the highest point was a structure built onto the sides of a thin cracked peak pointing up into the sky. Unlike a fortress, the edifice appeared much more like a collection of horizontal conk fungi clustered all the way around an old dead tree stump. In the highest of these flat platforms clinging onto the mountain peak, a bright light flickered and caught the eyes of Chug and Thorik.

Chug naturally adjusted his wings and started turning toward the light.

"Chug, we're not heading that way."

The sad expression in the brown dragon's face was clear.

Sighing, Thorik nodded. "Okay. We can quickly investigate seeing that it won't take us much out of the way." Patting his dragon's side, he could hear Chug's heavy breathing. "Besides, you're due for a rest anyway."

The extra excitement could be felt with Chug's heavier wing flapping to speed them up.

As they grew near to the structure, the radial extensions appeared to be specifically placed to see past ridges and peaks. Stairs extended from the rugged mountain stone face without a railing, connecting each of the structures together. It was now clear that this was a place to observe events in every direction.

"That one, right there." Thorik pointed to the highest platform where he had seen the light flicking at them.

Chug veered and banked enough to approach a large open walkway extending from the peak before landing on it with his usual level of grace and daintiness.

Climbing down, Thorik patted the dragon on the side, thanking him for not bucking him off and killing him upon landing.

"I was told you were coming," said an unexpected voice.

Turning quickly, Thorik was surprised to see a woman with semi-transparent skin drifting his way. Her robes covered her feet, but it was obvious that she was moving far too smoothly to be simply walking. Her waist-length hair was of natural long grass and wheat stalks which swayed in the air at an unnaturally slow speed.

"Ovlan?" Thorik asked.

"Would you be Thorik Dain?"

"Yes. We've met before. In the Mythical Forest, back... back before we came here. So I've met you already but you haven't met me yet, if that makes any sense?"

"It does. I was told a Thorik Dain would arrive."

"By who?"

"My daughter, O'Gee informed me. Apparently she has grown to have the ability to foretell the future."

"Or she's been talking to Granna."

"A friend?"

"A family member. Listen, I'm sorry to bother you, we were on our way to Pwellus Dementa' to find my friend, Avanda."

"Yes, I know. That is why I signaled for you to come here. She is no longer accessible."

"Why is that?"

"She has damaged the most important creation Deleth has ever made, Lu'Tythis Tower."

"Oh, no. What has she done?"

"She has damaged the mighty crystal that is cradled in the tower's peak. We are not sure if Deleth is able to repair it, or if there is another Keystone crystal to replace it. Fortunately, it is still functional aside from some unexpected esthetics."

"The ribbons of lights?"

"Yes. Hopefully that is the only side effect from the fissure she created."

"Avanda, what have you done?" Thorik turned and looked back at the distant tower. What will Deleth do to her? How can I stop him?"

"There is no stopping Deleth from killing her if he chooses to do so for her crime. Although perhaps you can help me with a challenge I have."

"I'm sorry, but I can't give up on Avanda that easy. There must be a way."

"There is. If you can perform a task for me, the result may free Avanda at the same time."

With an awakening look of hope on his face, he turned back to gaze upon her. "Just name it. I'll do anything!"

"I need you to stop Ergrauth and Rummon from launching a war. You must use whatever means necessary."

It took a few moments for her words to sink in as Thorik continued to justify to himself that he had misunderstood her meaning. "You want me, a simple Num, to stop the giants Ergrauth and Rummon?"

"Yes, that is what I am asking."

"One is a giant Blothrud and the other is a fire breathing dragon! I am but an insect to them and will be batted away with ease. Please at least tell me that they are warring against each other."

"That would be a lie. There is a very good chance they will be working together on this venture."

"How...How am I supposed to accomplish such a thing? I've seen these two demons in combat and it took several armies to end their lives. I have no army. I have no powers such as you. Why must this fall upon my shoulders? The Notarians have abilities that could easily stop these two."

Tilting her head slightly at the comment, she gave him a slight smile. "Thorik, what do you know of the Notarians?"

"They have supreme capabilities and can do whatever they wish."

"Yes, we have grown powerful over many generations, and with that power the only way we were able to prevent us from destroying each other was to create a culture of doing no direct harm to another or to their property. Ergrauth and Rummon are Deleth's creations and his property. I cannot and will not violate our ways, but I can influence other species to do so."

"No offense, but hiring other species to do your bidding against one another makes your culture seem less benevolent."

"I am not hiring you to do anything. You came to me asking how to save Avanda. I'm informing you the best way to achieve this goal and how to save your species from extinction."

"Extinction? Ergrauth and Rummon are planning to kill the Nums?

"As well as the Humans and all the Ov'Unday species."

"And you Notarians can't stop this?"

"Can, but will not. I have already explained this. So it will be up to you to stop this lopsided battle before it begins."

"Why me?"

"You are the only leader that has come forward from the Ov'Unday side that has not been executed...so far."

"I think this noble action was meant for Gansler, not me. He was destined to lead and then die in this victorious battle only to go down in history as the Mountain King. Stories and songs would be passed down for generations of this brave and wise soul. His sacrifice of his own life to end the slavery of the Nums has lasted for thousands of years."

"I know not of this Mountain King, or this one called Gansler. Is he another leader among you?"

"Yes, he was. However, Gansler was killed in a battle in the city of Dolor. Now I have taken his role to lead these people to create a place of peace, not war."

"I understand, Thorik. These were also my intentions when I originally came here to Terra Australis."

"What made your people come here in the first place?"

"The Notarians live many years in the future; too many for you to grasp. We are over populated and have become so used to living in an artificial culture that many of us wish to exist away from civilization and back with nature. No place like this exists in our time, so we spent over a century developing a way to return to our past. We eventually were able to send four of our people here to build a paradise and Portibule for the rest to join us."

"You were one of those four?"

Ovlan nodded in her regal manner. "Yes, I created the Ov'Unday workers we would need to build our new home as well as Polenums to create civilized cultures. Feshlan created the Fesh'Unday and the florae to provide a balanced ecosystem. Deleth was the mastermind behind designing the structures, including Weirfortus, Lu'Tythis Tower, Pwellus Dementa', as well and the Temple of Surod which helped us breathe life and a soul into new species. Our fourth member, Humeth was the architect and builder of the

Portibule. Her talents will allow hundreds more Notarians to join us here."

"But why here in the past? Aren't you concerned about doing something that may cause your species or culture to never exist, just as I have?

"No. What we do here on this continent makes no difference to history."

"How do you know that?"

Ovlan gazed out over the valley and lakes that had once been an ocean inlet but now was a thriving flourishing landscape, "Thousands of years from now a cataclysmic event will cause the north and south poles to dramatically shift off balance. This entire warm and thriving continent that you see before you will shift to become the South Pole and will remain there for all time. A mile of solid ice will cover these lands and no one in the future will know that we ever existed."

"That doesn't sound much like paradise."

"It does to me, Thorik. I would gladly live a short life among nature than an eternity without it."

"I suppose." The Num struggled to imagine a mile of ice on top of his village of Farbank. "Prior to coming here, I had heard of you, Deleth, and Feshlan, but not of Humeth. Where is she?"

"She perished while using her own Portibule. Upon receiving a summons by Deleth, she attempted to travel to the Temple of Surod, on top of the Shi'Pel Mountain. Unfortunately, the Portibule misdirected her into a block of stone within the mountain itself."

"I'm sorry to hear that. I had no idea Notarians could die."

"We do not pass from age. Although, there are many other threats to us."

"I see, but why have you told me all of this?"

"So you understand that we are not different from your species. We each have our own unique skills and desires. Feshlan wanted this paradise to be free of civilizations with very few Notarians living in separate regions. My vision was to have minor civilizations and cultures thrive among each region's natural attributes while Notarians stayed distant and simply observed. In fact, I'm now to the point that I'm ready to leave with the others and live in the forests with the Fesh'Unday. Deleth made his goals perfectly clear. He wished to create a grand civilization that would serve the Notarians. Knowing his intents, Humeth created Humans to protect the passive Ov'Unday as well as the Polenums from potential threats by the Del'Unday."

"Humans were created to protect our lands?"

"That was the original intent, but without any threats they have veered off into their own culture." Ovlan touched Thorik's shoulder. "Now that Weirfortus and the other structures are completed, Deleth sees no need for the Ov'Unday. With Rummon ruling the dragons and Ergrauth controlling the rest of the Del'Unday, Deleth means to have these demons launch their attack against all Ov'Unday, Polenums, and Humans before the day of Advent."

"Advent?"

"Yes, that is what is being called the day we open the Portibule for all the Notarians who wish to join us. Nearly all of the Notarians have returned home one last time to celebrate their departure and say their goodbyes. Deleth should be heading back very soon, leaving Feshlan and me here to ensure all is well from this side of the Portibule. The day after Advent, we will be closing the Portibule to our origins forever. We will be severing ties with our civilization and will be on our own to thrive or perish in this new land of ours."

"So why is Deleth launching the attack now?"

"He knows that this must be done prior to having a larger collective of our species that would oppose such actions. He will have his demons strike, and they will strike soon."

"Even if I could stop them, which I don't know how I would, how will this save Avanda?"

"I do not promise to tell your future. However, your efforts to support my requests should increase your chances of her safety. Leaving Ergrauth and Rummon to their own path will inevitably cause the death of all your friends and family, including Avanda and yourself."

Chapter 22
Casualties

Wyrlyn pushed against the giant crystal with his E'rudite forces while Deleth attempted to regenerate the crystal's growth to fill in the fissure. Both stood on opposite sides of the Keystone at the top deck of the Lu'Tythis Tower as the winds picked up and storms gathered nearby.

"Hold it stationary!" Deleth instructed. The pressure he was placing on the object was immense and his level of detail was so precise that a minor vibration could cause additional degradation to the tall semi translucent stone.

"What caused the damage?" Wyrlyn spoke over the noise of the wind and his thoughts to maintain the Keystone's immobility. "My understanding from Irluk was the installation was a success."

"It was." Placing his hands firmly on the Keystone he closed his eyes and could sense the progress he was making hidden within the crystal. "Your Polenum friend that you allowed passage from Dolor caused this."

The answer caused an odd expression to flash across the E'rudite's face. "Clearly a Num could not cause such destruction."

"Not alone." He continued his focus before continuing. "Nevertheless, she was able to access your apprentice's book of spells."

The news immediately caused Wyrlyn's face to go flush. "Irluk still has that spell book?"

"She does."

With teeth grinding, he forced himself to keep his calm and focus on the crystal. "Where is my apprentice?"

"She has taken the Num to my home for now, until I can finish my work here."

"Irluk should be here helping with repairs!"

"No, her powers are not disciplined yet." His focus on the crystal caused him to move one hand slightly. "I might say the same about you."

Realizing he had allowed his own concentration to wander slightly, Wyrlyn regained his control over the enormous stone. "I have warned her about this concept of spells, Deleth. She explores new techniques before understanding and mastering the ones being taught. Irluk has been the most difficult apprentice I have had."

"You underestimate her creativity and have generated a rift in your relationship. In return she has come to me for guidance and I have provided her with a safe location to research and discover her potential."

Dumbfounded by the Notarian's words, Wyrlyn felt betrayed. "You have undermined the training to my apprentice?"

"Hold the crystal motionless!"

Wyrlyn did as instructed. "What right do you have to disregard my teachings?"

Deleth's voice returned to a calm uncaring tone as he attempted his repairs. "I have all the right. I am the ruler of this new land and you are but a player within it. If I am dissatisfied with your conduct I will simply eliminate you and pull in other resources."

As the master E'rudite over all others, this was the first time Wyrlyn truly felt threatened. "My creator was Humeth. I am her property. Your culture does not allow you to personally harm each other or the property of other Notarians."

Shifting his hands once again, he began working on a new location deep within the crystal. "I had no apprehension about ridding myself of Humeth once she attempted to obstruct my plans. What refuge do you conjure for yourself in reasoning that I wouldn't do the same to you or anyone else?"

A long moment of silence fell upon them as Wyrlyn pondered Deleth's strong words. The E'rudite had always speculated that there had been foul play in Humeth's death, but it was beyond belief that if could be caused by a fellow Notarian.

"There. Excellent. Keep it stable in this position." The Notarian caused new crystal growth within the Keystone. "Your time with your mentor Feshlan has corrupted your view of our occupying these lands. It is not to build a paradise as he and Ovlan continue to claim."

Confused, he asked the obvious question. "Why would they attempt to deceive us?"

"They did not. Our mission was just as they say. However, it took us nearly a century to build the Portibule to contact our people again in order for them to join us. During that time new leadership and agendas had emerged."

"In what way?"

"The Notarians are coming here to rule these lands as gods. You see, Wyrlyn, we are now the unprivileged from our time. We are no longer searching for a safe haven. Our focus has changed to claiming this new land with us being the rulers instead of the slaves. This is our escape from being oppressed to being liberated into the oppressors. It is time for us to be the masters."

The reality of his statements shook Wyrlyn at his core. His entire perspective of the future was changing before his eyes. "Why weren't Ovlan and Feshlan told of this?"

"They are not of that nature. Doing so would have caused them to revolt against this movement. Of course, if they had, their fate would have been much the same as Humeth after she found out and attempted to stop me."

Wyrlyn's belief of Notarians never harming one another was no more. Within this one conversation, he began to question everything he knew to be true. "And what of us, the E'rudites?"

"You will serve us and create what we need."

"If we refuse?"

Deleth took a deep breath and removed his hands from the Keystone. "I have admired your abilities for many years, Wyrlyn. You will either make a good slave or you will not exist in these new lands. It is as simple as that."

Knowing he could never defeat Deleth in a fair battle and that the Notarian could end his life at any unexpected moment, the E'rudite decided to bide his time and keep quiet until the circumstances were right. "Understood, Deleth."

"There, see how easy that is?" Placing his hands back on the crystal, he began his repairs again. "Once we finish this region of the crystal I no longer will need your assistance. You will then go to Weirfortus and assist your colleagues. They could use another E'rudite to help reinforce the dam until I have finished the final mending of the Keystone."

"Yes, Deleth." He held his tone, even though his teeth were clenched and his mind began to search for options of a better future.

"Once there, you will stay at Weirfortus until I call for you."

"Understood."

"I will know if you leave the dam, Wyrlyn. Do not test me."

Chapter 23
Rummon's Court

The cold air slapped against Thorik's face as he rode the brown dragon into the glacial entrance to Pwellus Dementa'. The chill of the ice cave felt good against his nervous body, calming his emotions of the unknown he was about to face.

Passing from glacial to stone tunnel, he could see the open cavern went on for miles past the city of Pwellus Dementa'. "Okay, Chug. I need you to really pay attention to me. We may need to leave in a hurry."

Nodding his head, the large dragon glanced about for something of interest.

Leaning to his right, Thorik prepared for a typical sharp corner to be taken by Chug. "Turn right!"

Chug banked hard to the left, nearly tossing the Num off his back.

"What are you doing?" he yelled while climbing back into position on the dragon's back. "I said right, not left." He pulled again to the right in his attempt fly the other way.

The dragon completely ignored him and began his descent to land in one of the open areas just outside of the city.

"Chug! Can you hear me?" Thorik continued to look over his shoulder at the area he had wanted to go. "What are you doing?" It was then that he realized that they were landing near an enormous red dragon. "Rummon? Chug, that's Lord Rummon!" Fear gripped every muscle in his body.

With his tongue hanging out of his mouth on one side dripping with slobber, Chug nodded his head with excitement.

"No Chug! No! Rummon has been ordered by Deleth to kill all Polenums." Pulling back on the dragon, he wasn't able to convince Chug to stop heading toward the dragon lord. "He's working with Ergrauth! Do you remember him? He's bad! They are working together to kill our friends."

Landing near the Red Dragon, in the typical chaotic way only Chug can do, Thorik was mesmerized by the Dragon in his early glory years. "Rummon?"

Watching Chug approach, Rummon nodded at the brown dragon who was now bowing back. "It would appear you have a parasite clinging to your back."

Chug turned his head around in an attempt to find such a creature.

Thorik, knew exactly what the mighty red dragon meant. "I am no parasite. I am Thorik Dain from Farbank."

"Get off his back, freeloader." Rummon's voice boomed without even trying.

Leaping off of Chug, he wished to show respect and prevent any conflicts. His mind was spinning on what he should say. "I have come in search of Avanda Frellican of Longfield. Could you assist us in this search, Lord Rummon?"

Still clearly agitated at the sight of someone using dragons for transportation, he glared at Thorik. "Gluic, is this the one you've been telling me about?"

"Yes, dear. He's the one." The voice came behind Rummon's ear as Gluic's colorful head popped up to have a second glance at her grandson.

"He has no wings. I don't trust creatures that can't fly."

"I know, dear, but he is my grandson, even with his deformities."

"I am not your enemy," Thorik added.

"Nor are you my companion. I know not if you are an ally."

"I hope to change that someday."

"You had best focus on simply not annoying me."

"Understood." Thorik was not here to cause more problems than he already had, and yet he found himself an opportunity. "I must ask, how is the Lord of the sky who wishes to be left alone being controlled by a creature not of the air?"

"Controlled? Never!"

"That's good to hear, Lord Rummon." He bowed slightly. "I had heard that Ergrauth had planned to use those of the air to do his bidding."

Growling at the thought, heated fumes rolled out of his nostrils. "That will never happen. We both have been granted the power to order all Del'Unday, whether they are from the air or land. However, we have an agreement not to cross those lines without prior approval from the other."

"Again, I'm pleased to hear it, because it was my understanding that his goal was to enslave your dragons once you helped him destroy his enemies." Thorik was very casual in his wording as though it was common knowledge, even though the story was of his own making. "You know that Ergrauth would never allow anyone to be his equal, especially not the mighty Lord Rummon. You would pose too large a threat to him."

In a loud slow clear voice, he leaned toward the Num and said, "There is no equal to me!" His voice pushed Thorik back several feet. "Why do you insult me with such rumors and wasted information?"

"I'm sorry, my Lordship. Please forgive me." He did his best not to show any fear to the mighty red dragon as his large deadly teeth were less than a foot from him. It was time to stop agitating Rummon. "I meant no harm. I simply came here to ask you if you have any information on a Num named Avanda Frellican of Longfield."

Slowly pulling his neck and head back up in the air, he observed his surroundings. "What is it you wish of her once you find her?"

"Only her safety. I fear she is either injured or in trouble."

"Perhaps both."

"I surely hope not. Do you know this to be the case?"

"I do. But I only give this information to you because you are the malformed grandson of the flyer named Gluic."

"I am grateful." Thorik grinned at his grandmother still casually riding upon the dragon's head. "May I ask where I can find Avanda?"

"Deleth has her. She has damaged his prized Keystone. Death will most likely be the punishment."

"NO! We can't let that happen."

"I can and I will. She is not a member of the air and I have no alliance with her or her kind."

"But I love her! Surely you're not callus to an injustice being done to her?"

"Who is to say it's an injustice? She very well may deserve what she receives as punishment."

"Punishment, yes, but not death! I know Avanda better than anyone. She may make mistakes and cause issues, but her heart is in the right place. She only means well or simply to explore. She is very curious."

"Her curiosity could possibly destroy this paradise. Deleth now spends every moment attempting to repair what he can on the Keystone before it causes the collapse of Weirfortus and the flooding of the land. The crystal will never be the same. His only hope is that it is salvageable."

"So he's not with Avanda?"

"If he wasn't detained by the Keystone's repairs, he would have already unleashed his verdict upon her."

"Then we still have time to reach her before he does. Where is she being held?"

Raising one of his large red eyebrows, he focused his view upon Thorik. "For such a small wingless creature, you are very tenacious about obtaining what you want and demanding of my time."

"I come by that of my grandmother, Gluic." Standing slightly more proud, he smiled at the orange and red feathered bird on the dragon's head. "And when it comes to my family and friends, I will stop at nothing to save them. I'm overly loyal in that regard."

"We dragons are loyal to a fault. Perhaps there is some winged blood within you after all. Safe travels in you effort to find her."

Chapter 24

Damages

Flying above the city upon his brown dragon, Thorik witnessed a celebration being held in the main piazza by all of the residents of the city. The Freedom Festival was fully underway as the Mognins, Polenums, Humans, Gathlers, and many other species all blessed the lands for the future with the arrival of the Notarians which would ensure endless peace and harmony for all.

Continuing on his flight path, the Num also noticed a large gathering of Del'Unday. Unlike the prior group, this assembly was dressed for battle and preparing for a slaughter. "Hurry, Chug! We must find Avanda and then warn the Ov'Unday before this massacre occurs."

Nodding his head in agreement, the large dragon casually searched the buildings for an obvious sign of Avanda, as though she would be waiting for them on an open platform. Showing no disappointment, he unsuccessfully continued his global visual sweep.

"Rummon said to look for the structure made of black marble with grand columns and white marble trim." Soaring by several black marble buildings, one eventually caught his eye. "There! That's the most majestic one we've seen. Surely Deleth would not allow any structure to be designed superior to his own."

Landing on the flat roof of the tall structure, Thorik leaped off and grabbed Chug's large wide head. "If something goes wrong, fly back to the piazza and alert the Ov'Unday of the approaching Dels."

Slapping a wet tongue against the Num's head was clearly his way of agreeing to his request.

Wiping the thick saliva from the side of his face and neck, Thorik turned and ran down the stone staircase which circled down several levels into the building. Slowing only for a moment at each floor, he was cautious not to walk in on anyone as he searched each level for potential holding locations for Avanda.

Bold powerful strokes of artistic flair carried over into the architecture of the building, unlike of the often infinite details that Thorik was used to seeing with Notarian art. Unnaturally clean floors and steps lead the Num around the spiral staircase a few levels before it opened up into a large room with two very large doorways.

In an attempt to move quietly, he made his way to the smaller of the two double doorways and proceeded to listen for any noises that could help him determine if it was safe. "What does safe exactly sound like?" he asked himself while hearing a collection of various creatures in the distance.

Slowly moving the door wasn't his challenge, for he struggled to move it at all. Once the momentum had finally started, he was able to see what he needed to. It was neither safe nor dangerous. It was simply a massive room filled with various creatures held prisoner.

Pushing his way in, he took a moment to close it behind him to ensure that he wouldn't give anyone knowledge of his location. It was then that he turned around and realized the full extent of what was before him.

Creatures of every species were caged or chained up. Most had missing limbs or eyes or other critical features. New hybrid species had been created with odd deformities. Tables of various chemicals and powders had been spilled and never cleaned up. Bags and purses lay tossed about as magical components were exposed from within them.

One red purse looked very familiar as it sat upon a metal box. It was too similar to the one Avanda normally carried to be a coincidence. And there next to it was a large open book of spells. Thorik was no expert on these. However, he had seen Vesik enough to know that this was the book which nearly destroyed Avanda.

Picking up the purse of spell components, he was suddenly taken off guard by something jumping about inside the metal box. Dropping the red purse onto the open book, he stepped back from the table.

"Don't set it there, you fool!" the voice came from within the locked box.

Thorik stepped back from the table and gave the object a quick review. Aside from a slit on both sides, there was no way to know what was inside.

"What are you waiting for? Get those components off of Vesik!" came the voice again.

Seeing no risk in following orders, Thorik stepped forward and picked up the cloth filled with various items and pulled the drawstring tight before returning his focus. "Who are you?"

The box jostled on the table as the creature within struggled to free itself. "I'm going to be your worst nightmare if you don't release me!"

"I think not! You are not who I came for."

"You came for Avanda, correct?"

Stepping back again from the voice within the box, Thorik didn't know what to think about this unexpected creature knowing such things. "How do you know of this?"

Again, the box bounced about from the movement inside until it finally stopped just before falling off the edge of the table. "Let me out and I'll show you where she is!"

Tempted, Thorik thought twice about his actions. "Tell me where she is and once I verify your words are true, I will then release you."

One final movement from within the locked metal box sent it off the table and onto the floor. The metal ping resonated throughout the room for several seconds.

Waiting for the doors to swing open in response to the noise, Thorik hoped the boxed creature would simply tell him what he wanted to know.

A long pause held the Num's attention as he waited for a voice or even movement from the upside down box.

"Hello?" No answer caused him to approach and kneel down. "Are you still there?" Again, without any answer, he carefully moved the box so he could see inside one of the slits on one side.

Even with a partially lit room, he struggled to see anything inside as he tilted it. It was then that he noticed something on the other side. It looked like skin pressed up against the other slit. Slowly, he moved one hand down to touch the object to feel it. Once there, he could feel a scaly texture.

Before he realized it, the creature moved, spun about inside the box, and a claw reached out through the slit and grabbed Thorik's fingers. Pinched against the metal side, the Num's fingers were locked in place.

Yelling at the pain as well as the unexpected change of events, Thorik pushed the box with his other hand in an attempt to free himself. Unfortunately, the grasp on his fingers were too strong to break and the skin was beginning to turn red.

"Let me out or I'll cut your fingers off!" A tightening of the sharp claw started to dig into the Num's fingers, causing them to bleed as flesh slid to the side.

"Okay! Okay!" Thorik yelled out before losing the digits from his left hand.

"Then do it! The key is on the table!"

Lifting the box back up and then setting it softly on the table was not done for the comfort of the creature within it. It was in fact the only way he could accomplish it with causing the loss of any body part.

Grabbing a ring of keys, he began to search for one that would be the appropriate size.

"It's a small one with two teeth on it, each pointing a different direction!"

Nodding, Thorik pushed the keys around on the table to find it. "This would be easier with two hands."

"You might as well get used to only having fingers on one hand if you don't hurry."

"Got it!" Grabbing the key, he placed it up to the lock and then stopped. "I have your word that you'll take me to Avanda?"

The pinching increased and more blood dripped from his fingers. "Open it!"

Shoving the key in, he turned it and unlatched the metal box.

The lid snapped open, and a winged creature leaped from it as it released Thorik's fingers. Landing on Thorik's chest, it knocked the Num into a large wooden chair.

With his heart racing, Thorik grabbed onto his injured fingers and attempted to protect his head from any attacks. After a few moments he peeked through his arms to see the creature standing on him, growling and showing his teeth. Green scales cover the winged beast from end to end with yellow horns across his head and back. "Pheosco?"

"You didn't even notice I was missing did you? I've been held captive for months while you and your friends are just enjoying life. At no time did you happen to say, 'Where is our loyal companion that has saved my life on many occasions.' You never once even questioned my sudden disappearance!"

"You nearly cut my fingers off!" Thorik pushed the dragon back off him and onto the table.

"It would serve you right for abandoning me!"

"You shouldn't have just left without telling us where you went!"

"I'm not your child or your slave. I will go where I please."

"Then don't complain to me about us not looking for you! Your capture is your own fault. In no way would we wish this upon you, but we can't help you if you aren't willing to be part of our family pod!"

Pheosco raised an eyebrow and snarled at the Num. "You have the nerve to argue with me, Num? My razor sharp teeth and claws could rip through your flesh as though it was lard."

"Yes, I'll stand up to you. I do not fear you. And I don't need your help." Picking up a few items he had dropped, he began to wrap up his hand and fingers to stop the bleeding.

Pheosco grinned at the act. "It's about time. I couldn't respect anyone who wouldn't stand their ground...even when it was obvious I could surely destroy them."

Tying off the wrapping on his hand, he glanced about. "We made enough noise to alert anyone inside the building. We need to get moving. Where is Avanda?"

"She's in a cell, down that way," he said, nodding his head toward the far wall.

Several large dead creatures laid along the walls near a few doors opposite of the way Thorik entered this hall of terrible experiments. Pulling his shoulders back and his chin slightly up, Thorik marched forward.

Pheosco waited for Thorik to get close before grabbing the ring of keys and launching himself into the air. "You will need these."

Stopping just shy of the only closer and locked door, the Num turned and grabbed the keys from the green dragon. "Thank you."

"She's not well, Thorik."

He began trying keys to the locked door. "Sick?"

"No. She was tortured by Irluk for betraying her trust and violating her beloved book of magic. Avanda would be beaten down until she had no life left to give, and then Irluk would invoke the most evil act up her. She used Vesik as a painkiller to revive her, adding to her addiction and desire for it. Taunting Avanda with just enough of Vesik's power to fight for her life, Irluk would cut her down again. Now she has been left alone and struggles without having it. I do not know how she will act or if she can survive without the book. Do not get your hopes up."

Finding the correct key for the door, he snapped the lock open. "You're talking about the woman I love, Pheosco. I will accept her in any condition she may be in."

Swinging the door open, the soft light from the main room did little to show what existed within the small cell. "Avanda?"

The reply was a soft mumble at best.

"Pheosco, grab a lantern." Stepping in, past the doorway, he kneeled down next to the faint outline of a body he believed to be hers. "I'm here now. It's going to be okay."

A few weak dry coughs escaped the body before him.

Placing his hands upon her, he traced over her shoulder and then to her hair. Dry and dirty, the hair was filled with clumps of knots. His hand then moved forward to her face which had always been soft and smooth. This time, however, his fingers felt the cracking and pealing skin layers that snapped off upon his touch.

A beam of light made its way around the corner and washed into the room as Pheosco flapped hard to carry the full lantern before setting it down in the doorway.

Lying before Thorik was Avanda. Clothes were torn and burnt with fire and acids. Bruises covered her neck and arms from restraints and various blunt weapons. Skin flaked off from one cheek and the opposite eye was black and blue from a dangerous impact.

"Oh, Avanda!" Pulling her up to him, he cradled her in his arms. "Why would Irluk do such sadistic acts?"

"She didn't," Pheosco replied.

Thorik rocked her in his arms as she started to wake. "Then who?"

"Avanda. She became so infatuated with Vesik that Irluk would only allow her to approach the book if she caused herself pain. The more pain, the closer she reached out to it, sometimes even touching Vesik long enough to taste its essence. Eventually Irluk was called away and Avanda has been left to die."

Raising a hand to Thorik's upper lip, she gently traced it with her dehydrated fingertip. "I'm alive," she uttered as she began to sit up slowly.

"You must rest."

"No. Flee before she returns."

It was difficult to argue with her when she was clearly correct. They needed to escape before being detected. "I'll carry you." Reaching under her, he could tell every movement he made was causing her discomfort, and lifting her knocked the wind out of her. "I'll save you. I'll make you better."

Stepping over the lantern, Thorik slowly carried her out the cell's doorway and back toward the center of the room. It was there that she began struggling to free herself and eventually was able to cause Thorik to set her feet down.

Standing weak-kneed, she held onto him for a few moments to gather her balance before turning from him and start stepping away. She quickly slapped Thorik's hand away as he reached out to help. She wanted to do this on her own.

Thorik and Pheosco watched as she slowly stepped and paused and stepped again toward the table nearby, which the book of magic sat open upon it. "Avanda," Thorik began before receiving a clear halting from her hand.

Pheosco flew over to the edge of the table. "You don't need it."

Thin eyes darted his direction from her. She was not to be stopped and she approached the book with the appearance of a starving Tigra preparing to kill its prey. Placing her hands on the edge of the table, she balanced herself just inches from Vesik while breathing hard from the difficult journey.

Stepping forward, Thorik prepared to grab her and pull her away. His instincts were simply too late.

Lunging forward, Avanda grabbed Vesik in both hand and held the large book over her head and screamed. "I don't need you!" Throwing the book across the table and onto the floor on the far side, she let out an angry yell. "I'm stronger than you!" Holding onto the table again with one hand, she grabbed her purse of magical components and pulled them in tight before her legs began to buckle.

Thorik swung in and cradled her in his arms before lifting her up off her feet again and looking into her dazed eyes.

"I'm better than Vesik." Her muscles twitched from recent abuse.

"Yes you are," he replied as they headed for the double doors.

"I don't need Vesik to be strong." Her eyes were now closed as she mumbled variations of the same theme.

Thorik nodded as they rushed to open the door, only to find a large red Blothrud preparing to enter.

Weapons drawn, the eight foot tall Del'Unday was preparing to enter and Thorik had saved him the task of opening the large wooden door. His hairless wolf-like head on the human musclebound torso rested on massive wolf legs and dangerous spikes extended from his elbows and shoulder blades. Roaring, he let out a battle cry that shook everything in the room, including the Nums and Pheosco.

There was no time to set Avanda down. No time for Pheosco to launch an attack. The Blothrud had been prepared and was immediately taking action against the invaders to Deleth's home.

Stepping forward he swung his enormous shiny blade forward to decapitate Thorik and slice the green dragon in half.

As he swung, a large brown mass dropped from above, crushing the unexpected Blothrud. Bones could be heard snapping as the mighty warrior was quickly transformed into a pile of flesh and broken body parts underneath a large brown dragon.

A large slap of Chug's tongue knocked Thorik out of his shocked state, as Pheosco leaped into the air and landed on his best friend's head for an embrace.

"Excellent timing, Chug! Avanda is hurt, so you'll need to carry her upstairs," Thorik continued as he placed her on his back before leading them up the large spiral staircase up to the roof.

Chapter 25
Freedom Festival

Once on the roof of Deleth's building, Thorik hopped on Chug and held tightly to Avanda. "Okay, my friend, take us back home to the base of the White Summit Mountain. Gently, please."

Leaning Avanda's back against his chest, he pulled her in tight. Worried he was never going to feel her touch again, he treasured the moment with her before Chug began his typical jolting takeoff. Closing his eyes, he rested her head in the curve of his neck. "I will never let you go, my love. I promise."

Pheosco flew back from the edge of the roof after a quick scouting. "No one is around."

Avanda's energy had been completely depleted and she had fallen asleep against Thorik. Even Chug's bouncing around prior launching them all into the air didn't stir her slumber as she coiled up in Thorik's arms.

Pheosco flew near them, spying below for threats. "It would appear we're overly fortunate that so few guards have been placed around Deleth's keep. In fact, I don't see anyone in the streets."

Thorik nodded. "They are all at the Freedom festival."

"Festival? The only thing being freed today will be their life from this world as genocide wipes out their species."

"No. They are celebrating the new start for the Notarians."

"And while they have all returned home to plan their invasion of our lands, Deleth has ordered Ergrauth to have the Del'Unday kill every non-Del'Unday before they return."

"That makes no sense. Why would they create us if they wish to destroy us?"

"Your species, like most, was created to build this paradise for them. Deleth created the Del'Unday to dispose of you. Then Deleth would have an army at his side and finally be able to take control over the Notarians."

"You've spent too much time in that locked box speculating on things you have no way of knowing."

"I was in that box because I found out the truth from Ergrauth himself. Only he had no plans of becoming Deleth's slave, so he wanted me to convince Lord Rummon to help defeat Deleth after performing the planned genocide. I refused, and was promptly placed in that small tomb."

"So Rummon never got the message?"

"Of course he did, using his own Blothruds to give it. But if I know my Lord Rummon, he will not listen to those not of the air."

"That is true, but we still have to stop this massacre from happening. When does Ergrauth plan to attack?"

"That's what I've been trying to tell you. The Notarians are now all gone and all the non-Del'Unday are together at the festival where they will easily be rounded up and slaughtered."

Looking down at Avanda, he knew she could not help, but she could withstand waiting a bit longer before returning. Sizing up his options, he could see the distant celebration in the food harvesting area at the edge of the city as Del'Unday began to file down streets for their attack. "We need to stop this!"

Pheosco sized up the size of the Del'Unday army. "I'm not one to run from a fight, but this is suicide. What spell are you under that causes you to think this is possible?"

"None." Thorik took in a deep breath, filling his lungs fully before slowly releasing. "The right thing for me to do is step in and perform the tasks that the Mountain King would have."

"You're going to get yourself killed. You are no King, Thorik."

"I'm not saying that I'm actually him. But I must do his bidding at this critical junction in our history. If I don't, all will be changed and lost forever. I may not be the one that legends are told about, however I can carry out his tasks and act courageously on his behalf."

"If I recall your stories, your King dies at the end of the battle. Are you going to live up to that act as well?"

Seeing the distant celebration of locals unaware of their fate, he nodded slowly. "If that is what's called for." Searching the local grounds he knew he had to come up with a plan quickly. "Legends say that the King stood his ground and fought his enemy in hand to hand combat."

"That's idiotic. You'll be trampled over."

"If it worked for the King, then it should work for me. To ensure we're successful, I need to play this out just as he had." Patting the brown dragon on the side, he pointed forward. "Chug, land on top of that building."

Music played and the crowd celebrated and ate. The large sloth-like Gathlers slowly moved their head from side to side, while the Nums danced together in groups of two, three, and four. When not eating, the giant Mognins were either playing their bamboo instruments or making percussion music with the stomping of their feet or slapping of their hands. Humans blew horns and rang bells or joined the Nums in their twirling and hopping about. Other species joined in as well. Joy was in the air, just as they had planned.

Holding onto Avanda as they landed on the flat roof on the very edge of town, he waited until they had come to a complete stop before leaping off and pulling several blankets from a clothesline to make a quick bed for her. Returning to Chug, he lowered Avanda off the dragon and into his arms. Wrapping his arms fully around her, he ever so gently carried her over, placed her on the top of blankets, and then kneeled beside her. Brushing back the hair from her face, he kissed her forehead before standing up again. Looking down over the ledge at the celebrators between the city limits and the growing fields of food, he knew they would easily hear him under normal circumstances.

"Residents of Pwellus Dementa', give me your ears!" He waited for a response, but received none from the crowd as they played music and cheered for their future happiness.

Realizing he needed a better platform, he climbed back upon Chug and glanced at the smaller green dragon. "Watch Avanda. I need to grab their attention." They lifted off and headed to the center of the festival, landing directly in front of several Mognins playing music on long bamboo instruments with strings spanning from the top to bottom of them.

Landing with the thud, Thorik proudly nodded at the way Chug could make an entrance and gain their attention. "Please! Everyone! Stop the music and talking! Your lives are in danger!"

Less than a fourth of the citizens near him stopped to listen. The rest returned to their long awaited merriment of this day. "We are no longer slaves and workers for others!" one of the Ov'Unday shouted at Thorik. "Today we are all free individuals! Our lives which were filled with dangerous work are behind us."

"The Del'Unday are on their way here to dispose of you! Yes, you are no longer needed to work as their servants and as miners, therefore you are not needed at all. In fact, you are now a drain on their resources. You have all become a burden to them!"

A few of Gathlers and Mognins looked around for approaching Del'Unday but found none. "Such extreme acts only come from great fear." one of the Gathler's said in their typical slow patient way. "If the Notarians feel we will be a drain on their resources, we can arbitrate ways to prevent this. This is nothing that good communication cannot resolve."

"The approaching Del'Unday army doesn't care about the reasoning of the Notarians. They are following orders to slaughter everyone!"

"There has never been such an incident of this nature and no examples to validate such behavior. Truth be known, truth be said, we have no reason to believe this is the case at this time."

"But it just did in Dolor! Once Deleth found the Keystone, he had planned to destroy the city while the workers were still inside it. That is why the refugees from Dolor came here after escaping the city."

"Do you have evidence of these acts?"

"Evidence? The last time your elders asked me for evidence they were slaughtered at the city of Trewek before they could take any action!"

Waving the others off, so they could stop listening and return to their entertainment, the Gathler stepped forward and placed a gentle a hand upon Thorik. "You are not from here and it can be confusing to outsiders. We have lived up to our end of the agreement and labored to help build this land and cities. Now, in return, we will receive freedom and the opportunity to live here."

Frustrated, Thorik was ready to pull his hair out, knowing they only had a few moments left to discuss the issue before bad events would take place. "What will it take for me to prove to you that an army is on their way here right now to kill each and every one of you?"

"We would have to see that there is truly a threat."

Biting his lip, he wondered how the Mountain King handled this issue. Searching for a way to stop the festival, the Del'Unday took care of this task for Thorik.

Screams and cries erupted from the crowd as the Del army swarmed out from the city swinging blades and maces at the merrymakers. Releasing the Del'Unday to enjoy the hunt, Ergrauth stepped out to the edge of the city and allowed his soldiers to have full reign over the slaughter. No planning was needed for such a simple confrontation.

Blothruds led the encounter and were followed closely by the fully black armored Krupes who had thick human-like bodies that were never seen under all of their protection. They weren't fast or agile, but they were relentless and very difficult to harm. Making up a large portion of Ergrauth's forces, the Krupes never spoke and never questioned his orders. They were excellent followers which the demon used as thoughtless pawns in his war games.

"There's your evidence!" Thorik yelled over the shouts of war and horror.

Raising his hand to calm the Num, the Gathler turned. "I will speak to Ergrauth. There must be a misunderstanding." He then quickly faded into the crowd as the Ov'Unday, Humans, and Polenums began running away from the city and out into the fields.

"We are too vulnerable here!" Unable to gain anyone's attention, Thorik worked his way back to Chug who had his head deep inside a barrel once filled with apples. "Chug! We need to get above this so I can see how to manage it!"

Picking his head up, with the barrel still on his head, the now blinded brown dragon glanced around for Thorik.

Pulling the wooden container off, Thorik jumped up onto the dragon's back. "Up!"

Swallowing the mouthful of half chewed apples, Chug pushed his way through the crowd as he ascended above them.

Checking over his shoulder, Thorik made sure Avanda was safe upon the rooftop where he had left her. Seeing that she was, he returned his focus on the crowd below. "Hide in the fields until we can regroup!" he yelled. "Grab whatever farming items can be used to defend yourselves!"

Racing away from the city various items where grabbed, such as buckets, hoes, shovels, racks, forks and scythes. Shears for sheep and iron sickles for harvesting were collected as livestock were released due to the trampled fences.

Flying overhead, Thorik yelled instructions and warnings as the army freely invaded the area. "Mognins! Roll the barrels and wagons at the Del'Unday to slow their approach. The rest of you, grab those grain flails, rope, and the harrow soil cutters!" Snapping his head around in haste he was attempting to gather as much as he could to use as weapons before the Del army completed their mission.

Ergrauth crossed his arms and smiled at the activity as one of his Blothruds approached with a Gathler. "Welcome council member, Dilur. It is good to see that your people are putting up a fight and that this will become a hunt. I was concerned that a simple destruction of your kin would have not been fulfilling to my troops."

Limping forward from gashes in his leg and across his body, the Gathler which had been talking to Thorik a few moments prior, worked his way to the Del leader, "Ergrauth, what is the meaning of this? Surely we can discuss terms. You have been reasonable in the past."

"I have been reasonable when I had to be. That is no longer the case. With the Notarians gone, I am claiming this land for myself."

Attempting to raise his voice loud enough to be heard over the battle behind him, Dilur addressed the Del'Unday lord. "Truth be known, you have the strength and power to accomplish this. But to what end? When the Notarian's return they will see your misuse of power and end your existence as easily as they created it."

Ergrauth gave an evil smirk. "When they return, Deleth will be in full control of them with an army of Del'Unday at his command."

"Ovlan will not stand for this," Dilur said in the most emotional fashion a Gathler could muster.

Finally turning his head away from the battle to look Dilur directly in the eyes, the lord of the Del'Unday growled.

"Then I will be removing Ovlan out from Deleth's path to success."

"I must protest this act, Ergrauth. Truth be said, the council will take action against you."

"The council will be dead within hours. You, however, won't last that long." Swiping his massive arm out, the blade on his knuckles sliced across the stomach of the Gathler, opening up his chest and stomach.

In his last few moments of life, Dilur watched his own internal organs flow out of his body and onto the ground before him.

The Blothrud who had brought Dilur stepped back. "Is there anyone else you would like to speak to, Lord Ergrauth?"

"No. Go enjoy yourself. After this we only have the colony at the White Summit left. Your battles are limited so make the most of them."

"Thank you, Master."

"While you're there, take down that dragon flying above. Rummon must learn to keep his own out of my business."

"Yes, Master." With that, the Blothrud turned and ran into the fields to help his brothers.

Thorik continued to coordinate from the air, upon the brown dragon. "Hurry! They are working their way into the fields!" Knowing that nearly a fourth of the community had been killed by the army, the remaining three-fourths wouldn't last long during the second wave of attacks. His instincts told him to run and hide and return when they had the advantage. "I must live up to the King's valor to win this battle," he told Chug. "He would not run from this threat. He would charge in on the enemy with courage and fearlessness. I must do the same."

The farmland only extended so far before the open sand and rock floors covered the ground the rest of the way to the cavern walls. There were no more places to hide. It was here that they stopped running, unsure how to proceed.

Fear could be seen in the faces of the citizens, as they clutched onto the farm equipment they had obtained. Few had their wits about them enough to hold their items up as potential weapons.

"No predator can defeat a prey with their back up against a wall and nothing else to lose!" Thorik shouted over the crowd. They were words the mountain King had spoken according to his Uncle Brimmelle. "Now is the time you look at what is in your hands and determine how it can be used to defeat your enemy!"

He could see the fear in their body language. Several even dropped their farm equipment to the ground. Others shook their heads at the thought of killing anyone, even a Del'Unday who wished to murder them.

"Pick up your weapons!" Thorik had to become the Mountain King right here and now in order to save them. He needed to compel them to charge forward with everything they had. "We will win this battle! It's foretold in history as our turning point!"

The words confused some while others struggled to come to terms with either dying or going against their beliefs and killing others.

"I will not kill!" shouted a Mognin.

"Then you will die!" Thorik shouted back.

"We will not kill," said another, then another, and soon a choir of voices chimed in on the chant.

Watching the army of Del'Unday racing in on them, Thorik began to panic. "The Mountain King's army has to win! We have to defeat them!" Glancing down at the chanting by the majority of species, he knew it was too late for this battle to be effective. "If you will not fight, then we will escape the city! Mognins, grab the harrows and hold them in front of you! You will plow our way straight through the middle and back into the city. Once there, make your way to the Portibule and run through any opening available!" He knew that any place was safer than inside Pwellus Dementa'.

The wooden racks with metal blades for breaking up the soil were given to the giant Mognins, who then held them out in front of them as a line of defense.

"Mognins! Form the shape of an arrow and everyone else get inside that arrow!" Thorik could see from his high vantage point that they only had moments to prepare. However, even with the eight-foot high stalks of corn, the Mognin's could see what was coming as well.

Unable to wait any longer, Thorik gave the command even though only half of them were in place. "Forward! Blow a path out of these fields!"

The approaching Del'Unday were hunting defenseless and frightened locals. Between that mindset and the casual military hunting strategy, they were completely taken off-guard by the sudden rush of massive Mognins running through the fields with blades pointing at them.

The sight of them bursting toward them caused a few Del'Unday to miss their footing, only to be trampled by the larger Ov'Unday. Others leaped forward with courage and impaled themselves onto the harrows. Some even stepped back to avoid being rolled over. Those that fought had to do so while avoiding the stampede.

Breaking through the frontline of Del'Unday was a minor victory, but a needed one. Mognin's took long strides but they were not one of the faster creatures around. They had been designed to haul large boulders and slabs of giant blocks, not win a foot race.

The Polenums and Humans had no problem following the front of the herd, but a few of the Ov'Unday were quickly falling behind, such as the Gathlers.

As the surprise of the escape plan wore off, the various species of Del'Unday revived their battle training and collectively started attacking specific Mognins. This opened gaps in the strong outer row of their escape arrow formation.

Pushing forward, the Del'Unday continued cutting down the Mognins. By this time, they were also attacked from the back side of the arrow pattern created by the Ov'Unday. Chaotically, they slaughter the Gathlers near the back and worked their way forward to the rest.

Several Ov'Unday stopped to cover and protect their loved ones, only making it easier for the Del'Unday soldiers to kill them as well.

"Keep moving! The city is the first step to your safety!" Thorik continued to provide orders from above. "We can make this!" It was then that a spiked mace was thrown from below, slicing Thorik's face, leaving several deep gashes across his cheek and forehead. The unexpected impact knocked the Num off the dragon and into the field nearly twenty feet below, knocking him unconscious.

Chapter 26
Retreat and Death

The Blothrud who had been talking to Ergrauth earlier ran up to the Num. "Orders from the Master." Raising his large sword high over Thorik's chest, he plunged the sword straight down.

In the instant it took for the blade to travel the distance to Thorik's chest, the Blothrud dropped the weapon and grabbed his eyes. A small green dragon was latched onto his head, gouging out the Blothrud's eyes. Each time the now blind Blothrud reached up to swing at the small winged creature, it leaped out of the way.

Chug landed next to them taking out several rows of corn with his typical landing. Turning to help Thorik, his tail swung around, knocking the legs out from the Blothrud. He then nudged the Num a few times to wake him up, without any success.

"He's out cold," Pheosco told Chug as the Blothrud stood back up and prepared to attack once again. "Pick Thorik up and meet me on the roof with Avanda." He then leaped at the face of the Del'Unday to distract him long enough for Chug to fly away.

Doing as his friend instructed, Chug grabbed Thorik in his front claws and lifted up into the air. Flying past the escaping Ov'Unday, they headed for the rooftop where Chug could see Avanda recovering near the ledge, slowly healing her own wounds. Smiling, the brown dragon let his tongue hang from the side of his mouth, which dripped saliva onto Thorik's face.

"He's here!" Avanda voice was still rough and it burned slightly as she attempted to shout at the incoming dragons.

With all the noise from the battle below Chug, it was difficult to hear what else she was saying as she continued to wave her less painful arm to get his attention. Seeing friends waving at him was something the brown dragon always loved to view. Nodding, he increased his speed toward her. Lifting Thorik up with one claw for safety, Chug landed with a hard thud, cracking the floor of the rooftop and skidding with his back feet to the far side of the building.

"No! He's here!" Avanda's voice was still painfully stressed and difficult to hear. "Chug, lift off before he grabs you!"

Unclear about her meaning, he sat back on his haunches and presented Thorik to her.

Before he could do anything else, Ergrauth reached up from the far side of the building and grabbed Chug off the roof, dragging Thorik with him.

Ergrauth's Mognin-sized body was massive, but even he had his limits as the Chuttlebeast-sized brown dragon was pulled off the roof toward him. Unable to hold him in the air with one hand, he grappled with Chug with both hands and pressed him up against the side of the building, cracking and breaking the structure. "Who are you? Did Rummon send you?"

Chug held onto the small unconscious Num in one claw as Ergrauth demanded answers from the dragon. His attempts to free himself without dropping Thorik were futile.

Growling at Chug, the lord of the Del'Unday moved his entire body closer to the dragon as he pressed him even harder against the wall. "Your involvement in this affair was a mistake that will cost you your life."

Whether it was the words he had said or the pressure he placed against his body, a large brown cloud of vapor flumed out of Chug's backside. The acidic aroma would have made a Chuttlebeast proud.

It was this smell that caused Thorik to awaken from the blow to his head. As he did, he realized he was dangling from Chug's grip and pressed up against the Demon, Ergrauth. "Ahh!"

Pulling back from the winged creature, Ergrauth ignored the small Num and kept his hands firmly at the dragon's midsection and neck as he began to squeeze both with his powerful fingers.

"Let my friends go!" came a female voice. Avanda stood on the roof ledge, with various magical components in hand.

Ergrauth grinned on one side of his mouth. "Absolutely. Once I crush his neck."

Tossing her components at his chest, they immediately snapped and began to freeze his skin, spreading across his chest, up his thick neck, and to his face. The ice was deep enough to prevent him from being able to move those regions, and he released Chug in order to use his fists to start pounding the ice off his upper body.

Chug immediately fell to the street before leaping back up into the air to collect Avanda on the roof. Setting Thorik on the roof, he watched as his friend Pheosco returned from surveying the Ov'Undays' escape.

"They are spread out all over the city. We need to go!"

Still dazed, Thorik ran over to Avanda who was weak from performing a spell she barely had the energy to perform. "Hold on, I'm going to get you out of here!" He then helped her up onto Chug and climbed on right after her. "Okay, Chug. Up!"

As they lifted off they could see Ergrauth ripping the remaining ice off his body. He was free. Then again, so were they. However, the locals were not. Flying overhead, Thorik and Avanda watched as the Del'Unday hunted the Ov'Unday down the streets and murdered them. Horrific screams could be heard across that part of the city. Thorik immediately started yelling down instructions as to the safest routes to the Portibule. Back and forth they flew across that section of the city helping as many as they could. However, they were now witnessing more executions by the time they arrived and were no longer able to assist those that fell behind in the escape.

Tortured by the sight of the devastation below, Thorik tightened his arm around Avanda as she returned the silent gesture by squeezing his arm with her hand. They both knew it was time to leave if they valued their own lives and if they wanted a chance to warn those living at the base of the White Summit.

"Chug." Thorik controlled his tone the best he could under the savage conditions he witnessed below them. "Go to the park in the center of the city, where the crystal towers stem from."

Veering slightly, the brown dragon headed to the opening which was filled with more survivors than they had thought. Nearly a tenth of the original locals at the festival were now gathered together.

Unfortunately, they had arrived too late. Surrounding the entire area, the Del'Unday tightened their noose around the remaining locals. Moving in on them, the residents began to be attacked and murdered as the military forces worked their way inward.

Ov'Unday near the middle of the piazza rushed onto the hexagonal platform from every direction, not caring where it led or if there would be a passage back to Pwellus Dementa'. Survival was the only instinct that applied as loved ones were swept away from each other by the crowds and pushed into the Portibule only to disappear from view.

The larger Ov'Unday such as the Mognins attempted to hold a strong perimeter against the Del'Unday, giving friends and family time to escape. Blothruds and Krupes were grappled and then tossed at other Del'Unday to push back the lines of battle. Unfortunately, without any real weapons or the desire to kill, the Ov'Unday could not hold their own against the blades and maces used by the predatory instincts and desires of the Del'Unday.

A gap was soon created between those escaping through the portal and an outer circle comprised of larger Ov'Unday species attempting to detain the Del warriors. It was into this rift that Chug set Thorik down so that he and Avanda could help.

Grabbing one of his Runestones, Thorik began to draw upon its powers. "We have to get out of here before Ergrauth arrives!" Holding the stone up above his head, surges of energy rolled out from it such as ripples in a lake from a fallen rock. Each ring of energy increased in size as it rolled across the courtyard and through everyone within it. As it did, the recipients slowed down as if time moved at a different pace for them. Humans, Polenums, Ov'Unday, and Del'Unday slowed in speed for a moment each time a wave band hit them.

Pulling out her own purse of spell components, Avanda quickly said a few key words and tossed a walnut up into the air. Those facing in toward the nut were provided with a momentary light show. Three quick blinks of various colors were followed by a blazing white light that caused temporary blindness. A large portion of the Del'Unday stepped back from the battle to adjust to the sudden lack of vision.

"Turn around!" Thorik yelled to the locals protecting the outer boarder. "Now is the time to escape before most can see again!"

It was more than obvious that most of the fighting had stopped, and seeing that the Ov'Unday wouldn't take advantage of the situation and pummel the aggressors, it was time for them to leave before the attacks continued.

Herding everyone into the Portibule was causing strange effects to the gigantic columns of crystals. A high pitched ringing could be heard from them and a low vibration was felt in the floor. The capacity of the portal gateway was exceeding its limitations.

Focusing back on the Runestone in his hand, Thorik directed the stone's energy at the crystals that grew out of all six angles of the platform. In doing so, he slowed the time encapsulating these thin long minerals. "This will only delay the issue! Hurry! Cross into the Portibule."

Pushing in from all sides, Thorik could see individuals walking literally through one another on the platform as though they were ghosts. Somehow the opening they entered caused them to not exist in the same place as others standing in the same location. His hands shook uncontrollably from the amount of energy needed to reduce the speed of time for such a large location. Closing his eyes, he gave everything he had until he fell to his knees in exhaustion.

The next thing Thorik recalled was another flash of light given off by one of Avanda's walnut spells. Opening his eyes, he was being helped to his feet by Avanda and a local girl he had seen before.

"O'Gee?"

"We'll explain later," Avanda said. Pulling him into the Portibule before a large group of Del'Unday arrived wielding swords and spears. Once onto the platform, O'Gee directed them into one of the side passages where two Blothruds leaped in toward them.

Avanda and Thorik dodged the oncoming strikes, while O'Gee stood idle, unsure why they stopped. In doing so, the blades from the enemy drove straight through her body. One sliced across her neck and the other directly into her heart. Yet there was no blood, no screaming in pain, and no sense that it really happened.

"Hurry!" O'Gee waved to the Nums to follow her without wasting any more time. Turning she walked right through the Blothrud's bodies and between the columns.

Glancing at each other for a quick moment, Thorik and Avanda grabbed hands and charged the Blothruds in an effort to follow O'Gee. In doing so, their bodies occupied the same space as the Del'Unday for a moment before passing the crystal portal passageway and landing inside Wyrlyn's home on the far side of the White Summit Mountain.

Dozens of confused Pwellus citizens held each other in fear within a large hall carved out to appear as the inside of a whale. Many were hurt. Many more were simply stricken with grief over the loss of loved ones.

"We're safe in Wyrlyn's home!" Turning around Thorik watched to see if any of the Del'Unday would follow.

O'Gee glanced from Thorik to the blank wall they all just escaped from. "They won't enter portals that are only single paths. It could lead them to the far end of lands or even deep underground. It's too risky if they don't know where it leads. For all they know, we just stepped into a solid rock and killed ourselves."

Moving his sights from the wall to the girl, he gave her a puzzled expression. "What are you doing here, O'Gee?"

"My mother suggested I look after you."

"Where is Ovlan? She will be worried about you."

"No, she knows I'm safe. Feshlan and my mother planned to travel to Weirfortus for one last evening together before Advent begins. We said our goodbyes before I returned to Pwellus Dementa', where it has always been safe…up until now."

"If you were there, why didn't you use some Notarian powers to stop the Del'Unday?"

"I don't have those powers. My father was a simple Polenum and I am more Num than I am Notarian."

Avanda stepped in and changed the conversation. "Thorik, some of these people need help. Do you recall the way out of Wyrlyn's home?"

"Yes." Leading the way, Thorik lead the large gathering out of the main hall, through various irregular corridors, out into the front lobby, and then outside the into the fresh mountain valley air.

Chapter 27
Weirfortus

On the west side of the massive freshwater lake, known as Luthralum Tunia, there was a wall many miles in length and extended a few thousand feet above the lake's surface. It had been built by the Notarians, the E'rudites, the Ov'Unday, and the lesser known Aq'Undays which lived below the water's surface. Massive stone blocks had been quarried from locations such as the White Summit and then stacked on the ocean's floor until the wall rose out of the water and into the air.

Once the underwater stone wall reached the entire length between the ocean inlet's shorelines, the saltwater was drained from within, creating a new land for the Notarians to live. The ocean's pressure would have easily cracked and destroyed the massive wall if it had not been for the E'rudites who lived within the wall and diligently used their powers to give the structure the strength to survive. Their purpose was to keep the water at bay until the Keystone could be found and made functional within the Lu'Tythis Tower.

After all the saltwater had been removed from the new lands, enormous algae-filled rooms filtered out the salt from the ocean's water before filling massive reservoirs with fresh water to be released by the E'rudites into the lake when required. This was the Weirfortus Dam.

Rooms for sleeping, training, and community interaction littered the inside so that the E'rudites could live and take shifts to keep everything stable. Dry passageways allowed for movement inside the dam and stone docks were built against the outside in order to float at the lake's water level. These provided access to boats as well as excellent vantage locations for the strengthening of the wall itself.

Wyrlyn stepped out of Weirfortus onto one of the docks and glanced over at the distant Lu'Tythis Tower that he had just departed. His mind had been racing with alternatives to becoming Deleth's slave along with everyone he knew. After a long moment of thought, gazing at the top of the remote island tower, he eventually peered over to a young man on the dock who was focused on a pyramid-shaped crystal pushing a prism of energy against the dam's wall. "Hello, Schulis. It is good to see you."

"Why, what brings you to these parts? I thought Ovlan granted you a prolonged sabbatical after your amazing work on the coliseum." The E'rudite continued to stand in the center of the dock as he used his powers to strengthen the wall against the ocean's pressure on the opposite side.

"She did, my friend." Smiling, he walked over to stand near him. "I have been creating my own gallery of sculptures within an abandoned rock quarry since then."

"Then you must be here to inform us of the completion of the Lu'Tythis Tower. After all of these decades, it will be a pleasure to explore new opportunities for our craft."

Lowering his voice, his tone became more serious. "I wish that were the case. I fear we may have another issue to address. One of dire consequences if I don't notify others immediately."

The younger E'rudite's brow lowered with concern. "Then do so and we shall resolve it, just like old times."

Pausing, he considered the ramifications of starting down this path, knowing the option of saying nothing would haunt him forever. "We are on the crossroads of becoming slaves for a new order. The Notarians have chosen an alternative plan for our lands, one that will change this landscape from a paradise to a prison."

His words were clearly a surprise to Schulis. "Surely this is but a miscommunication."

"Deleth was very clear when he informed me. He did not mince words. We either obey or perish." Watching the young E'rudite's expression of fear come over him, he added to his thought. "I, however, plan to do neither."

"We must alert Ovlan. She will resolve this."

"No. We are not to leave this structure until Deleth instructs us. By then it will be too late."

"Wyrlyn, he can't enforce such a regulation upon E'rudites."

"It is not wise for any of us to test this order, my friend." Grinding his teeth, he contemplated the challenge before them. "But I have not lived my life avoiding risks and I do not plan to start now."

"I will stand at your side as usual, my master. What can I do?"

"Your ability to move forward in time is a great skill. However, it is the changing of recent past events that would be most helpful."

"Then when do we leave to right this wrong?"

"If any of us leave, it could mean the destruction of us all. He watches our movement through the Portibule."

"Then we all go together as a united front. What could possibly stop the power of all the E'rudites working for a common cause?"

"Deleth is no fool. He knows such actions would risk the Weirfortus Dam's strength and the end to everything we have worked so hard to create and protect. Even if we allowed the ocean to break through Weirfortus and flood these lands the retribution for such a crime would be at a level we have never seen before. No, my friend, our leaving to warn others will do more damage than good."

"If only we could send a messenger."

The idea sparked life back into his face. "Perhaps that would work."

"He is far too intelligent to allow messengers to deliver warnings of his plans."

"True. They would only be inspecting for notes that would be alerting others of the upcoming events."

"I thought that was the idea."

"It is. Warning the reader will tip my hand to Deleth. If he finds out, he will surely be prepared."

"How do you plan on sending your message without him finding out?"

"I don't."

Chapter 28
Temporary Reprieve

Dozens of Pwellus Dementa' citizens filed out of Wyrlyn's front doors. Various species within the Ov'Unday were slightly outnumbered by the total Nums and Humans. Regardless of their forms, they all appeared exhausted and weathered from the battle. Most had fresh cuts or other injuries that caused them to limp or protect an arm or rib. These were clearly refugees from a disaster.

Grewen happened to be at the top of the steps as he surveyed the progress on the new homes near the half-moon lake's outlet to the river. "We need medical help!" he yelled out toward the newly constructed homes, in an effort to draw attention for assistance. Turning, he quickly began helping those struggling to walk. "What happened, Thorik?"

The Num had just stepped out with the others as he helped Avanda. "It was a slaughter. Ergrauth's army of Del'Unday have completely eliminated all other species from the city. The city is now a scene of a mass murder."

Picking up several others in his oversized hands to help them down the steps, he continued talking to his friend. "What provoked this action? I can't imagine the Ov'Unday causing a threat."

Several White Summit citizens ran over to triage the casualties and begin treating them.

Thorik followed Grewen as they spoke, helping Avanda down the steps. "The catalyst for this action was the vacuum of authority and power by the Notarians. Once they were gone, this gave Deleth the power to have Ergrauth assassinate the non-Del'Unday without anyone stopping him. And the only one in history that could stand up to this attack was killed because of decisions I made."

"You can't blame yourself. I'm sure you did the best you could."

"No. That's the worst part about it. Somehow I felt that I finally found the purpose in my life, and it was to act as the Mountain King. I truly felt this was my calling, Grewen, and in playing out this foolish lie hundreds of people died following my orders."

"This is exactly what I've been trying to tell you!" Brimmelle had approached them as Thorik had been talking. "You could never be like the Mountain King. His abilities were vastly superior to yours. How many of us must die under your command before you stop having these delusions of superiority? You killed the Mountain King! It's over! There will now never be legends and the Words of Order. There will never be Runestone scrolls taught to the youth so they understand the difference between right and wrong. And there will never ever be a statue against that mountain quarry wall of a man who embraces the greatest virtues we have to offer and encourages generations to strive for those high standards!"

"I can't be the one that has taken all of that away from this world. I can't live with that, even if I must sacrifice my life to right this wrong. I thought I could to try to act as the King and regain gift to the future, but I have failed."

"You're a fool, Thorik, not a king. Get that through your thick skull before you get us all killed. Just look at what you've done to Avanda!" Turning to walk away, he nearly stepped right into O'Gee, who had been standing just next to him. "How long have you been listening?"

Smiling, she raised an eyebrow as she thought a moment about the question. "I would guess that I've been listening since the day I was born."

"That's not what I meant!"

"I know, but I didn't want to give you that answer."

The answer was a bit unexpected and Brimmelle wasn't sure how to respond.

Grabbing his hand, she began to pull him away from Thorik and Grewen. "Come tell us more about the Mountain King. We do so enjoy your stories."

Brimmelle had waited most of his life to hear such words, and he almost didn't believe them when he did. Spending most of his life forcing others to sit still and listen to the teachings had become so engrained in his demeanor that he nearly melted in the girl's hands as she led him away to a group of children waiting for him. For a moment, life was perfect for him and he cared not about Del'Unday armies and Thorik wishing to be King. The glimmer in the children's eyes as they impatiently sat waiting for him to speak about his favorite subject, the Mountain King.

Grewen carried the last few needing assistance down the steps before addressing Thorik. "Why do you still allow Brimmelle to get under your skin?"

"Because he's right this time. I had no business getting involved in this. I should have listened to my instincts and just told everyone to run. Instead, I was trying to make history…no, I was trying to recreate history, and instead I made it worse."

"It sounds to me like that was the problem. You weren't listening to yourself."

Thorik was still holding onto Avanda. They both looked terribly defeated. Even with the blood still running down from the cuts on his face, her bruises and marks looked more serious. "Thank you for saving my life back there."

"I could say the same to you." Her attempt to smile caused too much pain to complete it. "We sure do get ourselves in the worst situations. Why do you think that is?" Holding her jaw, she didn't realize how many muscles it took just to talk, but now she was feeling each and every one of them.

"I heard what happened with the Keystone. I didn't realize Vesik was back in your life."

Her eyes lowered. "You don't understand."

"No, I don't."

"Yes, she called to me and I answered. But at that point, there was a spell I was looking for."

"There's always just one more spell."

"Thorik Dain, I've made mistakes in my life, just as you have. So you have to trust me when I tell you that the spell I was looking for was actually for you."

"For me?"

"Yes. Well, no. For us."

"Us?"

"It was a spell to return us home. It was a version of the spell my master, Bryus Grum, used to swap places with his pet bird in the Guardian Mountains. But this time we were going to swap locations with a few creatures through time instead of location."

Thorik appeared skeptical.

"I just wanted to return home with you and start our lives together in Farbank. I wanted to have a family with you and watch our children grow up and get in trouble the way we used to."

"I didn't get in trouble when I was younger. That was your specialty."

"True enough." The unconscious smile hurt her facial muscles again. "I only wanted Vesik long enough to see how the spell worked.

"And did you?"

"No, she wouldn't give me the final components to the spell and when I attempted to force it, she attacked me and everything around her, including the Keystone."

They both sat there on the bottom step in silence, still exhausted from their ordeal. As they thought about all that had happened.

Avanda lifted her head slightly to see those who were being attended to. Thorik peered around as well. They eventually looked at each other before she made the obvious comment. "Apparently others look worse than us, seeing that no one is coming to our aid."

Thorik's body ached from every movement and the longer he sat the harder it was to start moving his overworked muscles. "Here, let me escort you to your bed so you can rest."

"That sounds lovely." She then waited for him to stand up and help her up. "Are you planning on doing this soon?"

"I've made three attempts to stand up so far. Haven't you noticed?"

"No."

"Hmm…I thought I made some headway this last time."

"Not noticeable from way over here," she said, sitting next to him.

Without warning, both Nums were picked up into the air. "I think it's time for you two to find a good place to rest." Grewen's voice was easy to identify even without turning around to see him. "I'll send in someone to assist you as soon as we can."

And with that, Grewen carried them off with no struggles or complaints and placed them in their own tents for some well needed rest.

Chapter 29
A Gift Never Given

Thorik's Log:
What a fool I was to believe I could be the Mountain King. Not only have I prevented the real King from coming to power, I have disgraced his name by attempting to be him. It seems the more I try, the worse I make it for everyone involved. I'm lost. I have no direction in life. Why am I here? What was I meant for?

Rain fell throughout the night and into the next day as waves of thunderstorms rolled through. It fit Thorik's feelings of disappointment and gloom over his failed attempt to play out the noble deeds of the Mountain King. He had finally had the perfect opportunity to prove his self-worth in history and he nearly killed everyone by doing so.

Still living in a tent, he wanted to make sure those with families received the first homes built. The rest could wait until later, if there was a later.

Taking a deep breath, he listened to the rain over his head as it snapped upon the tent's surface giving slightly different pitches based on the size of the drops and the area it hit. The sound helped him relax. Periodic flashes of lightning created unique shadows on his tent as he counted the moments that passed until the thunder followed.

Some images against the tent looked almost alive as flags and other cloths flapped in the breeze. One shadow looked like a statue of a man, another like a bat, then another like a large bird.

His tent door flung open, sending a spray of water onto Thorik. "Good morning, dear! Isn't it gorgeous out?"

"Granna, you're soaked!"

Stopping for a moment, she realized he was correct and quickly shook all of the water off of her. Of course, this coated everything inside the tent with a nice layer of water. "I've heard you were a bit down on yourself."

"And who told you that?"

"Let's just say a little bird told me. Okay, not so little." Laughing at her inside joke she gave up the secret. "Actually, the bird was me. I'm usually right about those observations."

"It's nothing new, Granna. I'll learn to deal with my mistakes as usual. This time however, I think I've learned the lesson I needed to keep myself humble and my ego in check. I'm nothing more than a simple average Num."

"There's nothing wrong with your ego. It's your self-doubt that is your problem. But don't take my word for it. There are a few people you need to talk to, dear."

Thorik sat up slowly onto the edge of his cot. "Not now, Granna."

Gluic's eyes spun in different directions as her long bird neck craned forward. "Pull out the Trust Runestone and focus on it."

Unsure of the purpose, and also knowing that arguing the point would only delay it from being adhered to, he pulled out the appropriate Runestone and showed it to her. "There are still several Runestones that I haven't been able to activate and this is one of them."

"Pacify your grandmother, dear. Just try again."

"I've focused on it several times and if it's performed anything, it was not apparent to me."

"Not all of your Runestones are simply activated. Some require you to be interactive."

Not sure what that meant, he held the Runestone in his hands.

"No! No! You must stand up and take this seriously."

Doing as he was told he stood up slowly as his back cracked as few times.

"Excellent. Now step outside and let's give this a whirl."

"It's raining outside."

"Are you afraid of the rain?"

"No, it's just uncomfortable."

"You will never grow if you always stay comfortable, dear."

Finally stepping out into the muddy walkway, Thorik stood in the rain and waited for instructions.

"It's not going to activate itself, you know."

Shaking off a sudden cold wet chill, he again grabbed the Runestone with both hands and allowed the electrical sensation to go up one arm, through his chest, and then back down the other arm, into the stone.

A sudden bolt of lightning followed immediately with a loud crash of thunder causing Thorik's legs to weaken and his knees to buckle.

Maintaining his focus while now on his knees, he felt he was in tune with the Runestone's powers. Opening his eyes, he could see Gluic's beak inches from his nose. One of her eyes darted about independently as the other stayed focused on Thorik.

"What are you doing?" Thorik attempted to stay calm and focus on the Runestone's energy as they spoke.

Gluic didn't pull back from his face. "It's your turn. The stage is set. You've learned what you needed to learn. It's time."

"Time for what?"

"Time for you to stop blaming yourself for actions you've taken. You must own them, but not blame. Your parents would be proud."

"My parents aren't with me because of my actions."

"Aren't they?" Pulling back her beak from the tip of his nose, both of her eyes focused on an object behind him.

Slowly turning, his eyes began to grow as he could see his mother and father standing behind him outlined in the rain. "This isn't possible. You can't be here."

And with those words, their forms both faded.

"Why did you send them away?"

Standing up, he jerked his head around to see if the images had moved. "Granna, who was that?"

"Your parents, dear."

"No. My parents died when I was young. They died near Spirit Peak back when I lived in Farbank, thousands of years from now."

"Yes, dear. Their life force has been in this Runestone since their passing."

"They've been trapped all this time?"

"No. They died, but their souls were stored in this stone for your use one day. They don't feel the passage of time."

"Why did you not tell me this before?"

"You were not ready for this before now. And we have a limited time now that you have drawn upon their life force. They will only exist so long before we will not be able to contact them again."

"How much time?"

"It depends on how much was absorbed and stored in the stone and how well the stone retained its memory. Fortunately for you these are good stones. But you may have a minute or an hour. I have no such knowledge."

Turning back away from his grandmother, he focused on the Runestone again and with seconds his parents both returned. It was the rain that he was actually seeing as it hit their invisible bodies and ran down their faces and bodies. But it was enough to give him enough clear details to know that it was truly them.

Their images brought tears to Thorik's eyes. His chest tightened and his lips pursed. "I'm so sorry!" His voice was shaky and higher pitched than normal. "I didn't mean for you to die." Drooping his head, he didn't know what to say.

His mother stepped forward and placed a gentle hand under his chin to lift it back up. "There is no reason for you to be sorry. We are the ones who need to apologize to you. We made the decision to follow Su'I Sorat in an effort to find the Runestones. We made this choice. As parents, we should have thought more about the risk of never being there for you as you grew up, but look at you now."

Thorik's father stepped forward, placing a strong friendly hand upon his shoulder. "You have grown to be a strong looking Num. Excellent stance and good posture. I see experience in those eyes. You must have had some amazing adventures to have grown so much from the young lad I recall who wanted to be left alone to daydream and draw maps."

"I have, father. I have grown, but I would give all that away to bring you back."

Shaking her head, his mother disagreed. "Life comes and goes. We are all here for such a short time and we never know when our last day will be, so we must be thankful for every day we are given."

His father smiled at Thorik. "We were so fortunate to have our lives cross paths with yours. Never allow our parting of ways to define you. Instead, cherish what we had and build upon it."

"I've attempted to do so. I really have. Unfortunately, I've messed everything up. My actions caused the death of the Mountain King. I thought I did the right thing by taking his place and fighting his battle for him to save his name. It was a terrible disaster. I fear that I've done more harm than good."

"You fought a battle for the Mountain King leading them as the Mountain King?"

"Yes."

"No wonder it was a disaster."

"I know I don't possess the skills-"

"It has nothing to do with your skills. It has to do with you being who you are."

"I don't understand."

Gluic stepped into the conversation. "Dear, haven't you ever wondered why your soul-markings were so slow to come in."

"Yes, it's taken most of my adult life. In fact, they are still weak compared to most Nums."

"Your entire life you've been trying to do what would please others or you attempted to act like someone else to accomplish an action. You need to start listening to your heart and do what feels right for your own soul. Just start being you, dear."

"To be honest, I've done this for so long that I don't know anything else. I play whatever role is needed at the time to fit in or to help."

Thorik's mother smiled. "Always looking to please others. You get that from your father. It's charming and it's helpful, but at some point in your life you must feel good in your own skin and be willing to say no when you don't want something. This is your journey. Isn't it time you take control of it?"

In his typical fatherly voice, he added to his wife's comments. "You failed as the Mountain King because you were trying to be someone else and live up to actions that were meant for them along their path. If you had just stayed Thorik Dain, you would have succeeded."

"Would being me be enough?"

"Yes. Always. As long as you truly believe in yourself and do what it takes to make your plans come true."

The rain started to seep through his parents and their forms were losing their details.

"Don't leave me!" Thorik cried out.

"We are always with you," his mother said.

"But it's time to move on and be the best you that you can," his father added.

Tears ran down Thorik's face and mixed with the rain sprinkling on his head. "I love you! I will always love you."

"We love you, and are more proud of you than you will ever know."

The last word faded off as the outlines of their images washed away.

Thorik fell to his knees and gave a strong hard cry, finally allowing himself the opportunity to make peace with his loss so many years ago.

Gluic gave a soft smile and patted his head softly. "It's time for closure today. Tomorrow you will start a new day as you lead these people to freedom...your way."

Chapter 30
Dark Moments

Black marble flooring glistened from the fires in the carved out divots filled with oil along the sides of the long straight corridor. White marble was perfectly inserted along the wall in the shape of various unknown symbols from an unknown language. The center of the corridor floor was lined with a single piece of marble spanning the entire length of the walkway.

Heavy steps could be heard stomping down the corridor as it led toward a round forum area. They continued until the creature creating them stopped just inside the opening, where a man stood silently waiting for him.

"Ergrauth."

"Lord Deleth?" The giant Blothrud stopped moving down the passageway. "It was my understanding that you had returned home with the rest of the Notarians."

"I have been detained." His voice was soft and quiet and yet was very clear, as though he stood next to him instead of down the hall. "Have you brought something for me?"

Puzzled for only a moment, the mighty blothrud demon pulled forth a folded up parchment. "A messenger came through the Portibule from Weirfortus with this request. I had planned to place it in your chamber for you to read once you returned from your celebrations."

Deleth levitated the slip of paper from the Blothrud's hand and flew it across the room, halting just prior to him. Unfolding itself in mid-air, the document unveiled its instructions that were meant for others to read. "Wyrlyn is reaching out for Ovlan and Feshlan's support to prevent our plans. They plan to coordinate their efforts in Carrion Mire."

"We can defeat them, Lord Deleth."

"We? Your self-worth and value to me are out of balance."

Raising his upper lips, he exposed his sharp teeth as he growled from the comment. "I have done everything you have asked. I killed for you. I protected your assets. I even brought this critical message to you. I am more valuable to you than you let on."

After appearing slightly amused for a few moments, Deleth took on a very austere stance. "Let me ask you, Ergrauth, were the Del'Unday created by me?"

"Yes, Lord Deleth."

"And were they designed to be warriors that could easily kill a passive Ov'Unday?"

"You are correct again, Lord Deleth."

"Excellent. For a moment I thought I had errored in some way."

"Never, Lord Deleth."

"I should think not. And yet I still feel I'm in some way responsible in that I trusted you to utilize these powerful warriors to simply kill the Ov'Unday. Simple enough. Surround them and then chop their heads off. Not even a challenge. Unless, of course, you performed this event in the only place they can escape."

"I didn't think that-"

Cut short, Deleth talked over him. "You are absolutely correct. You didn't think. You have strength and courage, but you lack the intelligence of one of Feshlan's wild boars."

"We killed the majority of them and will hunt down the rest."

"Hunt down? They're scattered across the lands and are now hiding behind rocks and trees so that your patrols don't spot them. They'll propagate and multiply like a virus, infesting everything and then bursting out of hiding at the most inopportune times."

"We will find them all and they will die."

"I find that unlikely."

"A mistake was made. It will not happen again. My Blothruds are strong and smart. My Krupes are unwavering and fearless. The enemy won't be able to outwit us."

"Smart? Outwit? Do you know what I found when I returned from patching and reinforcing the damage to the Keystone? No, of course you don't. Aside from returning to find out about a relatively simple attack on the citizens of this city had failed, I also came back to find out that my prisoner had escaped. You know the one, don't you? The only prisoner I have? The one that nearly destroyed one-hundred years of work by cracking the Keystone? The weak little Polenum female that was being guarded by one of your strong and smart Blothruds. Does any of this trigger any memories in that hollow brain cavity of yours?"

Seething at the insult and humiliation, Ergrauth was shaking in anger. Towering twice the height as Deleth, he could easily crush the Notarian with a single blow, unless the Notarian saw it coming. If it was a frontal attack, he knew Deleth would use his powers to crush his body in the blink of an eye. And so he stood there and took the abuse.

Intrigued as to how far he could push the creature before him, Deleth waited quietly for several moments to see if the beast would snap. When Ergrauth didn't, he continued. "Travel to the last remaining work camp and destroy the remaining cluster of Ovlan's unneeded creations."

Ergrauth grinned, knowing that he had caught him in a mistake. "Don't you mean the last two work camps?"

"It's so rewarding to know you are staying cognizant of these events."

Feeling slightly vindicated, Ergrauth pulled his shoulders slightly back.

Walking up to the creature, Deleth waved for Ergrauth to lean down so he could talk to his head instead of his crotch. Once Ergrauth bowed down, Deleth spoke softly. "I destroyed the Dolor work camp a few months ago. There is now only one work camp remaining. If you had used the Portibule to arrive inside of Dolor for an invasion, you would have sent your entire army into solid rock and ice from the collapsed walls and glaciers. I just saved you from killing your entire military force, so in the future I suggest you resist the temptation to prove your intelligence around me. I already know your weaknesses. I created them on purpose."

Fuming from the verbal thrashing, Ergrauth's upper body shook with anger. "Why didn't you kill the citizens? Was it a moment of weakness?"

"No. Unfortunately Wyrlyn was nearby. Killing the citizens could have been detected by him and he could have tipped my hand to the other Notarians as to what my plans were. By keeping this quiet, all of the Notarians have returned home without any worries. I now have no risk and no weaknesses." To prove a point, Deleth took the opportunity to turn his back on the creature and see if he would let loose his fury.

The idea raced through Ergrauth's head several times, but he knew it was a trap. He would have to wait for a time that the Notarian did not feel threatened. "About the Portibule…"

"Yes?"

"The mass exodus damaged the crystals. It will only allow a few of us through at a time and requires time between each use. Additional use will surely damage it more."

Deleth finally showed his anger and without a single movement, the oil flames lighting the corridor immediately went out and a sound of Ergrauth in violent pain echoed throughout the building.

Chapter 31

Directions Given

Thorik's Log:
The legends of the Mountain King and his army have spread, embedding a sense of hope for our future as well as fear of the pending battle. I have no doubt that this will be a difficult challenge to survive, let alone win. Perhaps the faith in my uncle's stories will be enough to help us succeed in our goal of being free.

Sitting in the open grassy area, Brimmelle and Narra schooled the children on everything from the Mountain King to how to count and read. They had become the natural teachers of the White Summit village and took the opportunity to expand their time with the local youth to provide helpful skills. After a bit, Narra rounded some of the children up to instruct them on how to weave baskets, while Brimmelle headed to the hills to collect berries with the rest of the children. Fir Brimmelle had learned from his first experience with the berries to stay clear of the staining juices and urged the children to be careful.

Holding and swinging Avanda's hand, O'Gee led them to the children sitting near Narra. She quickly sat down to listen to the lesson while watching the children attempt the weaving for themselves. Reaching over for a chance to hold Narra's infant, O'Gee was full of cheer to hold and cradle the little boy. Making various goofy sounds with her lips, she made the baby laugh and giggle.

Avanda slowly lowered herself to sit near her. Still aching from head to toe, she eased her bottom onto the ground and sat cross-legged before she stretched her back with a controlled arch.

ZiXi popped her head up from under sleeves, cloaks, and blankets. She, like the rest of her species, was extremely nimble and hard to detect until she chose to present herself. Once she was out of sight it was difficult to know if she had left or was hiding.

Landing behind them, Gluic spread her wings to prevent herself from tumbling forward onto the children. "What do you think of our newest member, Avanda?"

With a pleasant expression upon her face, she reached over to collect the child for her opportunity to play. "He's adorable and he is the first of this new era." Playing with his cheek, she made him smile. "We'll have to take special care of him."

"You should. He's your greatest of grandfathers, dear."

Squinting at the thought, she craned her neck to look back at the orange and red colored bird. "Gluic, what are you saying? Are you suggesting that this child is a distant grandfather of mine."

"That's what you said, dear, not me." Her eyes spun off in different directions as usual. "Although it's true."

Narra's and Avanda's eyes met with a newfound interest in each other. "That would make her…" they both said in unison. However, neither finished their sentence as they reached over to hold each other's hand for a moment as to accept the new bond.

Placing both hands under the infant once again, Avanda lifted the boy up to her face. "Welcome to the family!" Her happy words were returned with a series of bubbles and drool from his mouth. "Yep! We're related." Laughing at her own joke, she held the baby up to show Grewen as he led most of the villagers toward Wyrlyn's home. "Grewen!" she yelled. "I'm his great, great, great granddaughter!"

Glancing over, he grinned. "I think you missed a few 'greats' in there."

"Why thank you!" Avanda said with a smile as she returned to play with her new relative instead of getting involved in the daily update announcements.

Walking up to Wyrlyn's massive stone structure, Grewen met Thorik who was already standing at the top of the steps. The White Summit citizens were a collection of those remaining from working at the quarry, the Dolor citizens, and those who had just escaped from Pwellus Dementa'. The Mognin had been able to ensure that Thorik's vision of the new town was being built while the Num had been training or traveling.

The progress in construction of new homes had started to come together. Jobs had been assigned for everything from cutting down trees, transporting lumber, cutting it into the sizes needed, as well as building the floors, walls, and ceilings. Other duties of ensuring food and water were also tasked. Most migrated to a task that they were best suited for or had some training in.

"It's about attitude, not size." Grewen tried to coach his Num friend before his planned speech.

Slowly glancing up at the Mognin, he chuckled. "That's easy to say when you're two to four time taller than every other species."

"Tell me, Thorik, would you jump from a spider that fall upon your arm?"

"Of course."

"Why? They are smaller than the size of your foot. You could easily crush them. Shouldn't they be the ones intimidated by you?"

Watching more villagers show up in the courtyard at the bottom of the steps. "Alright. Alright, I understand what you're getting at. Although for me to pull this off, I hope Ergrauth is just as afraid of Nums as I am of spiders."

"You just need him to be intimidated by one Num, you."

"Correct. How hard could that be?"

Standing on the top step of the wide staircase in front of Wyrlyn's home, Grewen waited until nearly everyone had left their homes and job sites, walked across the grassy area, and then gathered in the open courtyard. "Thank you all for working together on our new life here at the base of the White Summit. It inspires me to see all of our various species working so well together to help build a new future for ourselves and our children. However, Thorik has some news that will change our lives, so please move in so you can hear."

Thorik stepped up next to the giant, making the Num look even smaller than his species really was. "Thank you, Grewen. You've performed an unbelievable task in starting the community for a free society." Noticing that several of the villagers where slightly distracted, he gave a questioned look to his friend.

Bowing slightly at the compliment, Grewen reached over and removed ZiXi from the Num's shoulder before stepping off to the side and sat down on a wall nearly as tall as Thorik.

With a voice not as powerful as a Mognin's, he still needed to show a level of authority after following his friend, so he stood tall and projected the best he could to everyone before him. "You have spent most of your lives as slaves. Some of you had more challenging tasks with more brutal masters. Those few that had a peaceful existence as they served will have the hardest time understanding and supporting what I am about to say."

The crowd looked at each other as well as Thorik and Grewen with confused expressions.

"What I have found is that the Notarians had created all of us to serve various purposes. Some were to mine the blocks for Weirfortus and other structures. Other species were created to provide trivial duties to make life easy for the Notarians once they have colonized these lands. And some, such as the Del'Unday, where created to control us when needed, prevent us from overpopulating, and even butcher us if we are no longer needed."

Reading the faces before him, Thorik continued. "What they didn't expect was that we became more than drones and tools for their needs. We became self-willed and have the ability to develop our own culture and our own ways of life. This new-found power of ours has created fear within Deleth, so he has ordered Ergrauth to eliminate all of us from these lands prior to the Notarians returning. This, my friends, is the real Freedom Festival. It's a cleaning of this world by exterminating us. He wishes to purge us from existence because we are no longer obedient to his ways. So, he has sent Ergrauth on his way here with his Del'Unday army to finish this task."

"We'll run!" A voice came from within the crowd before several more chimed in. "We'll hide!" said another. They erupted with ideas. "They can't find us all if we scatter!"

"No!" Thorik raised his arms in his attempt to settle everyone down. "Running is no way to survive. I know. I've done it. My dear friend, Ambrosius, ran for a while. It never works. We must face our fears head on. We must stand up for what we believe is right. We must not allow them to destroy us simply because they do not need us or want us around."

"We are but miners!" a shout was heard. "We can't fight an army!" yelled another. "They are stronger than us!" The last one to speak was unaware that there was a Quix resting on his hat.

"Yes, they are!" Thorik shouted back attempting to not let the Quix break his concentration. "They are trained with weapons and given strength and ability to wield them. I will not argue this. They could walk in here today and kill every one of us. However, that is what we must play on if we wish to win this battle. The future lies with those who can overcome challenges, not to those using their strength to prevent change."

The crowd was completely confused. A Quix head popped out of a Gathler's cloak long enough to be seen by Thorik from up front.

Grewen, however, looked intrigued. "Thorik, what is your plan?"

"We change everything we know about a battle. First of all, we fight them here, on our ground. Let them exhaust themselves racing down the mountainside and across the valley floor. Then once they arrive, we end their attack before it even starts."

Grewen wasn't going to let the Num off that easy. "The Ov'Unday would rather die than kill oncoming attackers. It is not in our nature or our beliefs to murder."

"There will be bloodshed, my friend. It is a battle for our lives and for the future of our species. I can't promise that we will all survive. But I can even up the odds and I can give us hope to survive as a new culture in this world. Our other option is to scatter and allow them to hunt us down a few at a time. Dolor has been destroyed! A massacre has killed most in Pwellus Dementa'! They are now on their way here! We need to stop this here and now!"

Many in the crowd began to nod their heads in agreement. Dozens of quirky Quix had even come out of their hiding places to look at one another with concern. ZiXi popped out from Grewen's robe and looked about at her fellow species and then back at Thorik. "What are you asking from us?"

"Who will fight with me to save our children, our lives, our existence, and our future?"

Several cheered at the words and the passion Thorik put behind them.

"We will fight as the Mountain King army! We will win the day and we will end their plans of genocide forever!"

The Summit Valley citizens applauded for their new leader and his words.

Chapter 32
Details and Logistics

Fresh cool winds blew down the southern face of the glacial mountainside into the lake valley below, picking up the fragrance of pine trees before it flowed down the river valley. Sweeping across the warm mineral spring lake, the air absorbed just enough moisture to enhance the pine scent before brushing across the faces of hundreds of laborers grooming for war.

Males and females of various species worked together preparing for a battle against the well-trained Del'Unday warriors. Basic bows were made and arrows were shot at practice targets. Crude shields were constructed and nets were woven from twisted twine. There was no time for any fancy designs; it was all about function as time was at a minimum. Everyone who could work was working, aside from Brimmelle who quickly became the master of child care... as long as they would listen to his stories and not wipe berry juice on his clothes.

"We need more twine!" Thorik shouted as he surveyed the progress of his army. The deep cuts across his face from the Pwellus Dementa' attack were scabbed over but would never fully heal. "Reinforce those spokes to carry a heavier load!" Thorik's head shot back and forth as he coordinated everyone's efforts as he walked through the busy streets of the village. "Cut down enough trees to build the framework for a portable bridge!"

Seeing Luva in distress over the dismantling of his mural on the community center, Thorik gave him a pat on the back. "It's for a greater cause. We appreciate you sacrificing your artwork for this endeavor." Watching the Mognins pull the walls apart in order to use the resources for battle, Thorik made one last comment to the Gathler before moving on. "I look forward to seeing your next painting after we finish this battle."

Walking alongside Thorik while he did his inspection, Avanda was clearly not pleased. Her bruises and scars were clearing up nicely, so her expression had nothing to do with past injuries. Having had tried to interrupt his hollering of commands multiple times, she attempted it once again, this time more forcefully. "Can we talk about this?"

Avoiding eye contact, he continued to walk and inspect everyone's work. "There's nothing to talk about, Avanda."

"I disagree. You're leading this passive community into a war against an aggressive army of Del'Unday."

"Yes. That's correct." Picking up one of the wood cutting axes being converted to a war weapon, he pointed to the grip. "Put leather straps on these so they don't slip out of our hands."

Struggling to retain his attention, Avanda continued. "To what end? Even if you are capable of performing the legendary acts of the Mountain King, do you remember what happened to him?" Stepping in front of him, she caused him to finally stop and look her in the eyes. "He died!"

"I'm not trying to be the Mountain King and I'm not going to die." Stepping to the side he continued to walk and perform his inspection. "Pull those ropes tighter around those beams!" he shouted up to a few men building a platform.

"So, not only are you going to accomplish what the greatest Num has ever done, you think you can top it by surviving the battle as well?"

"I have to do this, Avanda!"

"Why? Because you are responsible for Gansler's death? Has Brimmelle pushed enough guilt into your heart that it controls your actions?"

The words struck him hard, forcing him to stop and turn to face her. "I accept that I'm responsible for the real King's death, but that no longer matters and it no long controls me. What I'm doing here is leading us to victory against extermination. I refuse to run and hide in the shadows of these lands."

"Why is it so wrong to leave this valley to live another day?"

Tension melted away as Thorik stepped closer to her and held her in his arms. "What happened to my adventurous little lady who had no fear, who charged head-strong into the unknown?"

Avanda slowly looked up at him. "I don't wish your child to be without a father." She let that sink in before continuing. "Yes, Thorik Dain of Farbank, I am with child."

"I'm a... I mean you are... we are..." He couldn't finish a sentence if he wanted to.

Her smirk calmed the moment. "Yes, on all accounts."

"But we have a battle to win. You can't be out here in the sun while people are working." It was clear he was flustered and struggling to compile a clear thought.

"I'll be just fine." Pulling him back into her, she regained his focus. "I want to settle down and finally enjoy our lives together."

"But they are coming for us." His thoughts began to return to the battle at hand.

"You know I support your reasoning. I trust and love your conviction for what's right. It's your strength against the steel blades of Krupes and Blothruds that frightens me. Your eyes are as strong and clear as any Num, but even they can't see the invisible Brandercats. And what if Ergrauth himself arrives to join the battle? How does one take down a demon of such power without another demon fighting for us? This is not even a battle that the Mountain King could win."

He then gave her a devilish smirk. "True, but I am not the Mountain King, which gives us the advantage."

Chapter 33

The Mountain King War

A dark hue began to fill the distant mountain passage up in a cradle of two sharp peaks, as though grey smoke was flowing into the valley. Thin and dense at the pass, the coloring thinned out as the smoky presence widened under the tight route. Unfortunately, it was not smoke. It was an army of Del'Unday breaching the valley's boundaries and beginning their invasion. War had arrived in the valley whether Thorik would play the King or not.

"Prepare for war!" Thorik yelled to his people. "Brimmelle! Move all the children and your assistants into Wyrlyn's home! Grewen, tighten the catapults!"

As the Del'Unday worked their way down the mountainside the grey misty mass appearance gave way to individuals. The closer they came the more details could be seen; the size of the creatures, the species, the armor, and the weapons they carried. Less of a wave in movement, they approached as a swarm of bees as many raced out in front to start the conflict before the others arrived.

They would first have to travel down the hillside and into the grass fields of the valley which were littered with large boulders that had rolled down from the upper outcroppings. Threading the needle between the lake and the river, they would then have to cross the bridge spanning the lake's water outlet before reaching the village settlement. It's at this next point that the combat would begin. Once they departed the village and approached the open courtyard that led to the steps of Wyrlyn's home, they would encounter the last remaining Ov'Unday community and the final battle to remove them from the world would begin.

Halfway between Wyrlyn's home and the small village, Thorik stood upon a platform and gave orders to stay calm, while he himself was trembling inside. "Execute the plan just as we practiced! No changes to our plan unless I give the order! We are fighting for the Mountain King and we are fighting for our own survival. We will be victorious! The King's army will prevail!"

He could feel the nervous tension in those around him. His soldiers shifted their weight from side to side and frequently glanced back and forth from Thorik to the approaching enemy. Anxiety caused many to continually re-grip the weapons they held before them. Even the normally calm Mognins and Gathlers were showing signs of stress.

Fading in and out from Thorik's vision, several Brandercats were racing out in front of the rest. These large mammals were not coated with hair as most cats were. Instead, they had scales that bent light, allowing them to hide in plain sight.

After reaching the base of the valley the cats headed directly for the bridge that spanned the lake's water outlet, which fed into the fast moving river downstream. Without any obstacles it wouldn't take them very long to travel across the overpass and into the structures built for the locals to live in.

Thorik could feel many eyes on him as they reached the bridge. "No action! Hold your ground!" He pulled his chest up and wore confidence in his face. Everything he did from this point on had to be performed as planned. He could no longer have the emotional attachments and self-questioning doubt that Thorik Dain of Farbank had over the years. He had to trust himself and his instincts. "Prepare the catapults!"

Over the bridge and into the streets of the small village, the Brandercats were no longer visible to Thorik and his defenders. He would have to wait for them to make their way through before they could be visible. In doing so, they could easily turn themselves invisible. The short distance from the village to the King's army gave little to no time to react to seeing footprints in the dirt.

More Del'Undays reached the base of the valley and approached the bridge as more continued to flow through the tight mountain passage. Their numbers continued to grow and there was already one Del'Unday for each member of the Mountain King army.

As expected, the large invisible cats burst out from behind the homes for face to face combat against them, but they were still unseen by Thorik and his followers due to the Brandercat's invisibility. As they leaped forward a series of twines crossing their paths were triggered, causing buckets of smashed berries to rain down upon them while exiting the paths between the homes.

Coated with dark sticky juices, the cats were now clearly visible as well as unmistakably angry. Attempts to shake off the staining liquid were pointless, and they stopped trying as they gathered together for a collective attack.

The frontline of the Mountain King's army was a straight line of Nums and Humans holding large shields which butted up against one another to make a five foot high fence. Each shield had a spike at the bottom which they had driven into the ground for stability. The shields also had a notch three fourths the way up on the back that was used to place one end of a short staff or stick while the other end pushed in the ground, strengthening the shield-made fence.

The Brandercats rushed the shields at a full run.

"Hand Nets! Now!" Thorik ordered to his front line.

Leaping up over the shields, the Brandercats would easily breach the frontline.

Behind the temporary fence was a row of Mognins who towered over the others. Standing twice the height as the Humans, several of them swung nets at the oncoming attackers.

Captured in the nets, the Brandercats fought to free themselves before the net was fully wrapped around them as Mognins placed hooks on the net's corners. Once the hook was placed, the large cats were shot up into the air. The hooks were attached to ropes that were anchored to large beam-sling weapons, similar to trebuchets. Once airborne the nets fell open and the cats plummeted into the raging river, quickly carrying the creatures away from the area. Steep river-cut cliffs along the shoreline prevented their escape for many miles downstream. It could take days for the Brandercats to make their way back to the battle.

More nets were tossed and more Brandercats were snared, just as the first ones had. Brandercats were ejected from the battlefield as quickly as the Mognins could catch them in nets and send them on their way. Without a single life taken on either side. the campaign was a success and small pockets of cheering could be heard.

More Del'Unday raced down the mountainside, along the river's edge, across the bridge spanning the lake's water outlet, and into the temporary refuge of the villager's homes. This time it was Blothruds, who would not be taken so easily as the Brandercats.

Waiting for the right moment, Thorik knew that others felt he had allowed too much time to be played out. "Prepare for the bridge! On my mark…" He waited until the bridge was at its capacity to the point that the enemy had to wait to squeeze into line to cross. "Release the bridge!"

Gathlers pulled on ropes that wrapped through several pulleys and then attached to the bridge, causing the planks to give way. Those on the bridge immediately fell through the structure as though the ice on a frozen lake had given way, trapping them up to their chests. However, before the Del'Unday were able to react, another set of ropes were pulled and the entire bridge snapped off from both shorelines and was pulled out into the main river before it began to freely float downstream with the majority of the occupants still attempting to break free.

Another victory cheer was heard as Thorik and his defenders were suddenly beginning to feel confident about their chances.

The Del'Unday who had made it past the bridge emerged from the homes and attacked with full force.

Krupes plowed into the shields, knocking holes in its fence line for others to enter. Blothruds leaped over the shields, swinging their swords at the giant Mognin. Nets were used but few were successful at throwing more Del'Unday out into the river. The King's army could not keep up with that tactic any longer.

"Hand to hand combat!" Thorik shouted, snapping his head back and forth as he attempted to keep an eye on all the activities below.

Krupes slowly and steadily fought their way forward, taking down all that resisted them. Blothruds chopped at the Mognin's nets before being snared and sliced their swords at their enemies, cutting off limbs and puncturing torsos and heads. The scene suddenly became bloody and wicked with hatred and malice, killing those only wishing to protect and defend.

"Overpower them!" Thorik cried out from above on his tower. "We outnumber this wave. Swarm! Just as we practiced!"

Thorik's confused troops pulled out of their fear long enough to obey his orders and they rushed toward the Del'Unday warriors. The first organized attempts at a mob attack were quickly cut down by the Del troops but soon they learned how to overpower and capture Del'Undays by using their collective mass and strength. Once disarmed and tied up, Mognins would carry the warrior to the cold swift moving river and toss them in.

However, the battle raged on as more broke through the shield fence. Some even fought their way free of the binding ropes and nets. Del'Unday had a fierce desire to fight to the death and would not be tossed out like trash by passive Ov'Undays. Each Blothrud and Krupe killed or maimed a dozen of the King's troops before being captured and restrained.

A large wave of Del warriors finally approached the now missing bridge after making their way into the valley. Blothruds ordered the Krupes into the water to start building

a living link to the far side of the waterway. It wouldn't be
long before the rest of Ergrauth's army would be upon
Thorik and his followers.

Thorik instructed his troops. "Uproot Shields! Hand
to hand combat! Archers ready!"

Humans and a few Nums pulled back on their bow
strings, holding their arrows as steady as they could. Several
strings snapped and a few arrows were dropped, but the rest
aimed toward the enemy and waited for the call.

Krupe after Krupe lowered themselves into the water
like a chain of army ants, except that these soldiers sank to
the bottom, over their heads. Following orders, they did so
without question as more piled upon them, creating a solid
bridge from the shields on their backs. It would only take
minutes before the remaining Blothruds would charge across
and finish the fight.

"Archers, Fire!" Slicing the air with a wave of a
single arm, he ensured all archers knew his intent to launch
their stone tipped wooden missiles.

A scattering of arrows filled the air just over Thorik's
head. Several, however, slapped the platform he stood upon.
He knew these weapons took years of practice and the only
value they would have was if the land before him was
saturated with targets, increasing their odds of hitting the
enemy. The somewhat random arrows wobbled through the
air at the Del'Unday on the far side of the new waterway
passage. Hitting their target was low in their favor, but the
sheer amount made up for it as they began to strike. More
than half struck something other than the ground, and half of
those actually caused some level of injury. However, few
caused any Del'Unday to end their ability to fight.

After assessing the ongoing hand to hand attacks with
the remaining Blothruds, Thorik turned back to see the
ramifications to the missile attacks. "Prepare for a second
volley!"

Back at the bridge, the Del'Unday ripped a few
wagons apart and used the timber to even out the path across

the backs and heads of the Krupes in the water. Soon the new bridge would allow the rest of the warriors and their wagons of supplies to enter the battle.

Pheosco sliced through the air and just over the enemy's heads as he spit out small fireballs directly into their eyes, causing them to lose focus. His aim was superior and his enjoyment of being involved in the action was far too obvious.

Following the green dragon through the air, Chug dropped his massive legs below him at just the right time to smack the unsuspecting in the head, knocking them over and often out cold. Unfortunately, his aim wasn't that of Pheosco's and he periodically slapped a Mountain King's troop member upside the head.

Thorik continued to give the King's army direction from a platform that once stood safe behind the front line, but was now surrounded by close range combat.

Nets occasionally worked, flinging the enemy into the river. Arrows impacted a few nearby Blothruds, and sometimes one of their own. A few giant Mognins were cut down to their knees before a mob was able to jump in and overpower the attacker.

Grewen quickly helped those he could reach and tied up those he wished to be removed, but he could not keep up with the amount of Del'Undays still fighting.

Swinging around for another pass, Pheosco flew toward Chug as he was ending his. A nod of approval to the brown dragon caused the typical response from the brown dragon when being praised, as a brown cloud was released from his backside. Unable to turn in time, Pheosco barreled into it and lost his heading. Upon escaping the fumes, a Blothrud had him at a disadvantage and struck him with his mighty fist, sending the unconscious green dragon plummeting to the ground.

By the time Chug turned around for his next pass, his friend was nowhere to be seen.

Considering pulling out his Runestones, Thorik knew that it would leave the defenders without a leader while he focused on the stone. In addition, any powers he used to hurt the Del'Unday would surely hurt his troops as well. So, instead he grabbed the sword he was given for battle and defended his platform from the remaining Blothruds while still yelling out orders.

It was then that he noticed that a new wave of warriors had rushed across the newly created living bridge and were now making their way through and out of the village's streets. Knowing that they would lose this battle if this new group reached their frontline, he shouted, "Avanda! Now!"

Within one of the structures inside the village, Avanda had been hiding and waiting for her name to be shouted. Finishing with the last component of the spell she had been working on, she stepped backward into a protective bubble, which she had created prior to the battle. Watching from within, she watched her spell infect everything around the clump of components on the ground.

Starting in the center of the village, the structures quickly turned a brownish green in appearance. Every stone, metal, plant life, and anything else with any physical matter suddenly began to decay, and mold, and rust away. Everything within its reach was affected and rapidly broke down in ashes. Even minor particles in the air felt its wrath as they broke down and floated to the ground like an unexpected brown rain shower starting only a few yards above the ground.

This infestation of death reached out in all directions, breaching the boundaries of the structures. Warriors within the area suddenly felt their skin being eaten away. Screaming from the acid-like feeling, green and black mold formed across their faces and down into their throats.

Those in midstride found that their legs literally cracked and shattered from the pressure of stepping on them. Within a mere moment all those who had been in the epicenter of the spell had fallen to a crumbing mass of rotten flesh.

The critical moment following was when the wave of the spell reached out to those just outside of the now destroyed homes. This included the living bridge and the warriors about to attack the King's army. The ramifications were the same, as the spell coated the Del'Undays with a fast acting plague, destroying the living and non-living alike.

Cries of pain were cut short as the victims of the spell rarely had the time to react before their vocal cords and many other internal organs turned to a liquefied state before hardening and crumbling away.

The spell rolled out across the ground in every direction, including toward the original frontline fence of shields. Then without warning it stopped. The following moments were filled with the sounds of the last few Del'Unday and structures falling down upon the dead grasslands. Once the spell had completed its task the only visible object between the far side of the missing bridge and the battle near Thorik's platform was a hovering sphere with someone inside it.

Looking out past the oily red and blue swirls of her sphere, Avanda could see the destruction in every direction. Her spell had worked and she had to wait for the light wind to blow away any remaining dangers. Once she felt it was safe, she stepped out of the sphere and onto the dead ground. Her foot sunk into the surface several inches as the top layer of the ground had lost its solidity.

Fearful of this new weapon, the Del'Unday on the far side of the lake's water outlet stopped in their tracks before risking taking any steps in the dead lands before them. They had just witnessed their comrades dissolve before their very eyes. It was time to stop and reassess their plans.

Knowing that no more Del warriors were crossing over, Thorik focused back on the battle just below his platform. Climbing down the ladder, he quickly started supporting the fight on the remaining Del'Unday. Their victory seemed to be at hand and Thorik knew he may have just saved the Mountain King's name and legend for future cultures.

Unknown to most, O'Gee had left the safety of Wyrlyn's stone fortress. She had been standing out on the top of the steps observing the battle as a curious spectator.

It was then that Thorik heard screaming from his own people. Instead of being up near the front line, where Thorik expected it to be, these cries for help came from the back, near Wyrlyn's home.

Sweeping down from the sky, dragons began attacking members of Thorik's defenders. Hundreds of flying beasts of various types and sizes had joined the battle. Some were as small as a Num Child and some as large as a Chuttlebeast.

The Mountain King's army scattered in every direction. They were no longer under Thorik's command. It was complete chaos as dragons attacked with sharp claws and biting teeth.

By this time Brimmelle had realized that O'Gee was gone and he raced out the front doors and down the wide stairway where she was still standing in amazement of the surreal events before her. Grabbing around her waist, he picked her up and ran back for the doorway, only to find he path blocked.

A large black dragon landed hard up against the tall doors, pushing them shut and blocking Brimmelle's path. It roared at the two Nums and moved forward for the kill.

In the distance, Brimmelle heard Thorik's voice making commands. Stepping down the stairs backward, the Fir tripped onto O'Gee and they rolled to the bottom of the staircase.

The black dragon followed them down and grabbed them in its front claws. Drool dripped from the creature's gums as it leaned over to bite their heads off.

Just then, Brimmelle could hear Thorik's voice once again, and then the black dragon roared in pain. Ridden by

Thorik, Chugs heavy body pounced upon the black dragon's back and bit into its neck. Rib bones snapped and blood shot out from the massive neck injury. A quick twist of Chugs head and the snap of the black dragon's neck echoed across the battlefield.

Hopping off of his brown dragon, Thorik pushed O'Gee up onto Chug. "The main doors are shut and only Wyrlyn can open them from the outside. I'll have Chug fly you to safety!" He then helped his Uncle onto the brown dragon as well.

Slapping Chug's side, he yelled, "Get them out of here!" Raising his sword, Thorik returned to the battle as his defenders were falling apart.

With battles all around them, Chug had to push over and step on a few other dragons before he gained any altitude. Once free of the ground, he fought several smaller dragons who were attempting to pull the Nums from his back. Slapping his thick tail and making a few maneuvers, which nearly knocked the two Nums off, Chug was finally able to break free with his payload intact.

A low pitched rumble echoed through the valley and the vibrations could be felt on the ground as well as in the air. Thorik had fought his way back to the platform to assess the situation, but upon hearing the low vibration, he peered up to the Mountain passageway. He could see an enormous Red Dragon perched on the peak. Rummon had arrived.

Upon hearing the low vibration, all of the dragons immediately stopped fighting and then bolted straight up into the air before they flew toward the lord of all flying creatures. It was a primal force so instinctive for all dragons that even Chug fell in line and headed toward Rummon with a blank stare.

Brimmelle shouted and pounded his fist against the side of Chug's body to make him snap out of the trance Rummon had placed on him, but there was nothing he could do. It wasn't a conscious choice, all dragons had been designed to follow Rummon's calling.

Thorik was horrified as he watched his friend carry his uncle and O'Gee away from the valley to who knows where. He screamed out at Chug in vain. It was hopeless.

Defeated, he moved his eyes from the events above them to the events on the battlefield. Dead bodies and scattered body parts littered the ground around his platform. Warriors still alive had limbs cut off and were quickly bleeding to death. The King's army wasn't in much better shape. The King's Army had survived but there was no winner here. No victory could be identified when death was scattered about their feet.

Thorik could see the Del'Unday on the far side of the lake prepare to determine a new plan of attack. With over half of his troops dead, he knew they had no chance of surviving a second attack.

By this point Avanda climbed up onto the platform and hugged Thorik with all of her might. "I thought I lost you. I didn't expect the dragons to support Ergrauth."

Holding her as well, he struggled to find the words. "I don't think Rummon was aware that Ergrauth has called upon them. I'm glad he called them back, but we lost Brimmelle and O'Gee in the process."

Standing next to him on the tower she could see the last of the dragons fly over the mountain range. "We need to save them."

"Agreed, but this battle is not finished. Are you ready for the next phase, Avanda?"

"I am. It appears Ergrauth has more Del'Unday than we expected. I wish I had enough components to cast the last spell again."

"So do I, but we still have enough of our people to drive the Dels from our lands."

"Will we have enough to drive them away?"

"When you and I are together, we can succeed at anything."

On the opposite side of the lake, Ergrauth yelled at his troops for the failed attempt to destroy the villagers. Most of them never even made it to the lake's outlet that fed into the river before having to turn and run from Avanda's spell. It had stopped the battle for them and gave them concern about reentering it again. "We are strong warriors! They are passive slaves! This should be easy for you!"

The giant Mognin-sized blothrud leaned against a boulder on top of a hill near the river and glared out across the valley at the various species still alive on the far side of the lake. "They still have most of their larger beasts with the strength to restrain our troops. The error was to attack on their terms. This time, it will be on ours!"

Smashing his fist into a supply wagon, he let out his anger. The side of the wagon exploded upon the impact as bags of food and barrels of water went flying. "Set up camp! We'll sleep here and then attack before first light of day."

Chapter 34

Final Stance

Night fell upon the valley and dozens of small little Quixes worked their way through the tall grass into the Del'Unday camp. Lead by ZiXi, they carefully avoided being detected as they all had tasks to complete before Ergrauth's army would have an opportunity to wake up and attack before sunrise. The six-legged marsupials carried the ends of long twine until they reached their destination. Once there, they simply tied their end of the twine to the sleeping Blothruds before heading back out into the darkness of the surrounding fields.

After returning to safety, a loud thud was heard to one side of the Del'Unday camp. The noise caused all of the Del warriors to snap out of their slumber, only to find the sight of a Mognin standing at the edge of camp, nearly out of the subtle campfire light that barely brushed against the Ov'Unday, exposing him to all.

"Kill him!" Ergrauth shouted as he woke and spotted the intruder.

The Blothruds were much faster to start their attack than the more sturdy and less agile Krupes, so it wasn't surprising that they were the first on the scene. In fact, the Blothruds were so quick to respond that the Mognin never had time to react to the incoming attack.

Several Blothruds raced forward and leaped into the air at the same time toward their enemy. One after another joined the attack as the first ones hit their mark. To their surprise, the Mognin bathed in the soft campfire light was nothing more than Luva's mural painting of Grewen on flat pieces of timber leaning up against a boulder. Crashing through the wooden canvas and into the solid rock not only broke swords and bones from the full force of the Del's attack, but their weight rocked the boulder off its setting and down the hillside.

Screaming in pain, broken claws, arms, ribs, and jaw bones were plentiful for the first group who had arrived. However, a second choir of yells occurred moments later as all of the Blothruds began to be dragged out of camp and into the darkness by twine that had been tied from each of them onto the rolling boulder.

Unexpected cries for help filled the valley as dozens of the Del'Unday were dragged down the hill and then out into the river only to be washed downstream. The few that had cut themselves free quickly raced back up pitch black grasslands and into the camp.

Ergrauth roared in anger over the repeated elimination of his troops. "Hurry! Prepare for our final attack on the Ov'Unday!" He gathered his weapons as his warriors returned to camp to collect their own.

It was then that all the campfires unexpectedly exploded in size with tornadic flames that shot up in the sky with a blaze of changing colors before releasing a shower of glowing ashes. This light show was only the first event that took the Del'Unday by surprise. The newly brightened area revealed the entire Mountain King army surrounding all sides of their camp. Every Ov'Unday stood ready to hold their ground. Every Polenum and Human held their weapons ready for an assault. And every giant Mognin and Gather held open nets, prepared to capture the remaining warriors. And unseen by the enemy, Avanda stood behind the Ov'Undays and focused on her spell to control the campfire flames. The Mognins had placed their portable bridge across the lake's water outlet so they could reach the enemy's camp.

Growling at the scene before them, Ergrauth very casually gave his instructions. "Kill them slowly. Enjoy yourselves. Start with that Num in the front."

Hot glowing ash floated down upon the Del'Unday as they questioned the sudden change of events. They had never been on the defensive and struggled with how to react to the situations before them. Mustering their courage from Ergrauth's words, they slowly started moving toward the clear leader who stood closer in then the rest; the small Num who stood holding a Runestone in both of his hands.

"Wait!" Thorik commanded. "Ergrauth, I do not wish to cause more death and bloodshed than what has already occurred. If you leave us and this valley right now, there won't have to be any.

Amused, Ergrauth eyed the leader. "Are your plans to throw that small stone at me?" He chuckled softly along with his troops at the comical idea.

"The first time I used this Runestone was in the underworld of Della Estovia. It has the ability to allow the dead to return to this world long enough to transfer life for those who have it. Trust me, you do not want to be their victims."

"Trust? I trust no one but myself." He stepped forward as he prepared to launch his warriors.

"If you persist in your desire to destroy us, you will lose your army and possibly your own life! Do not go down this path. I'm warning you!"

Still prepared to attack, the Del Warriors waited for their master's response.

"And so I've been warned," the demon replied with a half-hearted laugh before changing his tone to a serious note. "Leave the Num for me. Kill the rest at your choosing."

Before the Del'Unday finished their first step forward, the blazing swirling flames of the campfires immediately extinguished, allowing the blueish glow from Thorik's Runestone to penetrate the area while the red campfire cinders continued to fall around them. A gasp followed, not from the change in lighting, but from all who witnessed the appearance of the ghost within the campsite.

Through Thorik's use of his Runestone of Courage, he had summoned the appearance of Mountain King soldiers who had fallen earlier that day, as they aimlessly walked about the site until they realized they could suddenly see and touch the living. Thorik controlled the Runestone's powers to protect his own people as the spirits moved toward the Del'Unday.

Ergrauth watched the sight before them to see what game was being played. "Stand firm! It is only an illusion. They cannot harm you."

At first, soft touches were made by a few of the ghostly forms against the Warriors, giving the Del'Unday slight tingles to the exposed areas. Once the spirits understood the feast available to them, began grabbing onto limbs of the Del'Unday. Each exposure to Ergrauth's army transferred life force from the living to the dead, causing their nearly transparent ghostly forms for become more solid, first with bones, then muscles and veins, and then skin. This quickly began to accelerate as more apparitions began to mob the Blothruds and Krupes, while their Del bodies turned grey and vacant of life. Limbs crumbled and easily fell from their torso. All who were touched were sucked clean of life until all the Del'Unday were nothing more than piles of ashes and armor, while all of the Mountain King's army had returned to the living.

Avanda continued her spell and the vortex swirls ignited again from the campfires, coating the area with bright lights, revealing that the Mountain King War had ended.

Only one enemy had survived. With dead skin marking his legs and arms, Ergrauth had weathered the storm of the formally departed. His damaged limbs caused him to stand at a slight tilt in order to prevent him from falling. His breathing was stressed and his power was deflated.

Thorik calmly removed one hand from the Runestone and placed it in his sack before stepping forward to address the massive creature approximately four times his own height. "This is over."

Limping one step closer, the demon would not accept it. "How can you stand there with such confidence in your words, knowing I could reach out and crush you with little effort. My strength is still a hundred fold that of yours."

"Ergrauth," Thorik said in a firm commanding tone. "Your strength is that of your personally attributes and that of fear upon those you reign over. That source of strength weakens with distance and time. It causes others to obey until they feel they can betray you. Your strength is shallow and pointless."

"Betray? No one would dare betray me! Deleth has created me to be all powerful and eternal in life. No, little Num. You will be long gone and I will win in the end. No one could betray me for I give no one my trust."

"Sadly, that is true. But the day will come when you trust one of your children and they will betray you to the point of your death. I know this to be true as I have seen it with my own eyes."

Forcing himself to quickly make one more painful step closer to Thorik, he roared at the comment. "A prophecy you give me? One of my death? Then I'll give you one in return." Standing up tall, towering over the Num, he breathed hard a few times before having the strength. "There are more Del'Unday I can collect in order to hunt every single one of you down. We will not stop until this mission is complete. My prophecy is this little Num… We will defeat you and I will then rule these lands."

Nodding at the comment, Thorik added. "Yes, you may win some battles and gain some lands, but we will always be victorious in the end. Our strength is our diversity of cultures and ideas, helping us in continuing to adapt to our surroundings and outsmart you with a drive for survival and freedom and a love for one another that you will never understand."

Still unclear why the small weak Num would have the audacity to talk to him in such a way, he finally had to ask, "Who are you?"

"I am the leader of the Mountain King army. My name is not as important as what I represent and what we all stand for; freedom from the oppressors, such as you."

Furious, Ergrauth raised his own blade.

The Mountain King army around them stepped closer. Each and every one of them were ready to protect Thorik and prevent the demon from causing any more harm.

Ergrauth scanned the united strength of Ov'Unday, Nums, and Humans before him. Grewen and a dozen more tall and strong Mognins stood the same height as the demon. Together, they could rip his limbs off in his weakened state. This was not a battle he could survive. "You have won this battle. But I will rebuild and the day will come when I will rule all of these lands. You may survive as generations of species, but I am eternal. Your kind will forever be hiding under rocks and in caves to escape my wrath." Turning, he began his slow march out of the area toward the mountain pass.

"Perhaps," Thorik replied. "However, you will always have a nagging lack of confidence that your people will at some point betray you. Always looking over your shoulder, always increasing the fear level, always wondering who will be the one to attempt to assassinate you in order to take control. It will be a long and terrible life to live for you. One I would not wish upon my worst enemy. I pity you on this path you have chosen. No good will come of all that strength and power you possess."

Chapter 35
In the End

Tears of joy rained down their faces for their fallen friends and family who had been brought back to life and reunited. The White Summit villager's were rejoicing about the defeat of the Del'Unday army and the beginning of a new era.

"You are surely the Mountain King's army!" Thorik shouted out to the White Summit villagers. "We have established a foundation for future generations to live upon. We should honor our lost from prior battles, respect our fellow citizens of old and new, and be proud of ourselves for what we have accomplished."

Grand cheers, pats on the back, and hugs filled the courtyard at the bottom of the steps leading to Wyrlyn's home.

"Although I do have to say that was the worst painting of a Mognin I have ever seen! Please put pity on me and never add me to your mural!" Thorik could barely get the words out of his mouth as he laughed.

The crowd roared with laughter.

Luva slowly bowed to the group before standing up tall to address them. "It was the finest portrait of Grewen I've ever created. For those who don't believe me and didn't have the opportunity to view it, go jump in the river and see it for yourself." A slight grin was seen for the first time on the Gathler's face. "And just for the record, at least I know what a belt is."

Pertched on Grewen's shoulder, ZiXi stood up on her back legs and shouted, "I was in a hurry! We were only given a few moments to tie the twine to something! There was no room for error in being caught! Sometimes you have to improvise!"

Luva nodded. "Truth be said, Truth be heard. However, if that Blothrud survived the river, he will never walk properly again."

Again, the crowd laughed, before someone shouted, "And we won't have to worry about that specific Blothrud growing the Del'Unday population!"

The fun and laughter continued for a while before Thorik glanced over to see Avanda walking into the area holding a limp green dragon in her arms. "No," he said to under his breath before hurrying down the steps. "Is he…"

"He's still breathing. He was not knocked unconscious during the battle."

"Bring him into Wyrlyn's home so we can tend to him."

Once inside, they inspected his injuries. It wasn't long before the dragon awoke in a groggy state and looked up to see Avanda and Thorik gazing down at him. "What happened?"

"We won, thanks to your help."

Blinking a few times as he began to shake his head clear. "Who did we lose? Where's Chug?"

"He's gone."

"Killed?"

"No." Avanda assured him right away. "Ergrauth called upon the dragons and then Rummon arrived and called them back. Chug followed. You would have left as well if you had been awake to hear his call."

Thorik added to her comments. "Brimmelle and O'Gee were riding him at the time the Dragon Lord summoned them. We don't know where he would have taken them."

Pheosco got his legs about him and stretched his neck. "Is Ergrauth dead?"

"No. He was last seen heading back up to the mountain passage."

"Then Rummon most likely returned to Pwellus Dementa' before he released his followers. He'll wait there until Ergrauth returns and then put the Del in his place."

"How do you know for sure?"

"You have your Mountain King legends, we have our Lord Rummon legends. There is about to be a battle between those two giants."

Avanda and Thorik looked at each other and then back at Pheosco. "Will Chug return here after Rummon releases him?"

"Most likely. Once Lord Rummon has led them away, he would naturally release them and send them on their way. Hopefully Chug will simply fly back here."

Chapter 36
Escaped, But Not Safe

Just outside of the icy entrance to Pwellus Dementa', two Nums began to traverse the foothills after escaping the underground city. The hills were steep but the road around the mountain was too long and was often used by the Del'Unday they were attempting to avoid.

"I still don't understand why Chug brought us here?" Brimmelle complained as he followed the child Num up another series of rock outcroppings.

O'Gee glanced down to ensure they were not being followed. "When Rummon summons his dragons, they have no choice but to follow him. I'm sure once they all returned home they were free to do as they pleased."

"You mean that fat brown dragon may have just left us here to die and headed back to the summit?"

"Perhaps. Rummon's call is strong and places them in a trance. Chug may not even recall bringing us here."

"Then we should have just stayed on him for the entire trip."

Laughing at the idea, the girl shook her head. "I can just about imagine Rummon's fury if he saw us using one of his followers as a flying wagon. He has little tolerance for that."

Slipping, Brimmelle caught himself after sustaining a few scratches. "Ever since I left Farbank I seem to be climbing rocks or running from danger. Or in this case, both."

"You really miss your home, don't you?"

"You have no idea." Brimmelle lifted himself up to the next ledge and looked up to see how many more they had before it changed back from climbing to hiking. "It was peaceful. Something I haven't had in a long time."

Sitting several ledges up from him, she swung her feet in a playful manner as she looked over the valley and waited for him to catch up. "Would you go back if you could?"

"Absolutely!" There was no hesitation in his voice.

Beaming from the answer, she added another question. "Would you take anyone with you?"

After getting a firm foothold, he stopped and thought about it for only a moment. "Yes. I would take my family back there so I could keep them safe."

"Does that include Thorik?"

Losing his grip, he slipped a few inches before regaining his placement. "He is part of my family, just as Narra and her children now are. Unfortunately, taking them all home is not an option, is it?"

"Perhaps not."

Pulling himself up to her ledge, he rolled on his back and rested for a minute. "I'm no fool, child. We are here to stay."

"I've figured out how to change one of the portals within the one-way Portibule to deliver you home to your time."

Snapping his head toward her, he was astonished by her words. "Surely that's not possible."

"It is, and by the stories you have told me about your home I was able to isolate its location in time. I even peeked through to see the Mountain King statue. It's amazing."

Moving next to her, he was still in a numb state. "When did you do this? How soon can we leave?"

"I had just finished prior to the attack by the Del'Unday, and you can leave at any time."

"Well why didn't you tell us!"

"Because I knew it would only disappoint you."

"How could such great news possibly upset me?"

"Because you now have no way to get to the Portibule to utilize it."

Silence followed as Brimmelle realized she was correct. It was maddening to know after all these years he was so close to returning home and yet it was just out of reach.

Standing up, she helped him to his feet. "We should keep moving if we're going to get over this ridge by nightfall."

Nodding, his eyes were glazed over with the sights of returning home to his own house and bed, where challenges included nothing more than judging pie contests and deciding what Runestone Scroll to read to his followers. His mind was many miles away as well as thousands of years.

In his state, it was not surprising that his focus was not on his actions. So, as he continued to climb, he slipped once again, this time landing hard on one leg and falling to the side from the pain.

O'Gee rushed back down to the outcropping he had fallen onto. "Are you injured? Did you break anything?"

Grabbing his left ankle, he grimaced from the pain. "I think I might have broken it or at the very least sprained it." His words were spoken through his tight teeth as he attempted to not scream, sending his voice out across the valley to any potential enemies below.

"Can you still climb?"

A quick attempt to stand quickly gave him the answer. "No. It doesn't appear we're going to get any farther today."

"Perhaps not, but tomorrow won't be much better unless we have something to help you."

Brimmelle shook his head. "There isn't anything out here that can help this injury. We may have to wait this out before making the trek back to the White Summit valley."

"I think I have a way to speed up your recovery. We have supplies in the city that I've seen others use. I can sneak back into Pwellus Dementa' and grab them."

"Oh no you won't! You'll be caught and captured, or even killed."

"No one knows how to hide in that city better than I."
Unpacking her food and water rations as well as her gear,
she started back down the rock face. "I'll be back before
nightfall."

"Unacceptable! Get back up here at once!"

Light on her feet and quick to climbing down the
hillside, she started making quick work of the descent. "I
shouldn't be long!"

Still arguing with her while she ignored him,
Brimmelle had no ability to stop her from doing as she
pleased.

Thorik's Log:
The dead have been buried, the wounds have been bound.
The Mountain King's battle has ended with a triumph of
freedom for peace. However, unlike the legends of the
Mountain King I remember as a child, there was no final
battle where the lord of the dragons, Rummon, entombed the
King inside a mountain, causing his death. Perhaps I was
finally able to change history for the better.

Waiting impatiently outside Wyrlyn's home, Thorik
eventually spotted his dear friend Chug flying into the valley
and toward Wyrlyn's home. "I see him!" Shouting from the
top of the wide staircase, he alerted others of the news.

Grewen and several others looked at Thorik before
searching the skies for the brown dragon. The sight they saw
was not one they had hoped. He had no riders.

Waving to receive Chug's attention, Thorik guided
him to land nearby so they could find out what happened.

Happy to be back with his friends, the large brown
dragon made his merry way toward Thorik in a roundabout
way. Once there, he landed with a thud and slapped Thorik
with his large wet tongue.

"I'm happy to see you too, my friend." Wiping his face clean, he could see Avanda and Pheosco arriving to greet him as well. "Where are Brimmelle and O'Gee?"

Continuing with his happy demeanor, Chug glanced about as he searched for them as though it was a game to find them.

"No, they aren't here. They were on your back."

Chug carefully turned his thick neck to see if anyone was on him without him noticing. None were there.

Pheosco stepped in. "Chug, do you recall the battle?"

Chug nodded yes.

"Do you recall being called by Rummon to leave the battle?"

Thinking a moment, he then shook his head no.

"Do you recall where you were after the battle? The location where you flew from to come here?"

Again, he nodded yes.

Thorik was pleased by the answer. "Excellent! Take us to that location!" He then proceeded to help Avanda up on the brown dragon before climbing up.

Pheosco circled them until they were ready and Chug lifted up into the air. "Lead the way, my flatulent friend!"

Chapter 37
Carrion Mire

The valley of Carrion Mire was filled with geothermal vents and pools of boiling water. Streams of scalding steam shot into the air at random intervals from open pores within the surface. Sulfur filled the air with a sour smell that wafted across the lifeless landscape of colorful terraced pools as syrupy mud-stained oily paths marked snake-like patterns downward.

Small dams of crystalized minerals terraced the landscape from one end of the valley to the other, creating various pyramid shapes throughout. Each clear water reservoir had vibrant colored bases of blues, greens, reds, or yellows, providing vitality to an inert rocky basin.

It was near the center of the valley that a small vortex began to spin around, collecting the steam of the nearby pools. Swirling about, it grew in width to several yards before turning sideways and expanding the cone of the swirl angled backward.

Stepping out from the now dense cyclone, Deleth was followed by Irluk and the panther, Pantera, onto the harsh land before the swirling event faded away as though it had never existed.

Wyrlyn's former apprentice gazed about the new location. "Are you sure they are coming here?" Exposed holes vomited thick bursts of burning liquid and sulfur into the air. No plants could grow in such surroundings and no animals could survive long within it.

"They are already here," Deleth corrected. "There is no point hiding, my companions."

Before them, the images of Feshlan and Wyrlyn shed their invisibility and revealed themselves. The two stood at a slight distance from the new arrivals as Wyrlyn gave Irluk a disappointed glare, causing her to step slightly closer to Deleth.

Pantera growled at the sight as she hunched down for a possible attack. A necklace was visible around the panther's neck with a large piece of metal jewelry hanging below. Upon the item was a symbol of a hand with several rings and a mouth in the hand's palm.

"Steady," Irluk said to calm the large cat. It was clear that she now had control of Wyrlyn's pet.

"Irluk, you are at the crossroads you cannot return from. Do not go down this path."

Shaking her head with disbelief, she responded to the comment. "This is of your making, Wyrlyn. You have forbidden me from following my passion. Your path is one I see as a slow death of my soul."

The E'rudite and his apprentice stood firm on their beliefs. Neither were about to bend on them and there was no point arguing the fact once again.

Placing a hand upon Wyrlyn, Feshlan calmed his thoughts. With semi-transparent skin, it was clear that Feshlan was a Notarian. However, unlike Deleth's dark robes or Ovlan's gown made of living vegetation, his attire consisted of continual changing body suit of insects. The majority of the insects were on his skin, but it was visible that some moved from under it as well.

"Feshlan, it's unfortunate that you were brought into this."

"Deleth." he bowed his head slightly. "Ovlan and I just so happened to have planned to rendezvous at Weirfortus when I ran into Wyrlyn."

"How serendipitous." Deleth's soft polite tone was able to carry across the way and was clear to hear over the noise of the water geysers and spouts.

"Yes it was. Fortuitous, one might say, for he tells me of plans for our land unknown to us. Perhaps you can enlighten me."

"I would be honored to, Feshlan. Perhaps if Ovlan were here, I could clarify the situation to you both at the same time."

"She is not aware of the situation as of yet. She is still in her tower."

"Ah, always gazing out upon her lands from a distance instead of being part of the culture and future before her. No problem. I will deal with her after we finish here and once our people arrive to occupy these lands."

Rolling her hands in a slightly nervous manner and mumbling to herself, Irluk was clearly not focused on the conversation at hand.

Wyrlyn stood firm and prepared to defend himself and Feshlan against any attacks from Deleth or Irluk. However, Feshlan calmed his nerves with a simple head nod.

"Wyrlyn tells me of changes to our scope from this paradise being a rare gift for us to exist in, to a land we will rule and enslave. If this has been communicated to us, why wouldn't Ovlan have been informed, seeing that she is the lead on this endeavor?"

"Only in title," Deleth said. "She is so focused on her own personal view of this undertaking that she couldn't handle such a dramatic change in scope."

"You don't know that. Besides, she should have been given the opportunity to bring this dispute to the leads on the other side to see if she could sway them into understanding what we had accomplished here and to enable us to continue our original mission."

"Humeth talked that way, when I informed her. And when she was denied, she made plans to recruit you and Ovlan to prevent the rest of our people from joining us."

Feshlan thought for a moment before replying. "I do not recall her ever speaking of this."

"She informed me of her plans. She had to be stopped…and so I did."

Again, Feshlan thought before speaking. "Deleth, it is against the core of our culture to harm another Notarian or their property. Are you implying that you had an influence in her death?"

A cold calculated smile rose upon Deleth's lips. "I am not implying anything. I clearly influenced her by instructing her to enter a Portibule I set up to send her into the solid rock of the Shi'Pel Mountains."

"Deleth, she was Notarian!"

"She was my mate! I had to choose between fighting our people for the sake of these creations we have made, or to fight with them to become the ruler of this land! I chose to rule, even at the cost of my love, Humeth!" His voice thundered across the valley now as he spoke.

"Have you abandoned everything we are?"

"I have embraced the future, Feshlan. Something you will never do!"

"I will not permit you to carry out these plans. I will inform Ovlan and we will place a delay on today's day of Advent. We will not allow the crossing into these lands until this dispute has been resolved."

"Only a Notarian can prevent their passage. Ovlan knows not of this conversation and I have no plans to stop them. You are the only variable here, my old friend, and you will not be allowed to leave this place to interfere with their arrival."

"Even if they arrive, Deleth, you will not succeed; especially once the truth is known about Humeth's death."

Calming himself, Deleth glanced at Irluk and waited for her to nod back before taking in a deep cleansing breath of sulfur-laced air. "Ah, and this is where we run into the challenge." Slapping his hands together, a rush of energy exploded in all directions, knocking Wyrlyn and Irluk to the ground.

Feshlan stood firm and his insects fluttered in the violent waves as they clung to his body against Deleth's forces, many of which burrowed under his semi-transparent skin to prevent being blown away. The Notarian glared at his old friend with distrust. "Deleth, you have violated everything we stand for. Justice must be made."

"Your belief in the old ways has clouded your judgement. You're already trapped in a snare, and now I will bury you in these forsaken lands for eternity."

Feshlan attempted to step forward, and quickly realized he was blocked from making any movements. "Have you lost your mind? Notarians are not to ensnare other Notarians!"

"True, and yet I personally haven't. Irluk actually has, using a fine little spell given to her by her Num friend and enhanced with some of my own creative support. I have done nothing more than help Irluk, which is not my property. She in turn has captured you, old friend. What am I to do?" His evil grin influenced his tone. "Now that you are captured, it would be a shame to have you parish prior to informing the new arrivals of unsightly past history."

"Deleth, how can you speak of this? Notarians do not kill Notarians!"

"Again, true. However, should this valley suddenly gain a life of its own and devour your insect infested body, then I have lived up to your decree."

Endeavoring to use his powers, Feshlan realized he had been incased in a small invisible sphere. He was unable to walk toward him or use his abilities. His existence and his Notarian skills could not extend beyond his current reach. He was trapped.

Wyrlyn quickly tried to help, but was unsuccessful at breaking through the barrier around him. Even his E'rudite powers could not penetrate the unseen cage. After several attempts, he snapped his head toward Deleth and Irluk. "You won't win."

"Ovlan is the only one that can stand in my way. I will be leaving now to hunt her down."

"No. The E'rudites will stop you."

Slightly nervous, Irluk began to cast one of her spells as she stepped behind her new master.

Glancing to his side, Deleth grinned at Irluk before returning to Wyrlyn. "I only see one E'rudite questioning my path, and you are not a threat to me. This battle is over before it has begun."

Wyrlyn raised one eyebrow and smiled slightly off to one side of his lips. "Once you had the Keystone operational, we could feel its harmonics against Weirfortus. In your haste to repair it, you may have forgotten that by doing so the E'rudites are no longer needed there."

As the master E'rudite spoke, dozens of E'rudites came into view all around them. They had been cloaked and waited for Wyrlyn's cue to reveal themselves.

Deleth's right eyebrows rose slightly as he gave off a half smile. "This could be interesting."

Yelling out a quick phrase, Irluk caused a flash of light surrounded Pantera and herself before the disappeared from sight. Once completed, the black panther was now on the opposite side of Wyrlyn as she leaped forward to attack him.

A sudden blast of energy was thrust into the ground by Deleth, causing the geysers in the valley to erupt with massive forces, spraying everyone with scalding water, forcing most to protect their faces.

Holding the panther at bay with his powers, he had no desire to harm the cat that he knew was under her spell. Wyrlyn shouted over the increasing noise, "Irluk! Don't do this! You can still join us!" Holding back the panther with his mind and an outstretched arm, he used his other arm to grab the necklace and rip it from the cat's neck.

Once released from the necklace, the panther calmed and placed her paws over her eyes as she slowly transformed into Irluk. "Just a bit of Alchemy, my old master."

Furious at the deception, he reached up and prepared to spike the jewelry into the rocks to destroy it before a potential curse could be activated. "This is blasphemy against everything we stand for!" As his words activated the spell, he stopped himself from releasing the item onto the ground. Instead, he shook as he struggled to fight off her ability to control his actions.

Smiling up at Deleth, she nodded. "He's ours!"

As the E'rudites recovered from the momentary burning of searing water, a barrage of powers shot toward the center of the valley where Deleth stood. Bright rays of light clashed against beams of darkness while forces attempted to rip the Notarian limb from limb. The left side of his face began to age rapidly as Schulis attempted to penetrate Deleth's skull with his E'rudite power of time. Distortions of space, gravity, light, time, as well as the basic cohesion of the fabric of the universe were strained around the dark Notarian.

Irluk tossed various components into the nearby pool and chanted her magical spell. The oily mud in the base came alive in a serpent-like form and jolted out of the water toward the attackers, before a second and then third mud serpent rose to help join the battle against Wyrlyn's friends.

The real Pantera still wore her enchanted necklace and had materialized near the valley wall, behind Schulis. She quickly used her sharp claws to attack him while his focus was on the danger in the center of the valley.

Deleth's body warped into various forms as he fought off the effects and attempted to stay alive. Skin melted, burned, froze, became brittle, and even liquefied on various parts of his body. Bones warped, snapped, and pierced through the skin. Fingers twisted and broke off, while blisters grew and exploded yellow ooze down his face and neck.

The E'rudites were winning until the ground throughout the valley began to shake from Deleth's powers. The ground heaved and buckled, launching rocks, mud, and poisonous liquids from below the surface up into the valley.

Wyrlyn attempted to control Irluk's orders that were controlling his actions, without any advancement. Instead, he used his powers to churn the winds in the valley into a giant circle, striking all the E'rudites with violent sand and rock debris collected by his powers. "No!" was all he could shout out against Irluk's mind control.

At the same time the E'rudites were fighting Deleth's barrage of projectiles and Irluk's mud beasts, they continued their attack upon Deleth as large fissures began to open down the center of the high mountain basin as higher cliffs crumbled from the movement below.

E'rudites from all angles used their powers to protect themselves from the land as it came alive and attacked them from every side. New vents blasted open beneath their feet, outcroppings fell from above, and the ground rolled like ocean waves in a hurricane. Fighting the land they stood on, they continued to blast the Notarian with their powers.

One after another, Wyrlyn watched his companions fall to the attacks. Again he fought against the charm upon him as Deleth sent out another series of blasts against his friends.

Irluk continued to use Pantera and her mud creatures to fight the battle for her. "It is a new day, Wyrlyn. As you once told me, we must adapt to our environment. That is exactly what I'm doing."

Reaching in with everything he could pull from, Wyrlyn powered his way free of her spell long enough to stop her attacks on his companions. Turning, he made his painful journey toward her.

She used the charmed item to inflict pain upon him as it drove Wyrlyn to obey her thoughts, and yet it became more and more difficult to influence his actions. Ordering the closest mud beast to attack him, Irluk knew her restraint on Wyrlyn was slowly becoming limited.

Forcing his legs to move toward her, he felt himself also pushing himself backward against his will. Fighting for each and every step, he could see the mud creature approach from the side. It would easily knock him a dozen yards away from her, defeating his efforts. However, as it attacked with its thick rock and mud arm, Wyrlyn, raised his arm and crouched down.

The heavy strike from the creature slapped Wyrlyn so forcefully that it broke the man's arm, causing him to scream in sudden pain. The impact had also caused the jewelry to be knocked from his hand before landing into a hot spring at a safe distance.

No longer under Irluk's spell, he instantly ripped the mud monster into thousands of small pieces and then knocked his prior apprentice across the valley floor. Furious, Wyrlyn pushed his way toward Deleth, even against the Notarian's attempts to stop him. "We would rather die than become your slaves!"

Deformed and in pain from the ongoing attacks, Deleth's struggling voice carried even though most of his lips had been lost in the battle. "Those terms are perfectly acceptable." The Notarian clenched both fists and focused once again on the ground beneath his feet, as two more of his fingers fell from his hands.

Racing across the valley floor the small fissures linked together and snapped open like a giant mouth, swallowing everything that fell within it. Below the surface was a river of magma flowing through caverns filled with stalactites and stalagmites which acted as teeth to pierce everyone who fell into it.

Pantera made her way to Irluk as she clutched onto the cat while attempting to hold steady against the chaos around them. In spite of her own safety, she could see that Wyrlyn was on the offense. Irluk quickly grabbed her items and launched a series of flaming balls of mud to spit forth from the boiling pools around him.

The land aggressively rippled with intense waves, pushing the E'rudites toward the monstrous mouth, while the land Deleth stood upon was calm and without challenge. One after another, the E'rudites were forced toward the middle of the valley, as Feshlan stood helpless in his invisible prison until it too was rolled into the mouth of the land.

Avoiding Irluk's spells, Wyrlyn dodged several flaming mud-balls before using his powers to lift his beloved pet, Pantera, and toss her into Irluk. In doing so, he misjudged his footing and Deleth easily pushed him into the open fissure. Like many other E'rudites who had fallen, he was able to stop himself before landing in the magma river or being impaled by a stalagmite, yet he was now in the mouth of the land beast.

Gathering his footing, Wyrlyn could see several other E'rudites had done the same. He also could see Feshlan on a long boulder surrounded by flowing lava, still trapped in his unyielding invisible cage. As the Notarian fought to break free, Feshlan's energy was seeping into the stone below him, as it turned red and began to pulse like a beating heart. Deleth was giving the valley a pulse and self-sustaining life at the expense of Feshlan. Time was of the essence to regain control of the battle and end it once and for all.

Motioning to the other E'rudites, Wyrlyn prepared to have them all use their powers to leap up out of the valley's mouth and attack Deleth with everything they had. Glancing up, his heart sank as he could see Deleth pulling his normal appearance back together as he leaned over the edge and grinned at him.

Several more E'rudites were flung into the fissure before the entire length of it immediately slapped shut. It was not enough to simply trap them as Deleth used his powers to lower the ceiling of the cavern they stood within. Sharp stalactites moved down to chew their victims as the E'rudites worked together to push upward against the ceiling in a stalemate of powers.

Grabbing onto Pantera for stability, Irluk took a deep breath as she realized that her defection had meant the difference between being crushed with her prior allies below versus standing next to Deleth and surviving. She had made the right decision if she had plans to survive.

Deleth's body continued to regenerate as he kept a firm hand on the ground below them. Regardless if Ergrauth was successful in killing the Ov'Unday, once the rest of the Notarians arrived through the Portibule, he could release the

E'rudites without concern. He had won this battle and he would now rule these lands forever.

Chapter 38

The Tale's End

Chug led the way over the mountain peaks, past Ovlan's Tower, down into the glacier valley, and into the entrance to Pwellus Dementa'. Thorik and Avanda clung on and allowed the dragon to guide himself while Pheosco flew just above them to watch for any potential enemies. Rushing to save the Nums, they didn't notice Brimmelle as they dashed past the outcropping the Fir was leaning up against. Waving his arms and attempting to get their attention as they flew away, Thorik's uncle was too late. He was completely overlooked, even though he was one of the two they were searching for.

Racing into the glacier cave, they followed it to the open cavern which held an unnerving quiet about it. The glowing crystal columns still sprang up from the center of the city and glowing light still flooded the underground city with needed illumination, and yet the city seemed dead.

For the most part it was true. As they flew overhead, they could see the death of every species within the streets and open forums. It did not appear that anyone remained in the city. It would have been completely quiet if not for the various waterfalls slapping down into fountains, churning their fresh water into small pools. However, many now were tainted with the blood of victims from the massacre. Brimmelle and O'Gee were nowhere to be seen.

Thorik was uneasy about the situation. "This city has been abandoned by all, including the dragons, if they had truly returned here. Chug, are you sure you brought them here?" Receiving a nod from his brown dragon, the Num glanced to the center of the large city. "O'Gee knows how to use the Portibule. She most likely escaped through there with Brimmelle."

Veering to one side, Chug headed toward the long crystal columns that reached up from the piazza. The air in the massive cavern was far too quiet and still for his liking and concern showed within the dragon's facial expression. Something simply did not feel right.

Down on the street, O'Gee stepped out of a doorway with a handful of medical items to bring back to Brimmelle, who was still waiting for her outside the cavern. Seeing the brown dragon and his passengers fly past, she yelled up to them.

Gliding over the city, Thorik didn't hear the child's voice. Instead, a low rumble pierced through the silence, followed by loud voices in the central piazza.

Looking at each other, Thorik and Avanda nodded before ordering Chug to head that direction. And as they did, they could hear the fuming argument between Ergrauth and Rummon. Landing nearby, out of sight, they peered into the piazza to learn of the events unfolding.

"You betrayed us!" Ergrauth yelled as he circled the dragon ready for an attack.

"It is you who has deceived me! Sending my dragons into war without my knowledge is far beneath even you!" Standing firm, he craned his neck around to watch the creature.

"I sent a messenger telling you of these plans."

"I don't care if you told me these plans yourself!" The dragon roared with an anger that shook the buildings. "I never agreed to help you!"

"These orders were from Deleth. Do you wish to defy your maker?"

"I wish to be left alone! We of the air are not your puppets or Deleth's! We are Dragons!"

"You will be nothing once Deleth finds out you have betrayed him. He ordered those Ov'Unday killed, wiped off the face of these lands. This would have happened by my hands, but you willfully prevented it!"

"And I would do it again. Will you also reveal your entire plan to gain my support to kill Deleth once my following accomplished your battles with the Ov'Unday?"

"We could have accomplished this. Yes, Deleth is powerful, but he is also vulnerable. A powerful being such as yourself could hold him off long enough for me to attack from the back and end his rule over us."

"Perhaps." Rummon voice had a hint on skepticism. "And then who would be next if not those of the air?"

"No one. Once Deleth is eliminated than we do as we please. The other Notarians have no desire to control us."

"It would not be in your character to stop fighting until all are under your ruling. Those of the air would be next on your agenda. You would sneak in at night or when we are no longer fearful of your presence and then attack like the cowards you are!"

"Cowards?" Ergrauth puffed his check out at the comment. "We are fearless!"

"You are without honor and your words mean nothing to you aside from obtaining what you want."

"Being smart enough to play your advisor is a strong trait, not a vice."

Rummon raised his chin in defiance. "Fortunately, I know that I am and always will be your advisor."

"You don't have to be!"

"And you don't have to be a righteous dictator without integrity!"

It was on that phrase that Ergrauth leaped at his opponent. "You have cost us our one chance to rule this land!" grabbing onto the red dragon's neck, he dug his blades under his scales.

Rummon swung around, attempting to extricate Ergrauth from him. "I wouldn't rule this land or any other land with you!"

Pulling at the dragon's scales, he shoved his blades up underneath them and into Rummon's skin.

Bucking at the pain, the dragon slapped his body against a nearby marble wall, with Ergrauth in between them, crushing a few bones of each creature, and carving a slice out of the Del'Unday leader's torso. Yet it wasn't enough.

The Blothrud lord held on and applied more pain under the scales time and time again.

As debris flew in every direction, Thorik and his companions raced out of the streets and into the open area before the buildings fell upon them, only to find themselves in greater danger.

Both giant creatures rolled about back into the piazza, crushing various pieces of art and hitting the Portibule itself. Blood poured from open wounds on both of them. Coughing up blood added to the mix as they continued the fight.

Rolling onto his side, Rummon forced Ergrauth onto a metal piece of art in the form of a sharpened arrow, puncturing Ergrauth in the side.

A loud cry of pain echoed from the giant Blothrud. He had been severely injured and released the dragon before he rolled off to one side. "Go ahead and kill me! Now will be your only chance!"

The Nums and smaller dragons hit behind various pieces of art as they were able to race back into the city and out of the openly exposed area of the city.

Stepping back from the battle to take a breath, Rummon shook his head slightly. "You still don't understand. I don't want to kill you or to join you. I simply want to be left alone in peace."

Raising himself back to his feet, he held his side and blood poured from it. "You are a fool, and one day I will have you under my control." Limping slowly, he began circling the dragon once again. "It is only natural for there to be a single supreme leader, and I have chosen myself to be just that." Leaping unexpectedly, he landed on the back of the dragon. Injured, he played up his own pain more than it had truly been in order to gain the advantage of surprise.

Rummon bucked and shook his body, attempting to remove his rider. His legs couldn't reach properly so his tail was used to snap around and wrap around Ergrauth's thick neck.

Digging the long blades of his claws under the scales of the dragon's neck, he held on for the ride of his life.

Unable to pull the beast off, the dragon released his tail and leaped up into the air. Rummon then flipped upside down and crashed into a sturdy marble building, destroying large a section that rained down into the streets. Unable to remove the beast from his back, he raced himself across the piazza and flung his back at the crystal columns surrounding the Portibule.

Unlike the structures for living, the crystals showed no signs of the impact, as the powerful Notarian barrier protected it from any damage.

The same was not to be said for Deleth's creations. Both creatures roared upon the impact as bones cracked and heads knocked against each other, resulting with them plummeting to the steps of the Portibule.

Dazed by the event, Ergrauth wasted no time in resuming his attack from the back of the red dragon.

Shrieking from the newly applied pain, the dragon launched himself up into the air and through the city as he attempted to scrape the two-legged creature against the buildings to knock it off. Building walls blasted into pieces, crumbled to the streets, and caused many structures to collapse. And yet his rides was still firmly clamped onto his back.

Thorik, Avanda, Chug, and Pheosco raced for cover from the falling buildings, dodging most of the larger slabs of stone they were now coated with dust and pebbles from the battle above.

Without success, Rummon darted away from the city's center and continued toward the cavern's icy entrance. Once there, he flew high enough to shove Ergrauth's head into the glacier while they flew toward the exit until the giant Blothrud was finally knocked off of the dragon's back.

Soaring out of the glacial cave, blood flung from the red dragon's injuries into the air as he spun around and landed in the entrance, staring at Ergrauth. "You will never rule me!" Then, upon taking a deep breath, he raced into the cave and released a blazing fire from his mouth.

Ergrauth ran back toward the city as the fireball enveloped the entrance, chasing him back toward the cavern. Dodging at the last moment to survive the attack, his back was still scorched by the sweltering heat that had been released.

Sounds of rupturing glacial ice echoed through the entrance. The heat had been more that it could withstand.

Rummon let out another intense spray of raging heat at the Del'Unday leader, this time setting him on fire before turning and flying back toward the exit. He continued to spray his weapon of searing flames across the ceiling of the ice cave as fissures snapped open upon impact and chunks of ice broke free and fell to the floor.

The entire entrance was now unstable as it shifted and cracked, causing tremors in the mountain's valley.

Stopping at the exterior of the glacial cavern, Rummon turned once again and reared back before violently spraying out one final amazing stream of flames into the opening.

Still sitting up on the hillside, Brimmelle watched in horror as Rummon's attack melted the ice, causing a mudslide of rocks and trees as the side of the mountain gave way. The mountain shook as a wave of ice, water, and debris rushed over the entrance and into the river valley, closing the entrance forever.

Taking only a few moments to recover, Rummon turned and flew east over the forests and mountains to the distant deserts and badlands.

"The legend was true. The Mountain King defeated the Altered Creatures at the White Summit and then was trapped within the mountain by Rummon." As it sunk in, his realization changed its focus. "Thorik, Avanda, and O'Gee are trapped forever. My family. My friends. They entered to find us. Now they've sacrificed themselves to save me."

Meanwhile, the cavern shook as the mountain side collapsed over the entrance.

Thorik and his companions hung onto each other as the floor quivered beneath their feet.

Ergrauth raced from the entrance with everything he had left to give. He was furious that he had allowed himself to be in such a situation as he ran for safety. Ceiling rocks fell from above, landing near him during his escape into the city and then to the piazza. Blasting past the Nums, without even noticing them, he made his way into the Portibule before he disappeared through a portal.

Avanda nodded in agreement. "We need to leave as well."

"Not yet. Not as long as the Portibule is still operational. We must ensure it does not allow the Notarians to return to conquer this land as their own and keep us as servants."

More rocks cascaded from above as the tide of destruction moved from the obliterated entrance toward the city.

"Thorik, those crystals can't even be destroyed by Rummon and Ergrauth. You better have a plan to destroy the Portibule other than by strength and force!"

Placing his hand against one of the crystal columns he could feel the vibration which occurred when the Portibule was used by Ergrauth. "I do." His smile suggested a new level of confidence.

"Thorik," Avanda said with a grin. "Just tell us what we need to do, and fast."

"Avanda, I want you to cast a spell to write a thousand letters that say 'The Mountain King defeated Ergrauth and the Del'Unday' and then…" His focus changed to Pheosco. "If I recall, you can control the fiery breath of yours pretty well."

Spitting out a single burst of flames out the side of his mouth, Pheosco raised one eyebrow.

"Excellent. I want you to fly down as many streets as you can and light the candles on the messenger statues."

Chug waited for his instructions and lowered his head, feeling overlooked in having any part of the plan.

Thorik then turned to Chug. "You have the most important part of this plan, my friend." Once the large brown dragon perked up, he continued. "You need to place all of the letters somewhere on all the statues."

Avanda walked over and touched the crystal column and looked upward to take in the vast length all the way to the ceiling. Small rocks fell from distant ceiling due to the mountain slide in the front entrance. "You want me to create a loud enough voice to give the messenger direction, don't you?"

"I knew I loved you for a reason."

"Well, we better be quick about it because I'm not sure how long we have before the Notarians return or this ceiling caves in."

"Agreed."

Conjuring up a thousand letters took time as the green dragon was busy flying up and down the streets. Once the pile of letters had flooded the piazza, she started working on the new spell to send out an order to them in one loud voice.

Thorik and Chug grabbed handfuls of letters and began stuffing them into pouches and nooks of the statues. The brown dragon placed several notes directly onto the wet candle wax because they would stick faster, even though several of them caught on fire from being too close to the flames.

It was then that Avanda's voice echoed across the city. "Take this message through any of the portals in the Portibule!"

The statues came to life and began their journey toward the piazza while Thorik and Chug continued to place letters on those statues that stood motionless, waiting for their next orders.

Heading in different directions, Thorik yelled to his friends. "We need to get through the Portibule before too many of the statues clog the passage and overload its capabilities!"

Statues from every direction headed into the piazza.

"They're arriving!" Avanda yelled. "Time to go!"

Pheosco and Chug arrived back first and Avanda showed them which one to enter to return to safety, but before they could enter a large rock crashed down, blocking their path to the single direction portals as well as two of the others.

"Thorik!" Avanda yelled, still waiting to see him arrive. "White Summit is not an option! I don't know where the others go, except for Lu'Tythis Tower!" She pointed to the correct portal for the dragons. "Go on! I'll be right behind you!"

Pheosco stopped. "I won't go without you!"

"Only a few can go at a time. I have to stay to show Thorik. Now hurry. We'll be right there!"

The two dragons rushed through, causing the crystals to dim once again.

Statues started arriving at the Portibule and began entering it, draining the crystal even more.

Thorik finally arrived in the piazza. "Get through! I'm right behind you!"

The crowd of statues pushed Avanda up the steps onto the platform, but she fought back to prevent herself from being herded into one of the portals. Just in case she lost her footing she reached out and pointed at the correct path for Thorik.

As he approached he continued to yell. "Hurry. I see which one! Get in there! Before the Portibule losses power!"

Statues continued to flood the piazza and they bumped against each other as they each attempted to make their way in.

Once she felt he was only a few statues behind her, she leaped in and through.

It was then that Thorik heard a cry for help. Turning, he saw O'Gee, trapped under a statue that had been knocked over by the crowds of others. "O'Gee?" Without thinking twice, he pushed his way against the flow of the statues toward her. "What are you doing here?" he yelled upon reaching her after climbing over many fallen statues. "Where's Brimmelle?"

Attempting to pull herself free, her legs were wedged under one of the fallen statues. "He's safe! He's outside the cave!"

"Then why are you here?" He moved the stone messenger off her and pulled her up to her feet. "Run!" He didn't have time to find out her answer to his prior question. With some luck, he could ask her again once they were safe on the other side of the Portibule.

More slabs of rocks fell from the ceiling, crashing down onto the city and destroying large sections of buildings. The piazza was not immune from the cave-in as chunks of ceiling rained down upon them, flattening art sculptures, stone messengers, as well as blocking the steps up to the platform on the remaining sides.

Thorik and O'Gee were trapped.

"Up there!" The girl yelled over the loud hammering of falling rocks.

There was a gap perhaps big enough for a Num to crawl through, which led to the single-way portals. It was their last chance as the crystals began to lose their glow from the enormous over use and drain upon them. In addition, their weakened state caused cracks to snap open with each of the long crystal columns.

Dodging falling debris, they reached the boulder blocking the Portibule entrance. Pulling her up in his arms, he lifted her over his head and onto the massive rock. "Hurry!" he yelled. Get inside one of those portals the moment you're on the other side!"

She turned and nodded. "She was right. You did save me."

"Go! Now!" he yelled as the ground shook uncontrollably from the collapsing cavern.

Slipping behind the rock, O'Gee disappeared from his view. And a moment after that, the crystals dimmed again, but this time they lost all light from within.

Thorik scrambled up and worked his body into the small opening. However, his backpack prevented him from climbing through. Pulling back out, he removed the frail old pack and pushed his way back into the hole, pulling the pack in after him. His yank was the final stress required to rip the strap away from the rest of the treasured backpack, causing it to tumble back down the outside and out of his reach. Holding the detached fabric, he knew he didn't have time to climb back out to retrieve it. The backpack his mother had made for him and Runestones his father gave him were now gone.

The ground rumbled and shift as large portions of the ceiling slammed near the Portibule. Falling onto the platform, he quickly rolled to his feet and searched among the scattered stones and broken messengers. O'Gee was no place to be seen. "She made it!" he mumbled under his breath, coughing from the dust of the shattering rocks.

He didn't waste a moment as he rushed for a portal as he recalled which one led to Wyrlyn's home. Racing forward, he passed through the portal and into the boulder that had fallen on that side of the Portibule platform. He had not been transported anywhere. The portals were no longer functioning. It was now a simple platform, one that would be used to bury Thorik Dain of Farbank.

Not willing to accept this fate, Thorik scampered up the rubble, climbed back through the small opening, rolled down the other side, and then landing next to his ripped pack. Grabbing it, he reached for his sack of Runestones as he looked about him.

Cracks snapped within the crystal columns as they lost their ability to hold up the ceiling. Chunks popped off the sides of them sending glass-like shards down to the surface. Building sized sections of ceiling fell, crushing entire city blocks. Streets buckled upward from the pressure and waterways in the ceiling broke free, unleashing powerful waterfalls.

Smashing behind him, a large stone landed and blocked his path back into the single-way portals, but in doing so, it knocked the path to the Lu'Tythis Tower's portal back open.

Running for the new entrance, he leaped over debris before sliding to a stop at the correct portal. However, it no longer had the energy to work, as he continued to try while looking back out at the cavern. Reaching into his sack, he frantically searched for a Runestone that could possibly save him. The sound was so deafening that Thorik couldn't hear himself shout, "NO!" at the sight before him.

Pwellus Dementa' collapsed. The entire ceiling fell upon the cavern floor below, crushing everything within it. The city and the Portibule were no more. The legend of the Mountain King defeating the Notarians had been played out and was now established for future generations. Thorik had lived out his destiny, but now the journey had ended.

Chapter 39

Lost and Found

O'Gee rolled in the bright grassy open area until she came to a stop after escaping the dark Pwellus Dementa' through the Portibule. Her heart raced from the near-death experience as she gained her bearing on where she was. Pulling herself up, her eyes adjusted to the new light as she peered over the knee-high grass and gazed in amazement at the sight before her. There, on the far side of a half-moon lake, was a giant statue up against a carved away flat mountain wall.

She was at the rock quarry near Wyrlyn's home, but all was different. The extra blocks lying around had been carved into various Fesh'Unday as they surrounded the perimeter of the warm misty lake on the cool morning. The homes of all the workers were long gone with no trace of ever existing. And across the lake, leaning against the ancient rock quarry's rock face was an enormous Mountain King statue with a familiar face, that of Thorik Dain.

Rising to her feet, she gazed about for signs of life. To her fortune, Polenums were spread out around the lake in groups of two to four, all sitting calmly as though they were waiting for an event to unfold before them. Close to her, a Num couple sat near one of the statues along the shore of the lake.

Sitting across from each other, the middle aged Nums held hands, making a large circle with their arms as they peered down into a large flat silver bowl filled with a semi-opaque liquid.

O'Gee watched for a few moments before approaching the two. As she did, the sun light began to fade and the entire valley appeared to be having a sudden change from daytime to nighttime. Even more curious, the couple didn't seem surprised about the event.

Glancing up, the young Num noticed the moon was blocking the sun. It was the eclipse that Brimmelle had told her about. She had successfully set the Portibule to the correct time in the future for Brimmelle to return home, and yet she had been the only one to ever know it. Not even her mother, Ovlan, would know where to look for her.

The couple continued to peer into the bowl as they watched the reflection of the eclipse for themselves. As the apex of darkness coated the valley, a comet was very visible as it raced across the sky under the moon, showering the earth with debris.

Thousands of particles fell in an amazing lightshow display of shooting stars in every direction. The combination of the sun's flaming ring around the black moon and the glowing white fragments was a sight never seen before or ever again.

If it had not been for this onetime event, O'Gee would not have been able to pinpoint the correct time in the Portibule.

As the couple enjoyed the lightshow, they looked up from the bowl to see the shower of descending sparkles. Breathtaking at first, they were startled to find a young Num standing next to them. O'Gee had arrived.

"Why is everyone here?" O'Gee asked before they shook off the initial shock of an unexpected visitor standing next to them.

"Surely you know that we are all here for different reasons as we look for answers from the Mountain King on this unique occasion. Are your parents here looking for answers as well?" The male was broad and had a rough appearance, as though he had worked physically hard most of his life.

"No." O'Gee nodded her head calmly, stepped closer, and placed a kind hand on each of their shoulders. "What specifically are you two looking for?"

"My wife and I are here to make a critical decision in our lives."

His wife smiled at the forwardness and odd behavior of the youth. "We're asking the Mountain King if we should travel downstream to spread his words."

O'Gee smiled at the statue of Thorik as the sunlight slowly returned from the eclipse. "Yes, he wants you to do just that."

Mesmerized by the events of the eclipse, comet, and the sudden appearance of a child, the husband could only assume these were the greater powers they had hoped to reach out to. "You've spoken to the Mountain King?"

"Yes. He wants you two to travel south and start a family."

The wife lowered her head at the comment. "We are unable to bear new life."

O'Gee tightened her hand on the older Num's shoulder. "Then I will be your child."

Chapter 40
Hello Again, and Goodbye

The cool mountain winds ruffled Gluic's feathers as she worked her way up the mountainside. The smell of pine trees filled her lungs as she weaved back and forth around the tall treetops until her ascension on the mountain lead her past the tree line and into the nearly barren lands where only grazers roamed.

Her normally hectic flight path had been radically increased with the high elevation winds blowing at her sides. Veering from side to side she continued to slowly climb up to the peak where a series of giant fungi-looking platforms clung to the highest point and overlooked the lands in every direction.

With a sense of relief, she let the air currents push her up and over the platforms to have a clear view of the structures before she headed back down and toward the largest of them.

Landing was less than elegant, as usual. In addition, she was already busy searching for something before she had even gained her footing, causing her to trip and bump into a short wall that trimmed the open walkway.

Shaking off the slight crack on her head, she could see someone coming out toward her.

Ovlan's long gown flowed behind her as she glided out of the tower and into the open overlook. Her semi-transparent skin allowed Gluic to see faint images of her muscle and bone structure. She was clearly a graceful and sophisticated being.

After bowing her head, Gluic ruffled her orange feathers on the top of her head and controlled her eyes long enough for them both to gaze in the same direction. "I've been gone for so long that I forgot how beautiful you truly are."

Ovlan halted her approach and eyed the odd looking bird before her. "I see a lovely creature in my presence, and although a bird is viewed it is an elderly num that exists in its place."

"Dare to see beyond what others only view." Gluic waited for her to realize who she really was.

Ovlan took a moment to focus on the bird's aura. "You have a glow about you similar to my daughter, O'Gee."

"I dropped the 'O' from O.G. a long time ago. If others knew I was Ovlan's Gluic, I would not have been able to enjoy the experience properly."

Contemplating what was before her, she responded in a slow thoughtful tone. "You are not the child I am familiar with. Yet, I feel you speak the truth."

"Yes, mother. My child self has just left you on a very long journey in which I will explore the future and watch the Mountain King's birth and growth. My life has been such an amazing journey that has led me back home, to you."

Kneeling down, Ovlan gracefully touched the bird's head, pushing back its mess of feathers. "It is you. My child."

"Yes, dear. My grandson, Thorik, has destroyed the Portibule. As he did, my youthful-self escaped by leaping in and ending up in the future, a few generations before he was born. My son, Brimmelle never inherited any of your powers, but my daughter and grandson had a touch of it, and it was enough for him to utilize the E'rudite's Runestones."

Placing both hands on sides of Gluic's face, Ovlan used her powers to transform her from a bird back into the child she knew as O'Gee. "This is how I see you."

Smiling with her youthful features and color-rich hair hanging in front of one of her eyes, she nodded and treasured the vitality that she could feel throughout her entire spry body. "True. But it's no longer who I am, dear. I have aged and have matured and am very happy with who I have become."

Slightly disappointed that she would never see her daughter's adolescent face again, Ovlan could not hold back a tear from running down her cheek. "I understand." Ovlan looked one last time into her child's eyes. "Goodbye, my little O'Gee." And with her hands still cupping the sides of her daughter's face, she watched the Num before her gracefully age into a woman and then into an elder Num.

Stretching, she could feel all of the old pains return to her lower back, knees, wrists, and fingers. "Ah, that feels better," she said half-heartedly. "Although I will miss the ability to soar in the sky. I had just perfected my gliding technique."

Ovlan gazed at her full-grown daughter and wondered how she not only survived, but had actually blossomed and flourished in a world without her family and friends. She was a survivor who made the best of every challenge in her life. "I'm very proud of you, O'Gee."

Reaching up, the elder Num gently touched Ovlan's soft cheek. "I know, mother, and I of you."

"Surely not. It would appear that I have been absent from your upbringing."

"Never. You were with me every day of my life. Your love was eternal and I could feel it throughout time. Do you recall what you always told me each time we parted ways?"

"Yes, Gluic. I just recently told it to O'Gee."

Gluic smiled, pulled her mother's hands up near her now wrinkled Num face, and breathed in her scent. "I've lived by those words. Please say them for me now."

Gazing into her eyes, Ovlan smiled and breathed in deeply before saying, "Enjoy the Adventure."

"And I have so enjoyed it, mother. Thank you for giving me this life. It has been a gift I can never pay back."

"Then you have made your life worth living, my dear. That is payment enough."

Chapter 41
Birth of Kingsfoot

A large block of stone floated into place by the powers of Wyrlyn. There were many of these stones lying about after the Quarry was shut down. This one ton block of granite was thin, wide, and tall and was being set on its end in the center of a large hexagonal slab of marble with a Runestone design etched into it.

Coordinating the placements, Brimmelle waved his hands about to direct Wyrlyn's efforts. "I still don't understand why Ovlan didn't kill Deleth when she found him holding you and the other E'rudites captive."

Grinning at the Num's useless hand gestures, Wyrlyn calmly moved the stone into place. "Ovlan's moral compass has not changed simply because Deleth's has. She knew it would take all of his focus to keep us at bay, providing the Mountain King time to destroy the Portibule. Once she was informed that the passageway was destroyed, her arrival at Carrion Mire immediately ended his fight against us so he could return to Pwellus Dementa' to greet the new arrivals." Grinning slightly, he added, "I would have loved to see his expression when he arrived to find out that the other Notarians wouldn't be coming to his aid."

"Aren't you concerned about revenge?"

"He has been defeated. The Del'Unday armies have run off, Deleth's alliance with Rummon is now broken, and most of all, Ovlan and Feshlan now know they can't trust him. He holds no threat to us any longer."

Once the stone was in place, Brimmelle commented. "Perfect." He recalled how the courtyard was designed during his trip to the location several years ago, which would also be thousands of years in the future. Still struggling with the time traveling concept, he focused on ensuring each stone was set in the correct location. "This scroll is for the Courage Runestone. Like the others, it must be carved to appear that the scroll is unraveled and hanging from an invisible hand, high up above."

Wyrlyn raised a single eyebrow. "You do understand that if I place them in a different configuration then you will have seen them in the new order during your travels. Therefore, no matter where I position it, it will end up being in the correct sequence regardless of my placement."

Brimmelle didn't follow his logic in any form. "Just place this one here so we won't have to worry about it."

Laughing at the comment, Wyrlyn began using his powers to start chipping away at the stone so to make it appear more like an unscrolled parchment. "You should also double check the placement of which Runestone design I placed on each of the large hexagons of the courtyard. I think I may have swapped two of them yesterday."

Shaking his head, Brimmelle raised a hand slightly. "No need. I checked them again this morning and they are all in the exact arrangement I recall seeing them in the future."

"Case proven," Wyrlyn replied.

Unsure what that even meant, Brimmelle pulled out a parchment from his side pouch and handed it to Wyrlyn. "This is the exact words for this scroll. Do not change a word or the placement of anything."

"Again, you wouldn't know if I do."

"Oh, I would know. I have a perfect memory."

Laughing at the conversation, the E'rudite got back to work.

"And when you're completed with these..." Brimmelle gazed up at the carved out quarry mountain wall. "...There is a grand statue we must build. I have a debt to pay to my nephew that I should have listened to more often."

After assisting Wyrlyn with the design of the courtyard, Brimmelle returned to the class of children, many of which were playing various games and singing songs. Several mothers helped coordinate some various teachings of how to weave baskets, make twine, and many other useful skills. Standing firm, he watched over the group with pride.

A soft hand was placed around Brimmelle's waist as Narra snuggled up against him. "I'm so proud of you. This generation will never have to see the slave mines or quarries, but your stories will remind them of our fight for freedom so they will never forget to be thankful for what they have."

Fir Brimmelle took in a deep breath and stood up straight. "Let's hope that we never forget the Num that had the courage to rally us together in order to defeat our enemies and to prevent the Notarians from invading our lands." Noticing Narra's children had walked over and were listening to them, he smiled as he picked up the youngest who was now over a year old. "I'm sure you don't want to hear that old story again, do you?"

"Yes we do!" Revi answered for both of them. "We love hearing about the Mountain King!"

Her voice carried and the other children came running up to him. "We want to hear another story!" they shouted in various forms.

Laughing at the interest, he finally gave in. "Okay. Okay, but you'll have to sit down and stay very quiet."

It only took a matter of seconds before they all were sitting and ready to hang on to his every word. Even the mothers sat down, placing the younger children on their laps. Narra retrieved her son before sitting next to her daughter Revi, who was eager to play with the toddler.

Beaming from the interest, Fir Brimmelle couldn't wait to get started with another day of teachings. "As you know, the Mountain King saved us from staying in slavery, but what some of you don't know is that it was I that raised him. In fact, it was I that saved his life on many adventures and it was I that taught him many of the beliefs that are going to be etched in those stones behind me."

Children made soft sounds of amazement as they attempted not to interrupt his story.

"Yes, I had a hand in what he became, but it was he who actually saved me from myself. He forced me out of my shell of what life was about. He brought me to new lands and civilizations so I could experience different cultures and ways to address issues. He forced me to listen and to let go of my own fears. Truth be known, The Mountain King saved me from a solemn lonely life with no pleasure and gave me this paradise with a fresh start. I will always be thankful for this gift he gave me, and you should never forget what he has done for you and your families." Slightly emotional, he wiped a tear from his face and straightened up. "Today's story will be about the Mountain King's Responsibility Scroll…"

His perfect memory allowed him to recite the words as he once read them to his following in Farbank, but now it was filled with emotion. After each reading he would then have a group discussion of how each individual interpreted the words. After all those years, Brimmelle was open to hearing what the words meant to his students.

After his teachings ended, he felt another hand upon him, this time he had a sense it was from someone he had not seen in a very long time. A moment of fear crept in before he pushed emotion aside and turned around. There before him stood his mother, just as he remembered what she looked like when they lived in Farbank. Grey hair had replaced most of her brown hair and she had a range of colorful flowers and feathers tucked into her clothes like normal. Using a sturdy sunflower stalk as a walking staff, the flower itself hung just over her shoulder.

"Hello, dear. How have you been?"

His soul-marking faded to a hue nearly equal to that of his normal pale skin as though he was seeing a ghost. Without wasting any time, he grabbed his mother in a hug, lifting her off her feet as he spun her around in a circle.

Laughing without care of who heard him, he shouted with joy. "I knew you hadn't been turned into a bird! How did you get here?" Swinging her about one more time, he finally set her down gently. "I don't even care. I'm just so thankful you're alive and well!"

Smiling, Gluic nodded softly. "You have grown so much, dear. I'm so very proud of you."

Hugging her once again, he noticed someone approaching. "Mother, I want you to meet Narra."

"Your love?"

Smiling, he glanced over to her. "Yes. And these are her children."

"Yes, I know them, dear. However, you should introduce them to me."

Narra pulled her hand forward, dragging her daughter out from behind her. "This is my daughter Revi." Turning her head toward the infant in her other arm, she gazed down into his eyes. "And this is my son, Thorik." Looking up at Gluic, she continued. "Brimmelle wanted his name to be Thorik."

"Really?" Gluic appeared skeptical of the statement.

Her son nodded. "It's true." Turning, he glanced up to where the future Mountain King statue would be carved, bearing Thorik Dain's face. "In spite of his successes, I made so many mistakes raising him the first time that I'd like a second chance to prove I can do better."

Gluic nodded. "We all want that opportunity, dear. However, we only have one chance in raising our young. As long as our love is pure, we can only guide them, for they have their own journey to live out." Placing a soft caring hand in his, she smiled to herself. "They are the authors of their own stories, my son. Only they can change their adventures if they aren't happy with them. Just as I have allowed you to find yourself. This exploration outside of Farbank, my dear, was just as much about you as it was your nephew and myself."

"Thank you for being patient with me, mother."

"Of course, dear. Although, it surely took you long enough to get it though that thick stubborn head of yours."

Chapter 42

Fate of Avanda

Halfway up the hill, a single home was built overlooking the valley and river below. Stones made up the first few feet of the walls and the base of the home, then timbers were used to construct the remaining walls and roof. It was a sturdy house that would stand the test of time.

Opening the front door, Avanda stepped outside a few yards before stopping and gazing at the sight of green forests, grass plains, and a wide river surrounded by mountain peaks on either side of the river's valley. The fragrance of Spring's wildflowers carried in the gentle breeze, relaxing her mind and calming her soul.

A small blue crystal shard was pulled from her pocket and she gazed down at it as she recalled the first time Thorik gave it to her before escaping Della Estovia. It was a symbol of their love, one that had been strained and rebuilt so many times. A love that would last in her heart forever.

Smiling, she glanced up and watched her son reach out his arms as though he was flying while being carried by Pheosco through the air. Both Pheosco and Chug flew about the valley in the airways as they entertained the infant. The child had become their own responsibility in so many ways.

"Good morning, my love." Thorik reached around her waist and snuggled his chest against her back. Holding her tight, he rested his head upon her shoulder. His soul-markings were fully vested in his skin with dark swaths across his arms and up one side of his neck.

Closing her eyes while cherishing the morning hug, she reached back with one hand and ran her fingers through his hair. "Good morning. Do you recall what today is?"

"Hmm…Harvest Fest is in the Fall…But I'm sure it's some special day to someone."

"Really? Special to someone?"

"Yes." His smile grew from ear to ear. "It's very special to me, for one. It's the anniversary of the destruction of Pwellus Dementa'. If Wyrlyn hadn't taught me how to use the Runestones to create energy I would have never been able to force that portal to work again."

"I don't even want to think of what could have happened. You wouldn't have made it back. Your son wouldn't have a father." Taking in a deep breath she sighed at the relief of that never happening.

Watching the dragons play with the infant Num, Thorik called out to the green dragon. "Pheosco, did you hide my coffer and Runestones in the caves below Spirit Peak as I asked?"

"Chug and I did, first thing this morning." Giving the baby a quick spin in the air, his green scaled arms firmly held the child from any harm. "They are hidden for your parents to find in a few thousand years."

"Thank you." He took in a thoughtful breath as he visualized his parents when he was a young lad.

"Now with those hidden, do you plan to return to the village near Wyrlyn's home?"

Gazing out over the fertile valley and smelling the fresh air filled with the scent of the lower forest, Thorik treasured the calmness away from all the hustle of village life.

Avanda knew his feelings well and could read him like a book. "I'm so glad you suggested we not return to the White Summit, but instead build this home overlooking the future village of Farbank."

Keeping his body tight against hers, he looked down at the valley below. "Over there is where Fir Brimmelle will live, just a few doors down from the Mullenfrather's home. My parent's will be building our sturdy little cottage beyond that patch of trees and your home will be built a few minutes south of here."

"I recall when Uncle Wess and I tried to slide down that hillside on a large wooden Runestone sled and he ended up breaking it in half after crashing into the trees at the bottom."

"If I recall, you took the blame for the broken carving." He grinned at the memory. "Do you remember the Harvest Festival events that took place in that valley just below us? And the races we had up to the top of Dula Peak and back down." He stopped, looked behind him at their home, and then started to laugh.

"What's so funny?"

"I just realized that the old ruins we used to race through in order to reach to the top are actually the remaining walls of our current home. We just built those ruins of our ancestors."

She chuckled at the thought. "I recall climbing up here to play in these rock walls when I was a child. It was like our castle retreat away from our parents."

"I don't recall wanting to retreat from my parents. Although Brimmelle was a different story."

"I can understand that." Rolling her eyes at the thought, she couldn't imagine having to be raised by Brimmelle. "So, what are your plans today?"

Thorik took in a deep breath as he gazed out upon the distant White Summit. "I don't know. Perhaps I will save a kingdom, or lead a quest across a vast deadly landscape, or maybe slay myself a demon."

Nodding her head, she gave a slight smile. "Well, I hope you'll be home in time for supper."

"Oh, I suppose I could push those adventures off until tomorrow…or next week."

Pulling his arms in tighter around her, she closed her eyes and breathed in his scent. "You miss those days, don't you?"

"Oh, at times I think back at the victories we had and how wonderful it felt to succeed. But I also recall a lot of times we nearly lost each other. Times where the Death Witch nearly had our souls."

"And now? Can you live without those explorations and undertakings?"

"Trust me, every day with you is an undertaking." His smile gave his voice a clear sign he was joking.

"I would have to say that I take on most of the challenge just putting up with your so-called sense of humor."

"Well, it's clear that our journeys gave you a damaged sense of humor when you named our son."

"What do have against the name Ralph? It's a much nobler name than Thorik."

Releasing her, he spun her around for the two to face each other before wrapping his arms around her once again. "Really? Is that the proper way to talk to the Num who saved your life more than once?" His playful confidence caused his chest and chin to rise a bit.

"Shall we count up the times I've saved you to see who owes who?" Her devilish grin gave him a clear picture that she could play this game just as well.

"I've saved a kingdom, led armies, and defeated E'rudites."

"That's only because I let you."

"That's no way to talk to me. I'm now the rightful Mountain King."

Avanda smiled pleasantly. "Yes you are, and I'm the rightful descendent and heir to the original Mountain King, which by your actions caused his death. You owe me your allegiance."

Thorik paused and squinted his eyes at her. He didn't know how to trump her. "You always have to have the last word, don't you?"

She nodded before replying. "It took you this long to figure that out?"

"Apparently."

"Shut up and kiss me, my King."

CHARACTERS Pronunciation Guide

Ambrosius: aeM-brO-zee-ahs
Asentar: as-en-Tar
Avanda: ah-Van-Dah
Bakalor: Bah-Kah-Lor
Brimmelle: Brim-'ell
Darkmere: Dark-Meer
Deleth: deL-'eth
Draq: draK
Emilen: ehM-il-eN
Ergrauth: erR-gRahTH
Ericc: ehR-iK
Feshlan: FehSH-Lahn
Gluic: Glu-iK
Grewen: Gru-'en
Humeth: Hum-'eth
Irluk: uhR-luhK
Ovlan: ahV-lahN
Sharcodi: shAR-kO-dEE
Thorik: Thor-iK
Trumette: truhm-et
Wyrlyn: Wer-Len
ZiXi: Zih-XEE

LOCATIONS Pronunciation Guide

Cuev'Laru Mountains: Koo-ehV Lah-Roo
Cucurrian River: Koo-kuR-ee-uhn
Della Estovia: Dell
Doven: dO-ven
Eldoric Mountains: el-Dor-ik
Farbank: Far-bank
Govi Glade: Gah-Vee
Kiri: kE-rE
Lu'Tythis: Loo-Tith-is
Pelonthal: peL-ahn-THahl

Pwellus Demanta': PWehl-us DEE-mehn-tAY
Pyrth: perTH
Trewek: trU-ek
Wierfortus: wEer-fort-us
Woodlen: Wood-lehn

SPECIES Pronunciation Guide

Blothrud (AKA Ruds): BlahTH-Ruhd
7' to 9' tall; Bony hairless Dragon/Wolf-like head;
Red muscular human torso and arms; Sharp spikes extend
out across shoulder blades, back of arms, and back of hands;
Red hair covered waist and over two thick strong wolf legs.
Blothruds are typically the highest class of the Del'Undays.

Del'Unday: DeL-OOn-Day
The Del'Unday are a collection of Altered Creatures
who live in structured communities with rules and strong
leadership.

E'rudite: EE-roo-dIt
The E'rudite aren't actually a species. They are
typically humans that have been trained in the basic arts of
the Notarian mind control powers which makes them much
more powerful than others, but not nearly that of a Notarian.

Fesh'Unday: FehSH-OOn-Day
The Fesh'Unday are all of the Altered Creatures that
roam freely without societies.

Gathler: GahTH-ler
6' to 8' tall; Hunched over giant sloth-like face and
body; Gathlers are the spiritual leaders of the Ov'Undays.

Human: Hyoo-muhn
5' to 6' tall; pale to dark complexion; weight varies
from anorexic to obese. Most live within the Dovenar
Kingdom.

Krupes: KrooP
6' to 8' tall; Covered from head to toe in black armor,
these thick and heavy bipedal creatures move slow but are

difficult to defeat. Few have seen what they look like under their armor. Krupes are the soldiers of the Del'Unday.

Mognin (AKA Mogs): MahG-Nen

10' to 12' tall; Mognins are the tallest of the Ov'Unday.

Myth'Unday: Meeth-OOn-Day

The Myth'Unday are a collection of Creatures brought to life by altering nature's plants and insects.

Notarian: nO-tAr-EE-ehn

These thin human-like creatures have semi-translucent skin and no natural hair anywhere on their bodies. Their motions are smooth and graceful and they have incredible mental powers that appear to be god-like to the other species.

Ov'Unday: ahv-OOn-Day

The Ov'Unday are a collection of Altered Creatures who believe in living as equals in peaceful communities.

Polenum (AKA Nums): Pol-uhn-um

4' to 5' tall; Human-like features; Very pale skin; Soul-markings cover their bodies in thin or thick lines as they mature. Exceptional Eyesight.

www.AlteredCreatures.com

Altered Creatures Epic Adventures continues with the
following books:

Nums of Shoreview Series (Pre-teen, Ages 7 to 12)
Stolen Orb
Unfair Trade
Slave Trade
Baka's Curse
Haunted Secrets
Rodent Buttes

Thorik Dain Series (Young Adult and Adult)
Fate of Thorik
Sacrifice of Ericc
Essence of Gluic
Rise of Rummon
Prey of Ambrosius
Plea of Avanda

Made in the USA
San Bernardino, CA
25 November 2015